A GRAVE
WAITING

A GRAVE WAITING

A Moretti and Falla Mystery

Jill Downie

DUNDURN
TORONTO

Editor: Cheryl Hawley
Design: Jennifer Scott
Printer: Webcom

Library and Archives Canada Cataloguing in Publication

Downie, Jill
    A grave waiting : a Moretti and Falla mystery / Jill Downie.

Issued also in electronic formats.
ISBN 978-1-4597-0636-1

    I. Title.

PS8557.O848G73 2012   C813'.54   C2012-901548-2

1   2   3   4   5   16   15   14   13   12

We acknowledge the support of the Canada Council for the Arts and the Ontario Arts Council for our publishing program. We also acknowledge the financial support of the Government of Canada through the Canada Book Fund and Livres Canada Books, and the Government of Ontario through the Ontario Book Publishing Tax Credit and the Ontario Media Development Corporation.

Care has been taken to trace the ownership of copyright material used in this book. The author and the publisher welcome any information enabling them to rectify any references or credits in subsequent editions.

                                                            J. Kirk Howard, President

Printed and bound in Canada.

Visit us at
Dundurn.com | Definingcanada.ca | @dundurnpress | Facebook.com/dundurnpress

Dundurn
3 Church Street, Suite 500
Toronto, Ontario, Canada
M5E 1M2

Gazelle Book Services Limited
White Cross Mills
High Town, Lancaster, England
LA1 4XS

Dundurn
2250 Military Road
Tonawanda, NY
U.S.A. 14150

PART ONE

Stating the Theme

Chapter One

Day One

Death had come tidily to the body on the bed. There was very little mess, apart from a neat hole in the middle of the forehead, and a trickle of dried blood from the mouth, which gaped open as if the end had come as a surprise. The victim appeared to have been shot at some distance, which suggested a marksman, or maybe just lady luck — for the shooter, if not the target.

The setting cast an illusory patina of glamour over the grisly reality of violent death, as faux as the furry leopard coverlet on the circular bed with the gilt-edged mirror over it, the silk flowers on the desk — although the mahogany of the desk seemed real enough, as did that of the built-in entertainment console. Through an open door, Detective Sergeant Liz Falla could see a sybaritically equipped bathroom, gleaming with gold-flecked marble.

"Floating palace, eh, DS Falla?" Police Constable Mauger handed her a pair of latex gloves.

Remembering Frances Hanna

The grave's a fine and private place
But none, I think, do there embrace.

— "To His Coy Mistress," Andrew Marvell

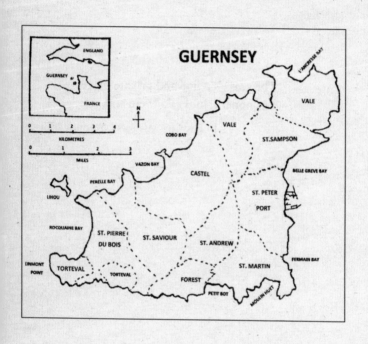

"A frigging marine mansion," Falla replied. "When did you get here?"

"About fifteen minutes ago. Chief Officer Hanley sent me straight over and told me to get hold of you."

As Falla bent down, the movement of the sleek Italian-designed yacht shifted the body on the bed abruptly. From the low rumbling outside it sounded as if the Condor Ferry was coming in to Guernsey from the south coast of England, cutting its engines as it came closer to its moorings, but still sending out a powerful wake of water.

Reflected in the mirror above the bed, the dead eyes seem to come briefly to life as the man's head shifted with the movement.

"Jesus! That made me — I mean, I thought —" Police Constable Mauger grasped the end of the bed with a latex-gloved hand.

"He's going nowhere. Who found him?"

"The cook. He's in the galley having conniptions. I've only had a brief word."

"Go sit with him, PC Mauger, hold his hand. I've got a phone call to make."

With a last, fascinated look at the body on the bed, PC Mauger reluctantly obeyed orders.

Liz Falla tried Detective Inspector Ed Moretti's mobile. She had already done so twice since the report came in, but no luck. Of course his mobile was off; he was on holiday. But this time she got a response. Third time lucky. Just as well, because this looked like a nasty combination of money, guns, and murder.

* * *

The thirty-foot tides of spring left even the lower shoreline exposed. The pungent tang of dulse, furbelows, and carragheen in the coral-weed rock pools assailed Detective Inspector Ed Moretti's nostrils as he approached Rosière Steps, overnight bag in hand. The first boat from Guernsey to the tiny island of Herm was arriving, a catamaran full of families and young lovers clutching cameras and baskets and bags and each other. After the car-less, crowd-less quiet of a couple of days spent on the island, which measures about a mile and a half across, the babble of human voices en masse — or comparatively en masse — seemed deafening.

The Massey Ferguson tractor, one of the few motorized vehicles allowed on Herm, was waiting at the dock to carry luggage up to the White House Hotel, so some of the visitors must be staying to swell the regular population of around fifty souls. From now on the crowds would build up until the end of August, but most would be day trippers from Guernsey, only three miles away to the west. Yet even in the height of summer you could walk with only the gulls for company between hedges of purple Hebe and New Zealand flax, buzzing with bumblebees and tortoiseshell butterflies, looking up at elderflower bushes as tall as trees.

"Back to reality," he said to his companion.

"Some reality!" Retired Commander Peter Walker grinned at Ed Moretti. "Little wonder you came back to the islands of the blest. What a rest it is for the old eyes not to look up at billboards and posters on every available space advertising every useless product under the sun. I like pretty women, God knows, but Christ I'm fed up with twenty-foot-tall semi-naked females trying to persuade me to buy mobile phones or motor cars or mascara."

"You can save your mascara-free eyes for sightings of rainbow bladderweed or butterfish."

"From Scotland Yard to the seashore. You're surprised."

The deceptively placid blue eyes examined the world from beneath a thatch of thick white hair, but the sixty-year-old who now spent most of his spare time studying the flora and fauna of the marine world seemed little different from the man who had changed the direction of Moretti's life.

"Not really. You've been peering into deep pools most of your adult life, Peter."

"And these are a bloody sight more pleasant, as you know."

"There's some pretty vicious infighting from what you tell me."

"I'll still take limpet and dog whelk over the scum I used to deal with."

"Fair enough. Phone me when you've had enough of marine life and feel like playing pick-up with us," said Moretti. "I won't ask for help with the villains, but you might like to sit in with the layabouts."

"That's what Fénions means? Good name for a bunch of musicians. That's a talented lot you're with, piano man — gifted sax player, and they're not easy to find."

"Garth Machin? Yes, he's good, but he chose money over music. He's a banker."

"Security over creativity. Like yourself."

"That's right."

Peter Walker looked at Moretti, sensing his withdrawal. Nothing new in that. They had first met in London, years ago, in a Soho jazz club where Walker played guitar when off-duty. He thought back to the first night Ed Moretti walked into the club, a small, dimly lit ground-floor space between a betting shop and an off-licence. One of the regulars had shouted out, "Where's the piano player?" and Walker had shouted back, "Gone AWOL, again. Is there a piano player in the house?"

"Yes."

A very young, very lanky man near the doorway walked forward. The scarf around his neck marked him out as a London University student, and Walker cursed to himself. What the hell had possessed him, asking such a question? There were few things he loathed more than half-cut women who thought they could sing like Lena Horne or Peggy Lee, and the untalented fringe of the student body who thought they could play jazz piano. It was usually piano, because they didn't arrive with an instrument.

"Ed Moretti," said the young man. Then, without further ado, he sat down and played Gus Kahn's "My Baby Just Cares for Me."

This student could play. It was to be the first of

many sessions and the beginning of a friendship that saw Ed Moretti change his career path to police work.

"Why?" Peter Walker once asked him.

"Because I never wanted to be a lawyer, but I couldn't think of anything else I wanted to do except play piano. Plainclothes policeman instead of lawyer is less of a disaster in my father's eyes than piano player, believe me."

"Shouldn't you be following your dream, not your father's?"

Moretti had shaken his head and said, "You don't understand, Peter."

He hadn't offered to explain, and Walker had not asked him to do so.

The catamaran eased away from Rosière Steps, and Moretti gave a last wave as Peter Walker's sturdy figure receded into the distance. It was a glitteringly clear day, and a sapphire sea creamed into a white froth around the islets of Crevichon and Grand Fauconnière, and the countless rocks that made sailing treacherous in these parts, unless you knew what you were doing. On Guernsey also, besides St. Peter Port Harbour, St. Sampson's, and Beaucette Marina, there were many anchorages around the island, but they all required knowledge of such things as low-lying rocks and neap tides, when the water was at its lowest point.

To the left of the catamaran, five hundred yards away, loomed the two-hundred- sixty-foot hump of the island of Jethou. For some reason it always appeared ominous to Moretti, forbidding in any light or any season. And yet Fairy Wood on the north side would be carpeted with bluebells and daffodils at this time of the year, and the island's past history was not as shady as that of others in this islet-dotted sea. On another, even smaller, island, a multimillionaire had for years run his business empire, thumbing his nose at the taxman. And on the island of Sark, a mini paradise, ruled until very recently by a feudal seigneur, many of its supposed residents were merely telephones with redirect facilities to wherever in the world the various businesses they served were to be found. A mini paradise indeed, for arms dealers, money launderers, and distributors of pornography, none of whom had ever set foot in the cathedral-like caves of the Creux Terrible, or gazed into the pellucid depths of the Pool of Adonis.

They were now out into the open, narrow channel that lay between the islands of Herm and Guernsey, passing Mouette and Percée and Gate Rock, heading for the harbour of St. Peter Port, the capital of Moretti's home island. Here, the wind strengthened and blew salt against Moretti's mouth. A small boat heading for Herm came alongside briefly, the man and woman on board waving at the children on the catamaran. They looked happy, carefree. Windblown. "I must get another boat," Moretti resolved.

He'd have time. It had been a quiet winter, with only the usual annoyances of civilized society: break-ins, burglary, car accidents. Domestic disputes.

Behind him Herm receded into the distance, and the curve of Guernsey's eastern coastline grew nearer. In the centre the houses climbed the terraced cliffs of St. Peter Port, behind one of the most beautiful harbours in the world, guarded by Castle Cornet, as it had been since the thirteenth century.

Old mortality, the ruins of forgotten times.

The fragment dislodged and drifted up from a buried repository of poems learned and texts committed to memory during his years at Elizabeth College, the private boarding school on the island. From mediaeval fortress to Hafenschloss for the occupying forces during the Second World War, Castle Cornet had survived the distinction of being the only castle on British soil bombed by the RAF, to become the keeper of the ruins of forgotten times. In the summer there would be open-air theatre and living history re-enactments. Seventeenth-century pikemen and eighteenth-century militiamen walked along Prisoners' Walk and past Gunners' Tower for the amusement of school children and tourists. And every day a soldier in Victorian uniform fired the noonday gun, the sound echoing across the harbour and the town.

The catamaran pulled into the moorings used at low tide at White Rock Pier, and its passengers marshalled themselves and their belongings. Moretti waited until everyone had disembarked and started to move toward the exit to the gangway. He'd drop into police headquarters on Hospital Lane before heading off home, see if his partner, Detective Sergeant Liz Falla, had got back from her gig on Jersey.

Not jazz for Liz Falla. Folk music. Acoustic guitar and a voice once described by a past lover of his as a cross between Enya and Marianne Faithfull. Was such a hybrid possible? Or even desirable? He had yet to hear her sing.

Something seemed to be going on over toward Albert Pier. Moretti could hear sirens, see the flashing of lights.

"What's up? Do you know?" he asked the catamaran skipper, a swarthy, bearded individual whom Moretti recognized as a not-infrequent patron of police hospitality after too many beers in local watering holes.

"Nope. But they were there when I left an hour ago."

Moretti took his mobile phone from the depths of his bag and turned it on. It rang almost immediately.

"Falla?"

"Guv?" His partner's voice was deep for a woman, with a singer's resonance.

"What's the problem down at the harbour?"

"I've been trying to reach you. Did you just come in on that catamaran?"

"You saw that? I only just turned my mobile on. Where are you?"

"Victoria Marina. There's been a shooting on a yacht."

"Where are the rest of the crew?"

"On land, apparently. The cook was scheduled to be first back this morning."

Liz Falla watched Moretti walk around the circular bed, examine the exact turn-back of the bed cover beneath the dead man, the position of his hands, the angle of his head on the satin-covered pillows. Ask him a question hours later about some tiny detail in the cabin and, snap, his photographic memory would provide the answer.

About a year ago she had not dared ask Chief Officer Hanley, but she *had* asked the fates, various colleagues, and sundry family members why she had been assigned to this laconic, introverted individual who had no small talk, and even less awareness of her as a member of the opposite sex of above-average attractiveness. Or so she had been given to believe by more forthcoming males with less in the way of looks and intelligence than Moretti. But she had got used to walking into his office, or picking him up in the police car, and having no comment made about a new hairstyle, or a new suit. The only acknowledgement he ever made of her femaleness was when asking for fresh insights or opinions her sex might give her. What she had first seen as a slight she now valued as commendation.

"This is when I wish we had a coroner on Guernsey. I assume the scene-of-the-crime people are on their way."

"Plus the pathologist on duty at Princess Elizabeth Hospital, Guv. We got here first. PC Mauger is sitting with the cook in the galley. He found the deceased. I've only had a quick word."

"Give us a chance to look at the victim before everyone gets here. You okay with this, Falla?"

His partner gave Moretti a long look from beneath a pair of straight, dark eyebrows. Old-fashioned, his mother would have called it. It was a look he was getting used to. And, after the first murder case they had worked on together, his question was ridiculous. Falla was no fragile flower.

"After some I've seen that have been in the sea a few weeks?" She grinned. "I'll manage, Guv."

Together the two officers bent over the body.

The dead man appeared to be in his late forties, Moretti reckoned. He was a big man, with an incipient corpulence that might well have gone on increasing if cruel fate had not cut him off before any further advance of middle age. But even in death one could see he had been handsome. His skin was tanned, his thick brown hair expertly cut, his features strong but perfectly proportioned. He was formally dressed in a suit of grey flannel, but casually accessorized: a silky, open-necked shirt, some light loafers in soft black calf on his stiffly extended feet. There was a damp patch between his legs.

"Shot from a distance," said Moretti, "probably from the doorway. Can't see any powder grains." Gingerly he got hold of the tip of a loafer and jiggled one of the flannel-clad legs. "Rigor still in the legs, but from the look of his jaw, it's worn off up top."

"Starts at the top and works its way down, doesn't it?" observed Liz Falla.

"Right. Then it starts to wear off after about ten hours or so. Longer fibres in the leg, so it hangs on. Do we know who he is?"

"Bernard Masterson, owner of the boat, says the cook. He's Swiss French — the cook, I mean. Name's a bit of a mouthful, but I've got it in my book. Jean-Louis Rossignol."

"Do we know where they were coming from?"

"Cherbourg, again according to the cook. It'd been an easy crossing, but they'd done a lot of entertaining in France, so he gave them all the night off. Even paid for them apparently."

"Interesting. Did you find out who 'them all' are?"

"Yes." Again, Liz Falla consulted her notes, reminding Moretti what a relief it had been to discover that this new, unasked for, female partner of his was as well-organized as he was. Better organized than he was. "Besides the cook there's a personal valet, a housekeeper, and two crew members."

"Where were they staying in St. Peter Port?"

"The Esplanade Hotel — that's a four crown. Didn't stint on them, did he?"

"Apparently not."

Stinting did not seem to be part of the victim's way of life, thought Moretti, picking up a set of ivory-handled brushes monogrammed in gold from the built-in dressing table between the entertainment console and the desk. Although Guernsey, second largest of the Channel Islands off the coast of France, had become a tax haven like the Cayman Islands or the Turks and Caicos, attracting billions of pounds, every bank under the sun, financial businesses galore, this particular high roller seemed an unlikely visitor.

Then there was the murder weapon. Guns were

also unlikely visitors, and this looked like a professional hit.

"Hello — what happened here?"

Liz Falla's glance followed that of her superior.
Moretti was looking at a heavy wooden magazine rack
that had tipped over near the bathroom door. Some of
the contents had spilled out on the floor.

"Could it have got knocked over in a struggle?"
she asked.

"What struggle? That's what's odd about it being
like that. Looks like someone took something out of
it in a hurry and knocked it over. Let's have a look."

Carefully reaching into the rack, Moretti pulled
out one or two magazines by the corner. They were all
of the *Penthouse*, *Hustler* variety, some more hardcore
than others. Liz Falla whistled under her breath.

"Dirty old sod, eh? Could this be about porn?"

"Too early to tell, but none of this stuff appears to
be illegal. What's this?"

Caught in one of the brass studs decorating the
rack was a fragment of glossy paper. Moretti extracted
it from the stud and held it up. Enough of the fragment
remained to show a fraction of a photograph and a piece
of printing.

"Looks like the prow of a boat, doesn't it. This
boat?"

"Don't think so. Different shape. Not a Vento Teso."

"Is that what this is? Can you read any of it?"

"'Dream big — you only live....' Ironic in the circumstances."

"I'll say."

"And there's something else: 'Offshore Haven Cred.'"

There was the sound of sirens outside the large oval windows of the master stateroom, a bustle of activity on the dockside.

"Here we go," announced Falla from the window. "The technical boys and the doctor have arrived. Oh, isn't that nice. It's the lovely Dr. Watt."

"Not a favourite of yours, Falla?"

"That's right, Guv."

She said no more, but more was not necessary. On an island that measured about twenty-five square miles, a high-profile professional man like Nichol Watt with an ex-wife on the island, another on the mainland, and at least two girlfriends got himself talked about. Moretti found his partner's love life to be something rich and strange, since her approach managed somehow to be both casual and committed, but as far as he knew it was always off with the old before on with the new. Such niceties didn't bother Nichol Watt.

Moretti stood up, pocketing the piece of paper. "Let's take a look around, Falla, then go and hear what Mr. Rossignol has to say."

The master suite in which Bernard Masterson had met his end stretched full beam across the prow of the yacht, and led into the dining room through sliding glass doors. On one side was the aft deck, set up as an outside dining area, and on the other was the kitchen.

Beyond the dining room, through more sliding doors, was the main salon that housed a huge, curved bar. There were dirty glasses still on the black-and-white marble countertop, a couple of bottles alongside them, one of Scotch, the other of champagne. The bottle of champagne was empty. Moretti picked up one of the glasses in his gloved hands.

"Lipstick. Falla, get Jimmy Le Poidevin on your mobile, tell him to come here when he's finished in the bedroom."

As Liz Falla made her call to the forensics chief, Moretti crossed over to the windows that faced Albert Pier. It was May, and the holiday season had not yet started in earnest, but the place was busier than usual. There was much rebuilding in progress. The three great travelling cranes and the one fixed crane on the very end of the pier that faced the Little Russel, the shipping channel that led into the harbour of St. Peter Port, were getting a major overhaul, and a new crane was being erected.

Not that the area was ever that quiet or deserted, since it housed the passport office, the ships' registry, the freight office, a bureau de change, a left-luggage office, a bicycle shop, and the offices of the various ferry lines: the Emeraude Lines, the Condor Ferries, and the high-speed catamaran service to France. There were always people about on the pier, so there was a fair chance of finding someone who might have seen or heard something. Hopefully.

And there was always the chance that someone on a boat might come up with something useful. The ambulance boat, the Harbour Authority boat, and the fisheries vessel were all moored close by, although there were fewer visiting craft than there would be in high summer. That, presumably, was how a yacht this size had found moorings in Victoria Marina itself, and not on a buoy in the outer harbour or up north at the privately owned Beaucette Marina near St. Sampson.

There was also the Landsend Restaurant not far from the Vento Teso's moorings. He'd have a word at some point with Gord Collenette, the owner.

"All set, Guv. Where now?"

"Upstairs."

A set of stairs in the main salon led up to the top deck, on which there was another lounge and a sky deck complete with bar, refrigerator, and another entertainment console with hi-fi, television, and a couple of pinball machines.

"Talk about over the top," observed Liz Falla. "How many bars has this thing got?"

"Three so far. This leads to the pilothouse, I think."

Set in a highly polished wood panel, the controls in the pilothouse looked like the dashboard of a very expensive car, with a cushy leather-upholstered swivel chair in front of the wheel. The bow deck was equipped with a Jacuzzi and yet another entertainment console.

"Everything seems to be in order." Liz Falla peered down into the empty Jacuzzi.

"It does. Apart from those glasses and the empty champagne bottle, you'd never know any of this had ever been used. Let's take a look below decks, where the steerage passengers, the staff that is, live."

On the lower level there were four crew cabins in the bow, and two guest suites. The guest suites were open and appeared unused, but the doors of the crew cabins were locked.

"That's about it, isn't it?" Liz Falla peered into a pristine guest suite.

"Almost. On a yacht like this there should be a garage."

"*Garage?*"

They found it. It contained water scooters, motorcycles, and a stunning silver Porsche. Diving equipment hung on the walls alongside two or three wetsuits. One suit appeared to be slightly damp.

"How the other half live, eh, Guv?"

"Other sixteenth *maybe*. Let's go and hear what Monsieur Rossignol has to say."

"Dear oh dear."

Gwen Ferbrache unlocked the front door of her house again, retrieved her shopping bag from the chair in the hall, went back outside, and relocked the door. No point in going into town and not picking up a few things while she was there, however pressing the main reason for her trip might be. Her preoccupation was such that it was fortunate she hadn't locked herself out, and the sooner she cleared her mind the better off she would be. *A problem shared*, she told herself as she hurried down the gravel driveway, particularly if you plan to share it with the son of your dear childhood friend, Vera Domaille, who happened to be a detective inspector with the Guernsey Police Force. Eduardo, whom she always called Edward.

She and Vera had grown up together on the same street, played together, shared secrets, including Vera's secret love for the Italian prisoner of war she had seen force-marched through the streets, to labour in one of the many underground structures built during the Nazi occupation of the island. Later, after Emidio Moretti had come back and married Vera, she had danced at their wedding, and mourned at their funerals.

They had not danced at her wedding. Her sweetheart, Ronnie Robilliard, had not been as lucky as Emidio. Enough of that. She had moved on, devoted her life to her teaching career and interests other than home, husband, children of her own. But Edward, with his father's dark hair and his mother's fine bone structure, held a special place in her heart. Pity he hadn't married that girl in England, but she was glad to have him back on the island.

Outside the twin whitewashed gateposts of her limestone cottage with its name, *Clos de Laurier*, painted in black on the right-hand post, she turned left past her hollybush hedge and descended the hill that led from Pleinmont Village to the coastal road near Rocquaine Bay on the western shore of the island. A quick glance at her watch assured her she was still in good time to catch the number 7A bus that would take her around the coastal road, inland past the airport, through St. Martin's, past Fermain Bay, and into the island capital.

There were fewer buses at this time of year, outside the holiday season.

Gwen was well into her seventies, but she could still keep up a brisk pace, thanks to years of walking the twenty miles of cliff paths on the spectacular south coast of the island, and the trainers she always wore on her feet these days. Not normally a lover of contemporary mores and modern inventions, she had quickly taken to the ubiquitous and practical footwear Americans called running shoes.

The day was clear and warm, and on any other occasion she would have enjoyed the feel of the spring wind blowing off the beach at Rocquaine Bay, sprinkling the surface of her spectacles with flecks of sand. She was briefly diverted by a flock of swallows and martins drifting high in the sky overhead, feeding off a swarm of midges over the tussocks of grass on the roadside. They did not necessarily presage a fine summer, but she was glad to see them. Briefly cheered at the thought of an excursion to see some of the birds who used Lihou Island as a stopover on their way north — flycatchers, wheatears, sedge warblers — she turned the corner past the clipped yew hedges of the Imperial Hotel, and crossed the road to the bus stop.

The sight of the classical frontage of the one-hundred-year-old hotel brought the purpose of her trip bubbling up again in her mind. *Bubble, bubble, toil, and trouble,* she thought. *They* had stayed there. All so harmless, perfect, so it had seemed at the time. They had met at the Water's Edge Restaurant in the hotel and she had felt no misgivings. Perhaps she was imagining things.

Along the curve of the coastal road, Gwen Ferbrache could see the bus passing Fort Grey, once known as Rocquaine Castle, used as a Nazi observation post during the occupation of the island, now a shipwreck museum, monument to the hundreds of lives lost in these inhospitable, rock-strewn waters. The Cup and Saucer, the locals called it, because of its shape, an inverted white mound above a wider grey concrete foundation. As the bus came nearer, she saw the driver waving and grinning. Lonnie Duggan — spring had arrived.

The reappearance of Lonnie Duggan in the driver's seat was as sure a harbinger of spring as the arrival of the first cuckoo. How he supported himself during the winter she did not know, but he was also a bass player with the Fénions, Edward's jazz group. The name meant do-nothings, layabouts and, although that didn't apply to Edward, it was an apt one for Lonnie, with his habit of semi-hibernation and air of cheerful lethargy. It was difficult to imagine him as a musician, even of an art form she found impenetrable, but Edward told her he was good. "Nimble fingered" was the unlikely adjective used.

"Hey there, Miss Ferbrache! Hop aboard!"

"Good day, Mr. Duggan."

Stifling mild irritation at being told to hop anywhere, Gwen Ferbrache climbed on board. About twenty minutes later, she and two other passengers were at the southern end of the Esplanade, trundling past the old dray outside the Guernsey Brewery, painted in the brewery colours of red and gold.

The bus terminus was a site, rather than a building, opposite Albert Marina. There was a kiosk for tickets, a public convenience, and a line of bus stops beneath a canopy of trees that included some sixty-foot-high turkey oaks that were under the threat of the chainsaw to make room for more parking, the subject of heated debate.

Picking up her handbag and her shopping bag, Gwen said goodbye to Lonnie, got off the bus, and headed toward the northern end of the town. As she passed the town church she noticed that there were two or three police cars and an ambulance leaving Albert Pier, sirens wailing. An incident on the cross-channel ferry perhaps, she told herself. A fight, someone taken ill, a drug seizure.

How the world had changed in her lifetime, and not always for the better. On Liberation Day, May the ninth, 1945, she had thought nothing could ever be that bad, go that wrong again. She sighed, waited for the light to change at the foot of Market Hill, and continued on her way to the police headquarters on Hospital Lane.

The morning sunlight shone blindingly off the stainless-steel appliances in the galley, lighting up in unflinching detail the bloated face and bloodshot eyes of Jean-Louis Rossignol. Hard to tell how much was caused by past excesses, or the shock of finding his employer's body. He was seated at a small, marble-topped table opposite Police Constable Mauger, his large hands clasping a mug of tea.

"Are you in charge?" he asked querulously, as Moretti and Falla came through the door. "Where 'ave you been? I sit 'ere and I am shocked, so shocked. *Mon dieu, c'est un cauchemar!* Did you *see* —?"

From the gust of liquor-laden breath that reached Moretti, the mug of tea contained something more than Orange Pekoe.

"Yes, I did see, Mr. Rossignol, and that's why you had to wait. There's not much space in here so, PC Mauger, could you wait outside?"

Moretti waited until the burly figure of PC Mauger squeezed past the three of them into the passage outside the galley, then turned back to the chef.

"Why don't you start by telling us how you came to be here, working for Mr. Masterson."

With a little whimper and a gulp of his toddy, the cook obliged. "I am cooking in Geneva, and I see an — ad, you say? — in April for someone to cook on a luxury yacht for the summer. Time, I think, for a change. So I apply, 'e 'ire me, and off we go, cruising to every port on the Riviera. I like it, always the change, and oh, the people I cook for!"

"Such as?" Moretti interjected.

"Big businessmen from Germany, Italy, France, America. Even sheiks — oh, the parties! And the women! Always pretty women from Mr. Masterson. Then suddenly 'e say we're going to the *Iles Anglo-Normandes.*"

"So this was unexpected?"

"Yes."

"Did he just say '*Iles Anglo-Normandes*,' or did he specify Guernsey?"

"Let me think — no, 'e say Guernsey, then 'e say where that is. Why 'ere? we all wonder, but the money's right, and 'e's the boss."

"Then what? Take us through yesterday and today. Were there visitors to the yacht when you arrived?"

"No. I think maybe tomorrow we 'ave company. Then Mr. Masterson say you all go ashore. Enjoy, 'e say. And for me to be first in the morning for 'is breakfast. Mr. Masterson is — was — Canadian. 'E ate a big breakfast in the morning."

"Did he speak French?"

"Yes, but not like me. Sometimes I 'ave the problem to understand. Adèle also, they speak French often together."

"Adèle?"

"Adèle Letourneau, the 'ousekeeper. Nice lady, never interferes with my kitchen."

"So, you came back this morning at —?"

"Nine, as 'e ask. I 'ave a key to the salon door, but that was strange. It was not locked."

"So everything would normally be locked up?"

"Yes. Mr. Masterson was so particular about that."

"Do you know who had keys?"

"Me, Adèle, and I think maybe that *petit salaud*, Smith."

"That would be who?"

"Valet to Mr. Masterson."

"You didn't get on, I gather."

"No one get on with that one. 'E once call me the friggin' fly in the fuckin' hointment."

A low burbling sound emanated from DS Falla, quickly suppressed as she bent over her notebook.

"I see. Now, what happened after you went into the salon. Describe what you saw."

"Dirty glasses I saw."

"You didn't move them?"

"I am chef, not valet. So I go through to the kitchen and there is no note. Always 'e leave a note for what 'e wants for breakfast. Often eggs and bacon, sometimes *crêpes* — 'e eat them with the sausage and the syrup." Rossignol gave a little shudder and continued. "At first I think maybe it is a trick by the *petit salaud*, but no, 'e is on shore, so I go to Mr. Masterson's cabin."

"Slowly now. Was the door unlocked?"

"A little open, that is also strange. It is always locked when 'e is in there, and for that cabin I don't 'ave keys. Then I see the legs. 'Mr. Masterson,' I say, and again I say it. Then I open the door and see — ah, oh, oh!"

Moretti pushed the mug toward the chef, who drank the last of its contents. Down the corridor outside the kitchen came the sound of a woman's voice, followed by that of PC Mauger.

"Jean-Louis! Jean-Louis!"

"Just a minute, ma'am. You can't go in there."

"Adèle!" The chef broke into a fresh burst of sobbing.

Moretti went out into the corridor. "It's okay, Constable. She can come in."

Adèle Letourneau looked nothing like any house-keeper Moretti had ever seen. Her lightly tanned features were expertly made up, framed by one of those deceptively simple hairstyles of heavy bangs and swinging, thick swags of bronze-highlighted hair that did not come courtesy of the little hairdresser around the corner. She wore jeans and a heavy navy sweater with a cowl neck. In one hand she carried a small overnight bag, and in the other she held a key.

"I didn't need this," she said, waving the key in front of her. "There's a policeman at the end of the gangway, ambulance, police cars — what the hell is going on?"

The housekeeper's voice was smoky with nicotine, her English accented. Close up, Moretti saw she was probably well into her forties and not her thirties, as he had first supposed. Before he could say anything, Jean-Louis Rossignol wailed, "Oh Adèle, Mr. Masterson is dead! Shot!"

"Dear God."

There was a thud as the overnight bag hit the ground, followed by the key, and then, almost, by the housekeeper. She swayed, and Liz Falla caught her.

"Here, sit down. We'll get you a glass of water."

The chef filled a glass with mineral water out of the fridge, and handed it to the housekeeper, who needed help from Liz Falla getting it to her lips.

"Sorry. This is a shock."

"Of course." Moretti gave her a moment, then turned to Jean-Louis Rossignol, who was whimpering softly on the other side of the table. "PC Mauger will see you to your cabin, sir, and I must ask you to stay there while forensics checks over the yacht. We will have an officer on duty at the foot of the gangway round the clock."

As the two men disappeared in the direction of the dining area, Moretti turned back toward Adèle Letourneau. The housekeeper was the colour of parchment, and her hand was still shaking as she took another sip of water.

"What happened?" she asked.

"Mr. Rossignol came in this morning, found no instructions for breakfast, went through to the master suite, and found your employer on the bed, shot through the head. Have you any idea why this might have happened, or who might be involved?"

"No, not as to who might be involved. But Bernard is — was — a wealthy man. I suppose theft was the motive. Was anything taken?"

"Nothing that we can see, but you will be the better judge of that. Did he have a safe?"

"Yes. In the bed-head."

"We'll get you to check, but there's no obvious sign of it being opened. Most thieves take what they want, and don't stay around to tidy up after themselves. And speaking of tidying up — there's a champagne glass with lipstick on it in the main salon. Is it yours?"

"No." Adèle Letourneau's hand on the glass stopped shaking. She had gone very still. Her guard was up, her shock controlled. "Bernard liked his babes, Detective Inspector."

"You think one of his babes killed him, Ms. Letourneau? Did you have any other visitors on the yacht I should know about?"

"No. But perhaps he arranged something in town, I don't know."

Moretti decided to change direction. "You called Mr. Masterson by his first name — had you worked with him a long time?"

"Yes." The housekeeper finished off the water in the glass, and reached over to take the bottle of cognac left by the chef on the stovetop. "If you don't mind, I'd like some of this, and a cigarette?"

"Go ahead."

Moretti watched as Adèle Letourneau poured herself a generous shot, and then pulled a packet of cigarettes and a lighter from the bag on the floor. The booze at this hour of the morning he could do without, but the thought of a cigarette and a cup of coffee filled him with longing. Surreptitiously he fingered the lighter he still carried in his pocket, and saw Liz Falla's half smile as he did so.

"To answer your question —" Adèle Letourneau lit her cigarette, inhaled deeply, and closed her eyes, "— we were once, what you might call, an item. When that was over, friendship remained, and trust. In his position, Bernard needed that, someone to trust."

"And what was Mr. Masterson's business."

"Bernard was a financier. He started off in Montreal, which is where I met him, but soon his business was as much in Europe as in North America. This summer his business was so scattered he decided to operate from the yacht. Besides, he enjoyed it."

"Financier, Ms. Letourneau. Can you be more precise?"

The housekeeper had surprisingly light eyes for a woman with her colouring, and they were fixed on Moretti like cold, pale marbles. "Bernard started out in Quebec buying businesses for rock-bottom prices when they were failing, turning them around, and selling at a profit. He built up a wealthy and influential clientele and contacts in North America and abroad, and gradually moved into being what he called a facilitator."

"A facilitator?"

Moretti watched Liz Falla write the word in her notebook, saw his partner's eyebrows disappear under the jagged line of her bangs.

"Can you give me an example?"

Falla's eyebrows revealed more than the housekeeper's eyes, fixed on him with apparent candour as she replied. "He was a middleman, putting together people who wanted to do business with certain goods in certain parts of the world. For instance, he just brokered a deal between Canada and Germany involving armoured personnel carriers."

"Impressive." Moretti pulled out the scrap of paper he had found in the magazine rack. "Would this have been one of Masterson's ventures?"

Adèle Letourneau glanced at the fragment and again her eyes met Moretti's, unblinking and candid.

"Oh, I don't think so. Bernard had moved far beyond this sort of business deal. But I know he was thinking of buying another yacht. This boat was proving a bit small."

Liz Falla put her pad away, and sat down opposite the housekeeper. "Did he have any family? Would you like to contact anyone?"

"There's only an ex-wife, no children. He inherited his first business from his father, and as far as I know he was an only child."

The housekeeper stubbed out her cigarette in a small metal ashtray on the table, and finished the last of the brandy in her glass. Moretti watched as the two women made eye contact, the housekeeper with that frank, straight look that revealed nothing. But maybe Falla could read her better than he could.

As he was mulling over whether to ask about guns at this point, or to wait until he spoke to Nichol Watt, Liz Falla asked another question. "Your chef says this trip to Guernsey was unexpected, Ms. Letourneau. You were more in Mr. Masterson's confidence than others. Do you know why he came here?"

Adèle Letourneau's gaze left Liz Falla's face and traversed the small galley as if in search of something neutral on which to settle.

"I have no idea," she replied.

As she looked at Moretti over the top of the housekeeper's shiny bronze cap of hair, DS Falla's brown eyes were far more expressive than those of the dead man's ex-lover.

Chapter Two

"**D**id you ever see anything like it, Guv?"

"Not in a bed-head I haven't."

"How much do you think was in that safe?"

"Depending on the current rate of the Euro, there had to be close to a million pounds, give or take a fiver."

"And she didn't even blink, did she?"

"She's good at that, not blinking. But I'd say Ms. Letourneau has undoubtedly seen many a million in cold, hard cash before today."

Liz Falla swung the police BMW through the gateway into the courtyard outside the police headquarters on Hospital Lane. In 1993 the Guernsey police force had moved its operations into the fine eighteenth-century building that had at one time been the workhouse. Popularly known as the Pelican, after the plaque high on the courtyard wall showing a pelican feeding its young on drops of blood from its own breast, it still carried the original name set in the brickwork: Hôpital de St. Pierre Port, 1749. In Guernsey, the past often serves the present in practical ways.

As they went into the building, the desk sergeant called out to Moretti, "Ed, there's someone waiting for you."

"Dr. Watt?"

"He phoned and left a message — here's his extension at the hospital. It's an elderly lady who says she's your aunt and needs to talk to you. Gwen Ferbrache."

"Gwen?" Moretti took the piece of paper handed to him. "What in the —?"

Liz watched this with interest. Her boss was not a man to reveal private emotions and personal feelings, and she once wondered if he had any. She knew better than that by now, having worked with him for a year, but she also knew he liked to keep his mask of cool detachment firmly in place. But he was looking anxious now, even startled.

"Seems a bit upset, so I put her in your office. Okay?"

"Your aunt, Guv?" enquired Liz Falla as they went swiftly up the stairs. "Do you want me to take care of her while you talk to Dr. Watt?"

"No, Falla, I'll talk to her. She's not really a relative, but she's the closest friend my mother ever had. This isn't like her, unless there's something really wrong. Normally she'd try to reach me at home, but I haven't been there for the past few days."

"That might explain it. My great-aunt Mabel gets agitated about the silliest things. She'll go on at my mother for days about getting a new dishcloth when she's got no need of another dishcloth."

Moretti did not bother to explain. This woman would not pester him about dishcloths, because she was more than capable of getting one for herself.

"But I do want to hear what Nichol Watt has to say, first, without an audience."

They went into another office near Moretti's that was temporarily empty, and Moretti made the call. At the sound of Watt's voice echoing down the line with its characteristic drawl, Liz Falla grimaced and silently fake vomited.

"Hi there, Moretti. Want to know something about the high-priced cadaver?"

"Time of death if possible, and something about the bullet that killed him."

"I'll know more after the autopsy, of course, but I estimate time of death to be somewhere between eleven and twelve o'clock, of a single gunshot wound to the head. Interesting bullet from what I can see, and I think they'll find it's a hollow-point. Everything looked neat and tidy on the outside, but it'll have done a hell of a lot of damage on the inside. I did part of my forensic training in the States, and saw some of these. Not the kind of missile I'd expect to find in the average British huntsman's gun cabinet, let alone on Guernsey. I think it should be sent straight to Chepstow. I wouldn't even waste my time sending it to the Jersey crime lab. We don't see many hollow-points around these parts."

Both of the islands had scene-of-the-crime labs, well equipped to identify drugs, analyze fingerprints, develop photographs, and take care of most of the basic needs of the island CID, but for some procedures the evidence was sent to the forensic labs in Chepstow, Surrey.

"Agreed. One other thing — he'd peed his pants. Before, or after death?"

"Before, in my opinion. I'll be able to tell you more tomorrow."

There was a click as Nichol Watt hung up the phone.

"I tell you, Falla," said Moretti, "he may be a shit with women, but Dr. Watt's great with corpses. You heard that?"

"He's never bothered me, Guv, but one of his harem is my stupid idiot cousin."

"Does she know about the others?" Moretti held the door for his partner and closed it behind them.

"Oh, yes, but it doesn't make one bit of difference. She thinks she can reform him. The love of a good woman and all that crap."

"Didn't read you as a cynic, Falla. You don't think the right woman can turn a man around?"

"No, I don't. Besides, I like the bad boys too. That's my problem."

Moretti was saved from any response by the appearance of Gwen Ferbrache in the doorway of his office.

"I heard your voice, Edward. I'm so sorry to bother you. I tried to reach you at home, kept getting your answer phone, and you didn't get back to me." She was smiling, but Moretti could hear the anxiety in her voice.

"It'd been a busy week, Gwen, and then I took a few days off. Went to Herm. But I'm glad to see you anyway. This is my partner, DS Liz Falla."

Liz found Gwen Ferbrache impressive. A pair of piercing blue eyes in a tanned face framed by short white hair surveyed her, and her hand was grasped in a firm handshake. She was wearing a skirt in a heathery tweed atop a pair of black and white trainers, and a quilted blue ski jacket over a pale blue turtleneck sweater. There was about her a sense of competence and self-sufficiency that certainly didn't suggest a tendency to overreaction, be it about dishcloths or anything else.

Introductions made, Liz Falla went to rustle up cups of tea, and Moretti took Gwen Ferbrache into his office.

"Now," he said, pulling a chair out for Gwen, and moving his own so they were both on the same side of his desk, "what's the problem? I know you wouldn't be here unless it was something serious."

"Well," said Gwen, placing her shopping bag on the floor and settling herself firmly against the back of the chair, "that's the problem, really. I don't know if it *is* serious, or whether it's my imagination, but I'd never forgive myself if I did nothing. You see, there's a child involved. No," she added, seeing Moretti's expression, "it's not child abuse — at least, I don't think it is."

At this point Liz Falla came back into the office with a tray, and cups of tea were handed out. When she made as if to leave the room, Gwen Ferbrache put out her hand. "Please don't leave on my account. Another woman's point of view might be useful, because this involves three women — well, a child and two adults."

"Go ahead," said Moretti, "have some tea and then start from the beginning."

Gwen Ferbrache took a good mouthful of tea and began. "As you know, Edward, I have a property in St. Peter's, the parish of St. Pierre du Bois, called La Veile. It's been empty for some time, mostly because it's at the end of a narrow lane full of grassy ruts that turns into a morass in the winter. Verte Rue, it's known as — green lane. Very difficult for cars, but it's a nice little cottage, fully furnished, which just needed the right people. And I thought I'd found them. Just over a month ago I saw an ad in the Wanted section of the *Guernsey Press* — I have it here." Gwen picked up her handbag, pulled out a scrap of paper, and handed it to Moretti.

"Desperately required immediately. House suitable for two females and a child, two years old," Moretti read out loud. "This telephone number they've provided sounds familiar."

"That's because it's the number of the Imperial Hotel, which, as you know, is quite close to my home. So I phoned and arranged to meet the two women."

"Go back a bit. Tell me your first impressions of the person you spoke to on the phone."

Gwen gave a little chuckle. "The first impression was that she had an American accent."

"American?"

"Surprised me too. But she was soft-spoken, not loud or pushy, so I felt reassured, I suppose. She said her name was Sandra Goldstein and she told me she needed accommodation for herself, her friend, and her friend's daughter, and that they would be on the island for an indefinite period. She said she was a writer of children's books, and her friend was an illustrator. I arranged to meet them at the Water's Edge Restaurant in the hotel the following day for lunch. When I got there they were waiting for me — the child as well."

"Describe them," said Moretti. "What age, how they were dressed, that kind of thing."

"Sandra Goldstein is late thirties, I'd say, and the other woman is somewhat younger. They sound alike, but they don't look in the least alike. Sandra Goldstein is olive-skinned, dark-haired, and quite tall. Her friend, Julia King, is fair-haired, shorter, and more rounded in build. As to what they were wearing — jeans, predictably, and quite nicely tailored shirts."

"And the little girl?" asked Liz Falla.

"A delightful child, very well-behaved and perhaps a little quiet for a two-year-old. But she clearly adores the two women, and clings particularly to her mother. Not surprising, I suppose. Her name is Ellie. What, if anything, it is short for they didn't tell me and I didn't ask. What struck me about her was her colouring, with such a fair-haired mother it was surprising, you see. She looks as if her father may be Hispanic, or possibly black."

"She could be adopted," Liz Falla observed. Moretti saw she had put down her teacup and was quietly taking notes.

"True. Oh, there are so many possibilities. And, after what happened, my imagination has run riot." Gwen sighed and twisted the handles of her handbag.

"Tell us what happened," said Moretti.

"They came with me the next day to see the cottage and loved it. 'It's perfect,' they said, more than once. They said they loved walking, and were quite happy to use the buses. They paid the deposit and a month's rent, and I gave them the name of a local taxi driver who knows Verte Rue and could take their luggage to the cottage for them. I left them to settle in and then, about two weeks after they moved in, I decided to pay them a visit. I went on my bicycle, because we'd had a dry spell and I don't mind bumping over the ruts, just as long as I don't get bogged down in mud."

"You didn't phone first?" interjected Liz Falla.

"There isn't a phone in the cottage, and they said they didn't need one. I imagine they use a mobile, I don't know. It was about three in the afternoon when I got there, and there was no sign of life. So I propped my bike against the gatepost and went to the front door. I knocked, there was no reply, so I peered in the window. The child was on her own in the front parlour, playing with a plastic lorry of some kind she was pushing around the floor. She looked up, saw me, called out 'Hi!' and came running toward the front door. I heard her trying to turn the door handle. Just then, Julia King came running from the back of the cottage — and I mean *really* running. But it was her face that gave me the jitters." Gwen Ferbrache shivered. "She looked terrified. And then I saw what she was holding in her hand — or, at least, what I think she was holding in her hand. Only it seems so unbelievable."

Moretti leaned forward and steadied Gwen's hands that threatened to twist the handles off her bag. "Tell us what you think you saw."

"A gun, Edward. I think that's what I saw. She was holding a gun."

Liz Falla stopped writing and looked up.

"Was it pointing at the child, or whoever was at the door?" she asked.

"At the door. She pushed the child behind her, and at that point Sandra Goldstein ran into the room. She saw my face at the window, thank God, and I heard her saying, 'It's okay, Julia, it's okay.' Then they let me in, and things became even stranger."

"In what way?" asked Moretti.

"They behaved as if absolutely nothing had happened. They gave me tea, talked about the delights of country living — spotting the first wild orchid, that kind of thing — said they were going to get bicycles, and then sent me on my way."

"Was there any sign of the gun?"

"No. Nowhere in sight."

"Have you been back to see them since then?"

"No! It was all far too unsettling, and I saw enough guns drawn during the occupation, thank you. But I thought I should tell you."

"You did the right thing," Moretti assured her, patting her hands. Liz Falla watched the gesture with interest. Demonstrative behaviour was not part of her boss's usual emotional toolkit. "I'll look into this — oh, don't worry, quite discreetly. I'll make some initial enquiries — child abductions and so on, they keep an international registry — and see what comes up. How did they pay you, by the way?"

"By cheque, drawn on a bank here in St. Peter Port. The account was in the name of Sandra Goldstein. There was no problem with it." Gwen had recovered her equilibrium. She removed her hands from Moretti's with an impatient shake.

"Can you think of anything else, however trivial, that struck you about them, or anything they said? Did they talk about America, or where they were from?"

"They said Connecticut, but that's about it. However, I did ask how they came to be in Guernsey, and Sandra Goldstein said one of their friends in the States had been here and showed them one of the tourist videos they give out at the tourist office on the Esplanade. They wanted a quiet spot for the spring and summer, because Julia King is recovering from a serious illness. Of course, at that point I asked no further, because I didn't like to pry. There's one other small thing, a comment Mrs. King made about the name of the cottage. She asked me what 'La Veile' meant and when I said 'Watchpost,' she said to Miss Goldstein, 'Isn't that perfect?'"

Gwen stood up. "I mustn't keep you any longer," she said, gathering up her bags. "Besides, I have some shopping to do before I get the bus back to Pleinmont."

"Would you like me to arrange a lift for you?" Liz Falla asked, preparing to open the door.

"Gracious me, no, young lady!" was the reply. "I like to be independent."

Just before she left the room, Gwen Ferbrache turned back and said, "Of course, Edward, my sight isn't what it was, and this could all be my imagination. They are two women on their own, used to living in a far more dangerous environment, and perhaps it was a stick, or something of that nature."

"Perhaps it was," said Moretti cheerfully.

Moretti and Falla watched the door close.

"Only it wasn't, was it, Guv," said Falla, gathering up cups and saucers.

"Oh no," said Moretti. "Not a stick and not her imagination. Not with this woman. Guns, Falla — we seem to have a theme going here, and it's not a common island theme."

"You've not got grounds for a search warrant, have you?"

"None. On our way out I'll round up PC Brouard and have him check those names you wrote down. We can do that for a start. I want him to look into a couple of other things as well. Gwen wondered if you might have any special insights. Have you?"

"Two, but they're not that insightful. First: how smart to mention a serious illness, because most people don't go prying at that point, do they? Second: whatever it is, one thing's clear. They are hiding from something, or someone, and they're scared — not just for themselves, but for the child."

"Agreed, but we'll have to leave it at that for now. You and I have got to go to the Esplanade Hotel. The crew are, I hope, safely corralled there, and I've sent DC Le Marchant to pick up passports and start to take statements. Come to think of it, I didn't notice what the yacht was called, did you?"

Liz Falla's grin always made her look even younger than her late twenties or whatever she was.

"Yes, Guv. My English teacher used to go on about dramatic irony, and I was never quite sure what she meant, but I think it might fit the name of Mr. Masterson's yacht. It's called *Just Desserts*. Only it's spelled like the pudding."

"Use every man after his desert, and who should 'scape whipping." Moretti held the door open for his partner. "And that was some whipping, Falla. Any thoughts on what we saw in the cabin?"

"All dressed up and nowhere to go, that was the first thing that came into my mind when I saw him."

"Right. Death was unexpected, but not his visitor. He'd literally cleared the decks, sent everyone, including his right-hand woman, on shore."

"*Petit salaud*, Guv — that's what the chef called the valet, right? What's it mean?"

"Little shit's close enough. Let's go and see what the *petit salaud* and the rest of the *Just Desserts* crew have to say for themselves."

The Esplanade Hotel is, in fact, not on the Esplanade at all, but tucked away on a hillside overlooking the harbour and the islands of Herm and Jethou. It is on a steep, narrow street that leads to Glategny Esplanade in the north of St. Peter Port, close to where Liz Falla lived in a flat in an eighteenth-century terraced house she had shared at one time with a boyfriend. The man was long gone, but the flat she had kept. She was fond of that part of the coastline, known as La Salerie after the ancient salt manufactory that had once existed there. It was away from the main shipping areas and marinas, yet close enough to the town to be convenient for work. Not that anything on the island was that far from anything else, but with the hours she worked it was useful to be only minutes away from police headquarters.

"Do you know anything much about the hotel?" asked Moretti, as his partner turned the BMW on to St. Julian's Avenue.

"Like I said, it's a four crown hotel. Not a five crown, I don't know why, but it's not that big. About a dozen bedrooms, I think. It's got great views and a super dining room, but pricey by my standards. Len and I had a couple of meals there on birthdays and such. Len's my ex, of course — well, one of them, but he lasted longer than most. Nearly two years."

Liz Falla gave a short, sharp laugh that had Moretti wondering if this particular episode in Falla's love life was not as easily disposed of as her occasional insouciant references to Len would have him believe.

"The owners live on Jersey, so there's a manager, from the mainland. Betty Kerr, she's called, and she's not lost time making herself at home. She's got a thing going with the head waiter, Shane Durand. Hope she knows what she's doing, because he's a lady's man, just like his dad. Here we are."

Liz Falla turned in through the gates and brought the BMW to a halt outside the pretty eighteenth-century

frontage of the Esplanade Hotel. It had originally been
one of the manor houses erected by the Guernsey privateers to reflect their dubiously acquired wealth and
house their ill-gotten gains. An extensive wing had
been added, but the original entrance and small tower
were still intact, and a beautifully maintained walled
garden descended the steep hillside.

Behind an imposing mahogany desk in the lobby,
embellished with flowers in a mammoth cut-glass vase,
they were greeted by the manageress herself. "Good
day, detectives. I'm very glad to see you, and I'm thank-
ing heaven it's not the height of the season. I'll be very
glad to get these people off our hands, and your officer
out of the corridor."

Betty Kerr appeared to be in her forties, well
coiffed, and discreetly dressed, as befitted her position. Her manner was crisp, suggesting steely efficiency
overlaid with a patina of professional charm. She did
not seem to Moretti to be the kind of female who fell
for womanizing headwaiters — but then, who knew
about women, and what *does* a woman want? If Freud
didn't know, was it any wonder Moretti had failed in
the only long-term relationship in his life?

"Understandable. But first, I'd like a word with
your night desk clerk. I asked if he could stay around."

"Bert De Putron. He's on the desk from eight to
eight."

Betty Kerr hit the bell on the desk, and a moment
later the desk clerk appeared. Bert De Putron was a
small man in late middle-age, who seemed only too
anxious to play a role in the drama.

"Shocking business, eh?" he said, with the smile of one for whom shocking business was a welcome relief from the nightly longueurs of desk-clerking. Moretti made a mental note to speak to the constable in the corridor about passing on information. "How can I help?"

"First, by telling me if anyone either arrived or left the hotel during the night."

"There's not too many guests at the moment, but there was a young couple who went out about nine, and came back around midnight."

"Give their names to DS Falla. How about the crew: Adèle Letourneau, Jean-Louis Rossignol, Martin Smith, Hans Ulbricht, and Werner Baumgarten."

"They all arrived just before I came on. Two of them left after dinner, and came back about ten-thirty. That'd be the Germans."

"Are you sure it was ten-thirty?" Moretti asked.

"Yes. One of the kitchen staff brought me a cup of tea as per usual. And I'm sure they were German, because that's what they were talking, and I know the sound of that lingo only too well. No one else left during the night. Allan Priaulx, who relieves me, says the fat one — that's the chef — left just before nine o'clock this morning."

"So who relieves you during the night? When you take a meal break, or whatever?"

"Well —" Bert De Putron's smile looked somewhat frayed, and his eyes avoided those of the manageress, "I have to take a break, right? So, around midnight I go to use the loo and get the meal left for me, microwave it, and bring it back to eat at the desk. But I'd hear anything, because of the buzzer on the door at night. It sounds through to the kitchen, and I couldn't miss it, I'm a hundred percent sure."

"Thank you, Mr. De Putron, that'll do for now." Moretti looked at Betty Kerr, who seemed a little more tight-lipped than when they had arrived. "Where are the crew members? In their rooms?"

"Yes. Ms. Letourneau has assured me she will cover the cost, and they had reserved a second night. In case it was needed, she said. But I thought I'd give you my sitting room for the interviews. It's further away from the other guests, and one of the crew is — difficult."

"I'll start with the difficult one. If you could show me your sitting room, DS Falla can fetch Mr. Smith,"

Moretti watched Liz Falla follow Betty Kerr upstairs, and made his way to the door she had indicated. The manageress's private space was comfortably but impersonally furnished, lacking individual touches such as photographs, suggesting someone who did not expect to stay around long. A few minutes later, he heard the strident approach of the valet, Martin Smith, and Liz Falla's imperturbably cheerful voice. "Detective Inspector Moretti will explain what has happened, sir."

"I should bleeding hope so!"

From the sound of the valet's accent, he was a Londoner. From his appearance when he hove into view, he would have been well able to defend himself in a tight corner, of which there were doubtless many, given his loud mouth. He was short, but built like a Tiger tank, with shoulders almost as broad as he was long, and biceps that strained against the thin cotton of his shirt. He was as unlikely looking a personal valet as Adèle Letourneau was a housekeeper.

"Why the hell are we cooped up like fucking criminals?"

His small eyes bulged out in rage beneath an overhanging brow highlighted by a ridge of scar tissue, trophy of some past fight involving knives, and he moved close to Moretti, his proximity as intimidating as any verbal threat. Moretti bent down until their eyes were level.

"Mr. Smith, your employer has been murdered, and you are here to help us with our enquiries."

He spoke quietly, but Martin Smith took a step backward as though he had been struck, and his monstrous shoulders slumped.

"Gawd, this is a friggin' nightmare. When? Where? The pipsqueak in the corridor told us nothing."

So the gossip was possibly confined to the night watchman. "Sit down, sir. The pipsqueak in the corridor did the right thing. Mr. Masterson was shot in his cabin somewhere around midnight. Where were you at that time?"

"Bloody here, wasn't I. He should have let me stay on board. I told him, farting around in some fancy hotel was not my idea of a good time, but he wouldn't have it. So here I was and here I stayed."

"Did you spend any time with other crew members?"

"Two of them some of the time, but they kept talking to each other and I couldn't understand what they were saying — they're German, you know."

"Yes. So, what did you do? Eat a meal, sit in your room — what?"

"The grub was good, I'll say that, and the booze was being paid for, so I went heavy on the single malt. Took a fancy to it when I was prizefighting in Glasgow. Then I watched television, Aussie rules football. Love those blokes." Martin Smith's eyes misted over.

"The housekeeper and the chef describe you as Mr. Masterson's personal valet. Is that another way of saying 'bodyguard,' Mr. Smith?"

If Moretti had expected the unlikely personal valet to weave and dodge the issue, he was wrong.

"If you mean was I watching his back, the answer is, yes."

"I see. Do you carry a gun?"

"I did. I had one in Europe, and then —" watching Smith, Moretti was reminded of a two-year-old deprived of his favourite toy "— Mr. Masterson took it from me, just before we made the crossing here. I told him he was doing himself no favour, and I was only messing about."

"What happened?"

"That ball of lard happened — the chef is who I mean. We had an argy-bargy, I pulled out my piece to scare him, just for a joke. He screamed blue murder, threatened to walk, and Masterson took it. For the time being, he said."

"What type of weapon was it, and do you know where he put it?"

"In his safe, I suppose, I don't know. It was a little beauty." The rasp in the bodyguard's voice became a caress. "Glock 17. Made in Austria. Very light, because it's made of plastic, see? Comes to pieces like a dream. Brilliant."

"Did you have a permit?"

"I didn't, but I suppose he did. I wouldn't know, not my problem." Martin Smith threw himself back in the chair, and its joints groaned in response. "I warned him. 'Don't let down your guard,' I said, 'just because you're in the back of beyond, that's when they get you.' He just laughed and told me to eff off. And look what's happened."

"Did he ever tell you what the threats against him were? Name names?"

"No, never, just told me to look out for anything. He was jumpier in Geneva, when the trip started, and then he eased up, more fool him. In his business, there's never a moment when you turn your back."

"His business?"

The expression in the bodyguard's eyes was now a little less candid. "Wheeling and dealing, that's all I know."

"Arms dealing?"

"So I heard, but I wasn't in on the midnight meetings, like his fancy housekeeper."

"Ms. Letourneau was present at business meetings?"

"In on everything, that bitch. In and out of the sheets with all and sundry, but she wouldn't give me the time of day."

"So she was in and out of the sheets with other crew members?"

"Hell, no! We were dirt beneath her feet, we were."

Moretti brought the interview to a close. "That's it for now, Mr. Smith. Since we're still examining the yacht, you'll have to stay here for the time being. Let us know if there's anything you need."

"Some clean clobber'd be good, and I suppose the krauts'll need some too."

"We'll arrange that."

As the door closed on Martin Smith, Liz Falla started to laugh.

"Little shit's right on the money, I'd say. But I know who he reminds me of. Popeye."

"Same muscle-bound walk, yes, but not so cheerful."

"Who do you want next, Guv?"

"The two crew members, separately, or, to quote Mr. Smith —" Moretti broke briefly into pseudo-Sondheim "— send in the krauts."

The two Germans, Hans Ulbricht and Werner Baumgarten, were very different from Martin Smith. Both were post-graduate students who had taken a summer job to help pay for further graduate work. Both were in their late twenties, both came from Hamburg, and had happened to be in Geneva backpacking when they had seen Bernard Masterson's advertisement. Only one of them, Hans Ulbricht, had previous experience sailing luxury yachts, but they were personable, and their intelligence combined with their physical strength and excellent English had appealed to Bernard Masterson, so he had hired them both. Moretti interviewed the experienced crew member first.

"I don't know much about handling a yacht this size. How easy is it for a crew of two?"

Ulbricht laughed. He was a good-looking, fair-haired six footer with a deceptively slim build and strongly muscled upper torso. "A piece of cake, Inspector. The yacht has a satellite-linked positioning system, an electronic chart program, and a laptop computer connected to an autopilot. It could almost run itself."

"Yet he hired you both. Was that something you specified as a condition?"

"No. I was pleased, naturally, but he told both of us to bring some decent clothes, since he might need us to talk to some of his guests."

"Who were those guests? Were they German?"

Moretti asked the same question of both men, and with both of them he was aware of evasive action of some kind being taken.

"Not all. Some. Businessmen, some petty bureaucrats — no, I don't remember the names — some pretty ladies who were probably high-class call girls, that kind of thing."

"Mr. Rossignol mentioned sheiks."

"Did he? There were some guests who may have looked like sheiks to Jean-Louis, but he knows more about shellfish than he does about sheiks."

"So there were none to your knowledge."

"None, but we hadn't been on board that long."

Werner Baumgarten was shorter, darker, and less sunny than Hans Ulbricht, but his answers were as pat and vague as his friend's. It seemed clear to Moretti they had agreed on what they would tell the police, and each corroborated the other. They had eaten with Martin Smith at the hotel, got some amusement out of insulting him in German to his face, then had gone for a walk in the town. They were vague about where they had walked, but this could have had as much to do with not knowing St. Peter Port as a deliberate covering of tracks.

What was really interesting was why they felt the need to be evasive at all.

"That Ulbricht's a hunk," observed Liz Falla as she scooped a sizeable portion of halibut into her mouth. "Almost too good to be true."

For such a slender person she can pack it away, Moretti thought, not for the first time. They had eaten fish and chips here together before, while working on another case, another murder. He liked the place, with its stunning brass fittings — the horses' heads around the bar, and the lamps along the windows that looked on to St. George's Esplanade, with Belle Greve Bay and the Little Russel shipping channel in the distance and, beyond, the islands of Herm and Jethou. There were a few locals in the public bar, who greeted Liz Falla as she came in and nodded at Moretti, but the lounge bar was quiet. They took a table near the window, away from a darts-playing middle-aged couple.

"An evasive hunk. Both of them were — evasive, that is. Why, I wonder."

"Could be they just don't want to be involved."

"Could be." Moretti drank some coffee and thought of the cigarette lighter in his pocket, and the packets of cigarettes on sale in the public bar. He ate a piece of fish instead. "I'd say from the exchange of glances between De Putron and the boss lady that he has been known to leave his post. I think we can rule him out as an alibi for the crew at the hotel, don't you? When we're done here, I want you to go to the harbour master's office and check into Masterson's arrival, how and when he cleared customs, whether they remember anything about him, or the rest of the crew. Then phone the station and give them details of the gun Martin Smith described."

"Right." Liz Falla pulled out her notebook. "Do you think he was killed with his own gun?"

"Possibly. What strikes me about that gun is that, if the little shit is correct, much of it is plastic, and it takes to pieces. Could be helpful getting it through customs. I'll have to find that out."

"But you'd think they'd pick that up on the X-ray machines, wouldn't you."

"Right. This weapon somehow skipped a customs inspection is my guess. And something else — did the CCTV cameras in the area pick up anything of interest last night? Let PC Brouard check the gun, Falla. You check the CCTV stuff."

Liz Falla put her notebook away and picked up her coffee cup. Her spiky, short haircut gave her an urchin, almost boyish appearance, particularly when she gave him her wide, now familiar, grin, showing the tiny space between her two front teeth.

"Let me guess, Guv. I'm looking for whoever might have left her lipstick on a champagne glass in the wee small hours."

"Right. And if she's not there, we have two other possibilities. That she came by boat, or she was already on board. You can drop me off at Hospital Lane, and I can take my own car from there."

"You're going back to the yacht?"

"No. It'll take the SOC people some time to get through there, so I'll stay out of their way."

Liz Falla smiled, thinking of her partner's rocky relationship with SOCO's head officer, Jimmy Le Poidevin.

"A bit of background on what Madame Letourneau called 'a facilitator' would be useful. Tomorrow morning I'm going to see someone who knows about guns, wheeler dealers, and million-dollar deals."

Chapter Three

Day Two

The parish of St. Martin, where Moretti was heading, is in the southeast corner of Guernsey, and contains some of the most spectacular coves and bays on the island. The coastline here is rugged and precipitous, the cliff faces sheer expanses of lichen-covered granite exposed to the elements, dotted in places with trees and undergrowth clinging precariously to an inhospitable terrain.

In 1940 an abortive attempt at a landing had been made by a group of Commandos at Petit Port, one of the little bays. In fact, that was all they had managed, to land and then strand three men who were not strong enough swimmers to get back to the destroyer that had delivered them.

Why there, of all places? And who planned such a cock-up? It was the kind of thing Moretti enjoyed mulling over with the man he was going to see.

Shape-shifter.

Dr. Ludovic Ross, classical scholar, fellow of Balliol College, Oxford, guest lecturer at Harvard and Yale, had taken for himself the name given by Homer to Odysseus the wanderer, the cunning No Man who could change his appearance and outwit the enemy, whether it be Lord of the Earthquake, or a man-eating Cyclops. Much of Ross's career remained classified, but from what Moretti could discover, the undercover work in which Ludo Ross had been involved had presented him with adversaries as dangerous and devious as any encountered by Homer's wandering hero.

Ross was not a Guernseyman. He had no true roots, he once told Moretti, because he was a colonial, and still thought of the country of his birth as his own. That country had now ejected foreign rulers from its soil, and he was *persona non grata* in a place no longer called by the same name. When he retired from academic life he settled in Guernsey, where his income would be taxed at a more modest rate.

"I've given enough to my country and I'm damned if I'm going to give back what I earned with the sweat of my brow and the perspiration of utter terror."

"You admit to fear?"

"Best way to deal with it."

It was Gwen Ferbrache who first introduced Moretti to Ludo Ross. She had run into him on Lihou Island, a small islet joined to Guernsey by a causeway at low tide. The priory that had been on the island had been the scene of a murder in the sixteenth century, but its appeal for Gwen was that it was on the migration route for countless birds on the wing to Western Europe. The three of them had a drink together one evening at the Imperial Hotel, and then one night Ross turned up at the Grand Saracen Club. He and Moretti talked about Charlie Parker and Billie Holliday, Oscar Peterson and other shared passions, and from time to time Ludo Ross phoned Moretti and invited him over.

Normally he would not go uninvited and unexpected.

"Always delighted to see you, Ed, but let me know if you're coming, won't you? There's a good chap."

"You're still cautious?"

"Habit of a lifetime, yes."

"How about postmen, that sort of thing?"

"It's the unexpected one looks out for. Though I don't like it when they change postmen on me."

What was it the *petit salaud* had said? Moretti turned his car into the narrow lane that ran above Ludo's house and braked to allow a startled rabbit in the middle of the road to make a decision. *Don't let down your guard just because you are in the back of bleeding beyond — that's when they get you.*

The rabbit opted for going back the way he came, and Moretti carried on, turning the corner that led to the steep lane down to Ludo Ross's house. But before that he caught a glimpse of the back of the house beyond an untrimmed hawthorn hedge entangled with blackberry bushes.

There were no windows on this side of the house, which was built against the slope of the cliff that led down steep, winding lanes to the coast. All the windows faced the sea, which could barely be glimpsed from them because of the wild profusion of trees and undergrowth that descended the cliff face. The house itself was curved, rather like a two-tiered cake of ivory plastered stucco. Beneath a steep-sided conical roof of pale grey tiles the upper storey was smaller than the lower, and a semi-circular balcony took up the extra space over the ground floor. No attempt had been made at taming the landscape, apart from a wide, paved courtyard outside the house, and there was no fence, wall, or gate. When Moretti asked why, he was told, "Because the kind of people I had dealings with don't have any problems with barriers."

Just before turning into the driveway, Moretti brought the Triumph to a halt, and called Liz Falla on his mobile.

"Anything on the CCTV cameras so far I should know about?"

He listened with pleasure to the low register of her disembodied voice. "Yes, Guv. There's all kinds of stuff, like people leaving the Landsend Restaurant and so on, but what's really interesting is the out-of-place person who shows up, if you see what I mean."

"Who is it?"

"Lady Fellowes, Guv. No mistaking her, is there?"

"None."

Of all the island residents who could have shown up on the CCTV cameras, none would have been more easily identifiable than Lady Coralie Fellowes. In the late 1930s there were few more recognizable faces, or bodies, than those of Coralie Chancho. She had first caught the eye when given a brief solo moment at the Folies Bergère, stepping out of the chorus line in a velvet *cache-sexe* and a headdress of ostrich plumes, to shoot at a straw-hatted Maurice Chevalier with a jewelled bow and arrow. The public demanded to see her again, and once they heard the unique voice with the sensual growl that came with the face and the body, Coralie Chancho became a star.

When that star declined, as is the fate of every fair from fair, thanks to the passage of time and nature's changing course, La Chancho made the career move every prudent woman in her position makes: she married money. How she came to Guernsey, Moretti did not know, but it was probably to do with holding on to that money.

"What was she doing?"

"Teetering along the deck, dressed up to the nines. The CCTV shows the time as one thirteen a.m. And she's the only woman on her own, anywhere near the yacht between ten o'clock and six-thirty the next morning."

"I've seen her at the Landsend, so perhaps she was there."

"Want me to check, Guv? I'm just on my way to speak to the customs people."

"Yes. I was planning to talk to Gord Collenette anyway."

Moretti finished his call and looked up. Ludo Ross was at the window of the Triumph, and alongside him was one of his Rhodesian Ridgebacks, Benz, his lips drawn back in a snarl.

"Put the window down, Ed, so he can get your scent."

As Moretti did so, the dog relaxed, and his master took his hand off the collar he was holding. "Park the car by the garage, Ed. Good to see you."

Ludo Ross was an imposing man, somewhere in his late seventies Moretti thought, who had held on to a fine head of grey hair atop a neatly trimmed white beard. The contrast was startling enough that it looked to Moretti when he first met him as if the undercover agent was still in disguise, with a fake beard hooked over his ears. But in no way did this bearded scholar resemble a jolly Father Christmas, with his hawk-like nose and light, uncommunicative eyes — eyes that now brought to mind the hard-boiled stare of the dead man's housekeeper to Moretti, as he drove into the paved courtyard.

"Good to see you, Ludo, and apologies for arriving unannounced."

"I was thinking of phoning you, as a matter of fact, to see if you were playing at the club tonight."

There were dark circles under Ludo Ross's eyes, as there often were, the loose skin looking bruised and discoloured. An insomniac who accepted his affliction as incurable and therefore, as he facetiously put it, not worth losing sleep over, he had once or twice persuaded Moretti to share his white nights with him after a session at the club. His record collection was exceptional, as was his wine cellar, but it was not a habit Moretti could indulge too often.

"Not a chance. That's why I'm here."

"So this is work related?"

"You could say that."

The dog ran ahead of them into the house, and was joined by his female companion, who made straight for Moretti.

"Hi, Mercedes. Remember me? I hope."

The ridgeback sniffed Moretti's extended hand and wagged her tail, then joined her mate. Together the four of them moved through the entrance hall on the right-hand side of the house, leaving a huge space to the left as a living area. This was covered by a pale blue Kirman carpet that extended the full width of the room. The décor and furniture were in spare, modern lines, the tones neutral, the paintings on the wall abstract. There were no photographs, no mementos of past lives or loves. The only indication of Ludo Ross's former academic occupation was the built-in mahogany bookcase that lined the walls from floor to ceiling.

Moretti accepted his host's offer of a beer, and waited until he came back, watched by the two dogs, who seemed relaxed, although they didn't settle until their master returned.

"So," said Ross, handing Moretti a glass of the Guernsey Brewery's Special Creamy Bitter, "what's up?"

"A body with a bullet in the head on a pricey Vento Teso in Victoria Marina, complete with a very pretty Porsche below decks, and a fortune in Euros in a safe in the bed-head."

Ludo Ross raised one bushy grey eyebrow. He surveyed Moretti over the top of his glass, took a gulp of beer, put down the glass, and smoothed his beard.

"Not your average Guernsey crime. What do you know about the body?"

"Bernard Masterson, a Canadian engaged in international deal making. Big-scale stuff, we're not talking widgets or ball bearings. According to his housekeeper, he just brokered a deal between Canada and Germany involving armoured personnel carriers."

There was a pause. Ross's hand on his beard stopped moving and for a minute Moretti thought he was going to tell him something. Instead, he asked a question. "What was a chap like that doing in Guernsey? Even if he had dirty money tucked away here, he didn't have to come near it."

"All the more reason *not* to come here. We are making enquiries, of course, through Interpol and Scotland Yard, and we may yet have to bring someone in, but I'd just as soon we didn't."

"Arms dealing."

Ludo Ross got up from the seat opposite Moretti and moved toward one of the long windows facing the courtyard. Ludo Ross always seemed to be on the lookout, whether he was standing talking outside the club, or on his own driveway, taking in what was going on around him — an unexpected noise, a passing car, a passerby brushing against him.

"You're in with some dangerous bastards there — at least, he was — many dirty and all of them devious."

"By devious I assume you mean dishonest."

"Depends what you mean by dishonest. In the world of these guys there is no black or white, and little grey. Morals of any kind are not part of the equation."

"No different from drug dealers."

"They *are* the drug dealers. Or they often are. Gone are the days when international security forces pursued separate entities that specialized in drugs, or prostitution, or gun-running. Now the world is criss-crossed with a vast, intertwined chain connecting drugs, gun-running, you name it."

"A perfect fit for Masterson. He was described to me as a financier, a facilitator, and a middleman. When I asked for something more precise, I was told about the Canada-Germany deal."

"He could indeed fit the frame. I'll give you an example of what I mean: Heroine from Turkey moves through the old Eastern bloc — Bulgaria, Rumania, across into the Czech Republic. From there it goes into Switzerland, Germany, France, England. The money the drug dealers make in the West buys Russian arms, which are then used by so-called freedom fighters wherever in the world there's a so-called freedom fight going on. One crazy-paving, interconnecting patchwork quilt, that's the kind of thing you're dealing with nowadays."

Moretti watched Ross walk back from the window, crouch down, and pat both dogs. He was wearing a navy Guernsey, putty-coloured slacks, and brown suede desert boots, his usual uniform, over a body a much younger man might envy.

"Thing is, Ludo, our dead man's arms deals appear perfectly legit. His right-hand woman was quite open about it."

"She's not going to talk about any deal he might have made with a proscribed government, is she? Someone killed him, which suggests there's something shady going on. We still come back to what he was doing here. It doesn't make any sense, not on a money-laundering, arms-dealing level. There's no doubt that Guernsey is part of a chain where dirty money is moved through London from Moscow, for example, but he could set up all kinds of shell companies to do that. Hell, he could be operating from a bank existing in cyberspace, run from a computer somewhere in the United States. Are you sure there's no personal reason for his murder?"

"Personal? As in a woman?"

"Who is this right-hand woman you mentioned?"

"Adèle Letourneau, also from Montreal. She describes herself as his ex-lover, now his housekeeper. His bodyguard — yes, bodyguard — says she was in on all business meetings. And she told me Masterson 'loved his babes.' She even suggested he might have been done in by some dangerous island femme fatale."

Ross gave a short bark of a laugh. "Damn few of those, but more likely to be a babe than an international arms dealer, or a babe set up by an international arms dealer. Won't be the first time they got to someone through his loins. A spy has no friends, which should include lovers."

There was an edge to Ludo Ross's voice, which suggested the awakening of personal memories. Moretti knew nothing about Ludo's private life, he had never mentioned a wife, or a family, or friends, and Moretti, who tended to be silent on the social context of his own life, was not about to ask.

"How does the housekeeper's alibi stand up?"

"Depends on whether you believe the night clerk at the Esplanade Hotel was doing his job."

Ross laughed, and this time it was the full, generous laugh that warmed his pale eyes. "Enough said. There is another possibility among many possibilities, and theft is still on the cards. Whoever your murderer is may not have been interested in traceable Euros, or put much faith in banks operating in cyberspace, but he may have preferred something else Masterson had in his safe, or on his person. Diamonds, for instance. They are portable, easily hidden, decidedly valuable, and a useful form of payment for less than squeaky clean deals. Have you found the gun? And what about the bullet?"

"A hollow-point, according to Nichol Watt."

"Nichol? He has experience in America, hasn't he? I think he told me he worked there for a number of years. I've always wondered why he left."

"In Nichol's case, probably to do with a babe. Like our victim, Nichol likes his babes." Both men laughed. "The bullet's gone to Chepstow for further tests, and I'll send divers down tomorrow if no gun turns up on the yacht. But I think whoever did this took the gun with him — or her. Why leave it around?"

"You're probably right. This kind of character often carries a gun himself. Did Masterson?"

"Yes, or his bodyguard did."

"That's right, you mentioned a bodyguard. So he expected trouble."

"Anywhere but here, apparently, because he'd sent him on shore for the night. The gun was a Glock

17 and it's disappeared. In your opinion, could a gun largely made of plastic that takes to pieces be smuggled through customs?"

"Highly unlikely in this day and age, and the bullets present another problem. It's more likely he got the weaponry he needed from sources close at hand, then discarded it. He'd have contacts, this chap."

Ludo Ross went back to the seat opposite Moretti and picked out a pipe from a rack on a nearby table. Pulling out a pouch from his pocket he started to fill the pipe and, as he lit up, the fragrant heady aroma of tobacco drifted across the room. Apricot essence and honey, some Oriental tobaccos, a touch of Turkish latakia. October 89, bought in bulk from the Dunhill store in London. Moretti put his hand in his pocket and touched the lighter he still carried.

"Sorry," said Ross, seeing the gesture. "Still on the wagon?"

"Clinging to the buckboard by my nails. Don't stop for my sake."

Ross smiled and put the pipe down. "I can wait. Where's that pretty partner of yours?"

"Is she? I suppose she is. Doing desk work, filling in forms, you know, all that shit."

"I heard her sing the other night."

"You did?" Moretti finished his beer. "What's she like?"

A sudden gust of wind outside the long windows of the living room shook the trees around the courtyard, blowing some loose twigs against the glass. Immediately the two dogs were up and over by the window. Moretti heard the male, Benz, growl softly in his throat. Ludo Ross looked toward the window and then back at Moretti.

"You haven't heard her? Shame on you, Ed. Not my kind of music, I thought, and then she sang Byron's 'So We'll Go No More A'roving.' Fair took my breath away, she did, and that's not easily done anymore."

"A friend told me she sounds like Enya with a touch of Marianne Faithfull."

Ross gave a short bark of a laugh. "Yes. The Enya is deliberate, but the Faithfull comes unbidden from God knows where in such a young woman."

His cool, pale eyes looked beyond Moretti, beyond the windowless wall, back to some past from which he had not yet detached himself.

Old mortality, the ruins of forgotten times.

"I nearly forgot —" Moretti pulled himself back to present priorities and took out from his pocket the scrap of paper taken from the magazine rack. "What do you make of this?"

Ross took the paper and walked over to the window. He looked at it a moment, then turned back to Moretti. "I assume there was something out of the ordinary about where you found this?"

"Someone had taken the trouble to remove whatever it was from a rack otherwise full of semi-pornographic magazines, knocking it over in the process."

"On the surface it looks like part of a brochure for high-priced yachts, but there *is* something unusual about it. See this?" Ross pointed at something in small print below the words *Offshore Haven*. The lower part of the letters had disappeared with the rest of the brochure, and it was virtually illegible. "That looks to me like 'limited partnership,' a phrase often used in business enterprises of various kinds, but not that often if you're just interested in selling a yacht. Looks like the middleman facilitator had something else on the boil, something that your murderer didn't want anyone to know about."

"We'll check. Shouldn't be too difficult if that's the name of the outfit."

"What about all those CCTV cameras? Did they pick anything up?"

Moretti thought about the ex-star of the Folies Bergère teetering, to use Falla's word, across the screen in the small hours. Better not, he decided. Lady Fellowes might have a perfectly good explanation, and she had friends in high places. As did Ludo Ross.

"I don't know yet," he prevaricated. "That's one of the jobs Liz Falla's doing." Moretti stood up, and the two ridgebacks were instantly alert. "I must go. Perhaps I could talk to you again, when we get more information."

"Of course. Let me know, anyway, when you're going to be at the club."

The wind was blowing hard enough to shake the lilac blossoms off the trees near the end of the drive, and somewhere a cuckoo was calling. Benz loped along by the Triumph until he reached the end of the property, then turned back to his master. In his rear-view mirror, Moretti watched Ross bend down to pat him, wave, and turn back into his house, closing the door behind him.

From the window beside the door, the one through which he could see out and those outside could not see in, Ludo Ross watched Moretti's car turn the corner, and listened until the sound of the engine was swept away by the wind. He walked back into the living area, crossing the blue stretch of Kirman, making for the wall unit that extended the length of the room opposite the windows. From an unlocked drawer he removed a folder, and placed it on the polished surface of the desk incorporated into the unit. Opening it, he shuffled through some papers, giving a grunt of satisfaction when he found what he wanted. It was a photograph, somewhat faded now, dog-eared, as if it had long been carried in a pocket, and often taken out by the wearer. Ludovic Ross smiled at the black-and-white image.

"He could use your talents," he told the face in the picture. "God knows I did." The smile turned to a grimace. "But then, could he trust you? Should he have trusted me?"

Holding the photograph by one corner, Ross started to tear it, then stopped. He placed it back in the folder, but this time it was not returned to the unlocked drawer. It was carried upstairs to the wall safe hidden behind the false bathroom cabinet, installed by a locksmith from East Sussex who had been flown in to do the job.

From the bathroom doorway, Benz watched his master stroke the cabinet mirror before turning away.

***

The rain was still holding off. Moretti thought about Liz Falla and the group she sang with, Jenemie. Why hadn't he made the effort to hear her? Not his type of music either, like Ludo, but that wasn't the reason. They had been together professionally for just over a year now, and he found her quick thinking, competent, and, from time to time, amusing. He wanted things to stay that way, compatibility with no confusion between the professional and the personal. He'd been down that road before, and it was a road that had brought him back from the mainland to the island.

Moretti headed back from the coast, picking up the main route through the parish of Forest toward the parish of St. Peter's, and the rented cottage owned by Gwen Ferbrache. She had pointed it out to him once when they made an excursion to some protected meadowlands nearby in La Rue des Vicheries to look at some wild orchids. Normally he would have asked Liz Falla to pay an informal call on the two women, on the pretext of checking on their personal safety. But since there was a gun and a family friend involved, making himself the target seemed the decent thing to do.

About ten minutes later he turned off the main road, drove past Torteval Church, with its conical nineteenth-century witches' hat of a tower, described in an old guidebook as "a supreme example of ugliness," and crossed over into the western section of St. Peter's. Slowing the Triumph to a crawl, he kept his eyes open for the menhir he remembered that marked the entrance to Verte Rue. The island was dotted with ancient stones and pre-Christian monuments, of which the most impressive was La Gran'mère du Chimquière in the gateway of St. Martin's churchyard.

Moretti had almost passed the stone when he caught sight of it, overgrown with brambles and wild-flowers. Campions, violets, and primroses ran riot in the hedgerows at this time of the year, before the obligatory hedge cutting in June, and only the weather-worn head of the stone peered through a coronet of white cow parsnip and nettles. Moretti stopped the car and backed up, turning cautiously into the narrow lane until he could see what condition it was in. To his relief the ground seemed firm, and ahead of him he could see a series of ruts leading to the cottage about a quarter of a mile down the lane. At least if he was in the car he had a better chance of escaping injury if they took a potshot at him.

It was a short, sharp switchback of a journey, the car wheels jolting alarmingly in and out of the ruts and over the occasional cross-channel made by escaping winter rains. By the time he got to La Veile, Moretti was more concerned with the car's suspension than with gunfire, and it was a relief to pull up outside the cottage and get out.

La Veile was a solidly built two-storey granite cottage, with a window on each side of the central door, set in a small porch. The two windows on the upper floor were framed by the tiled roof, which came down in an inverted triangle and squared off low over the front door. The place appeared deserted. Two bicycles, one with a child's seat on the back, rested against the porch overhang, and there was a multi-coloured beach ball perched in an empty flower box under one window.

Mindful of Gwen's experience, Moretti slammed the car door loudly, so that no one could be taken by surprise. As he did so, he saw a movement in one of the downstairs windows. Someone had pulled open the slats of the blinds installed in both of the ground floor windows. A moment later, the front door opened.

"Hello!" he called out. "My name's Ed Moretti, a family friend of Gwen Ferbrache. I thought I'd just drop by and introduce myself."

A woman stepped out from the darkness of the porch into the relative light of late afternoon, her long, dark hair swinging against her shoulders as she turned and shut the door behind her. Sandra Goldstein presumably.

"You must be the policeman," she said. "Hi, how are you? I'm Sandra."

She smiled at Moretti, but she did not extend her hand. As Gwen had said, she was above average height, but what Gwen had called an olive complexion looked more to Moretti like a fading tan. She was barefoot, wearing the jeans Gwen had called predictable, and a grey sweater with what looked like the logo of an American sports team on it, involving the head of a snarling jungle cat beneath the word *Panthers*. With her dark hair and intense, wary gaze, it seemed like a fitting logo for Sandra Goldstein.

"I'm a policeman," Moretti replied. "But this is just a courtesy visit to welcome you to the island and to make sure all is well."

"Of course it is. Why wouldn't it be in this perfect place?"

Sandra Goldstein laughed, and the sound was warm and happy. "Nice car," she said, nodding toward the Triumph.

"So you'll know who it is if you see it bumping and rolling up the lane."

I must at least see the child, thought Moretti, *even if I have to invite myself in.*

"Are you managing all right, so far from the bus stop, with your friend and the little girl?"

Sandra Goldstein laughed again, sounding genuinely amused. "After the States, Mr. Moretti, nothing seems so far on this island — heck, the longest bus ride is twenty minutes!"

Just as he was thinking he would have to make some excuse about checking the furnace or the door locks, the front door opened and a voice called out, "Sandy?"

Sandra Goldstein turned back to the house. "It's okay, Julia," she called. "It's Miss Ferbrache's policeman friend — you know, the one she told us about." Turning back to Moretti she said, "Won't you come in and meet the other inhabitants of La Veile? If you have time, that is?"

Standing in the doorway was Julia King, and what Gwen had not said was that she was remarkably pretty.

In appearance she was at the other end of the colour spectrum from her friend, with a porcelain complexion, wavy blond hair cut like a cap around her face, and a pair of deep blue eyes. She too wore jeans, and an emerald-green sweater that reached her knees and looked about four sizes too big for her. She smiled at Moretti, and there were dimples in her cheeks.

"So you are Edward," she said. "Miss Ferbrache is very fond of you, as she was of your mother."

"She's quite a lady," said Sandra Goldstein. "Come on in."

Moretti did not remember ever being inside La Veile, so he could not tell what, if anything, its new tenants had added to the décor. But the furniture in the sitting room to the right of the front door, and the armchair to which he was steered near the unlit fireplace, had a generic look about them. The place felt comfortably warm, and he saw a space heater against one wall.

"We don't light the fire until Ellie has gone to bed," Julia King explained. "She's much too fascinated by it. She's napping at the moment, but she'll be up again quite soon."

Accepting the offer of a cup of tea, so as to be around when the child got up, Moretti watched Sandra Goldstein leave the room and turned to Julia King. "I was sorry to hear from Gwen that you had been ill. You are convalescing here, I understand."

Julia King had taken the chair opposite him, and Moretti watched the colour rise up her neck and flood her face. "Yes, I feel much better than when I arrived. The rest has been good for me."

"You are an illustrator, so Gwen tells me."

"Yes." Julia King relaxed again, her face brightening. "I do illustrations for Sandy's books, but I do other work too. Would you like to see some?"

"Very much."

She got up and went over to a desk under the window and switched on the lamp, leaving the slats of the blinds closed, Moretti noticed. "Here we are, some of my other work."

"These are — exquisite."

Julia King's "other work" consisted of pen and ink drawings, some with a wash of colour, of country scenes, townscapes, shells, flowers, animals. None were bigger than postcard size, some tiny miniatures. The detail was painstaking, the control of her medium seemed to Moretti's untrained eye to be outstanding.

"Thank you. Your island has given me some great new material — see, one of your granite walls, bursting at the seams with flowers. I think they're just too wonderful."

From somewhere upstairs came the sound of a child calling out.

"That's Ellie. Please excuse me while I go get her up."

As she ran out of the room, Sandra Goldstein returned with a tray. "Julia's been showing you her work," she said, handing a mug of tea to Moretti. "She's very talented, and a terrific illustrator."

"Nice to have a friend as your illustrator." Moretti helped himself to milk, and refusing the offer of a biscuit. "Have you known each other long?"

"Since school days. I was originally a journalist, and when I thought up the characters of Warren and Wilma, I knew who I wanted to draw them."

"Warren and Wilma?"

Sandra Goldstein smiled broadly, lifting the slanting lines of her cheekbones. "Warren and Wilma Woodchuck. Julia and I are now doing our fifth book together."

There came the sound of a child's laughter, and a small girl ran into the room. She had curly dark hair, a skin like bronze satin, and huge brown eyes.

"Cookies," she said to Sandra Goldstein, pointing at the plate on the tray. "Cookies for Ellie. Please?"

Then she saw Moretti. She stopped and turned back to her mother, held out her arms, and started to cry.

From the door of the porch the two women watched Ed Moretti leave. The rain was just starting, and soon Verte Rue would be a nasty, messy, muddy, comfortingly impassable morass.

"Do you think he came because she saw the gun?" Julia King leaned against the taller woman.

"I don't know. He's got a difficult face to read. Not a poker face exactly, but you get the feeling he's looking at one thing and thinking another."

"It's an interesting face, isn't it? Didn't Miss Ferbrache say his father was Italian and his mother a Guernsey girl?"

"Yes. I was amazed at how quickly Ellie settled down. He must give off good vibes."

"What do you want to do with this?" Julia looked down at the card she held in her hand.

"Put it in the trash, I guess."

Sandra took the business card Ed Moretti had left with them, then saw the hand-written number on it. "On second thoughts, let's hang on to it, honey. Moretti gave us his probably unlisted home phone number. You never know."

"Then nothing will happen. Like an insurance policy."

"Right. Then nothing will happen."

The tail lights of the Triumph disappeared into the gloom. Julia King shivered, and Sandra Goldstein held her tight as she locked the front door.

Chapter Four

Liz Falla parked the police BMW outside the Landsend Restaurant and sat for a moment in the car, looking at the yacht. She could see it quite clearly, even though the floating dock and gangway were out of sight. The area of the pier along which Lady Fellowes had walked, perilously close to the edge, was in plain view, as was the police guard Moretti had ordered. Some of the SOC crew were still on board, and she had stopped off to ask if they had found anything of interest. Nothing, apparently. All the computers had been taken to Hospital Lane, to await the decision as to whether they, like the bullet, should be sent to Chepstow.

Liz had fond memories of the Landsend. In its earlier incarnation it had been little more than a glorified fish-and-chips café, her restaurant of choice when she was a kid. No hot dogs or hamburgers for her. Just lovely white fish in chunky golden batter, with a heap of thick-cut, greasy chips on the side and bottled tartare sauce.

But the Landsend, like Guernsey, had taken on another transformation. When money replaced tourism and tomatoes as the main income earner for the island, the Landsend moved upmarket, changing its menu and its décor. Gone were the wreaths of shiny plastic seaweed, the fishing nets hanging from the ceiling, one with a beautiful plaster-of-Paris mermaid trapped inside, clad in strategically placed seaweed and seashells, smiling seductively at the diners below. Gone was the five-foot-high statue of a cheerful lobster holding the Landsend's limited menu against his red-checked apron. Now there was a huge glass wall overlooking the harbour, white walls hung with sepia-tinted photographs, white linen tablecloths, single roses in crystal bud vases, fine china, and an ever-changing menu.

Gord Collenette was still the owner, but he had brought in a French chef and an Italian maître d'hôtel, and his carefully trained servers, both male and female, were chosen for their looks. It was certainly the sort of place where Lady Fellowes might well have dined, but it was hard to imagine she had stayed there until one o'clock in the morning.

Liz got out of the car and walked up the narrow tiled pathway between potted palms and hydrangeas to the main entrance. An elegantly dressed man, eyebrows raised, mouth pursed, stood on the other side of the glass doors, and watched her open them, making no move to help her.

"And what can I do for you?" he asked, the Latin lilt doing little to sweeten the tone, eyebrows descending as he scanned her dark suit, dropping to take in her shoes, with a quick flick back up to her wrist to take in her watch, Liz's only jewellery. Nothing sexual about it, but a rapid and skilled assessment of her potential as a paying customer.

"You can fetch your boss," said Detective Sergeant Falla, taking her ID out of her pocket and holding it up close to his face. "Tell Gord Collenette that DS Falla wants to have a word. Oh, and make it snappy, will you? This is police business."

The maître d'hôtel blanched visibly, turned on his heel, and disappeared behind swing doors. *Guilty conscience about something,* thought Liz Falla.

To Liz's right, through the narrow opening that had once been the Landsend lobster's kingdom, she could see the restaurant was doing good business with the suit crowd. Most of the diners were male, with a sprinkling of women who looked as if they were part of the same world as the men. Glass and cutlery clinked, an occasional laugh rose above the discreet murmur of voices, and Liz thanked heaven she was not the young woman sitting opposite the diner who bore a striking resemblance to the life-size lobster. The financial business had been the direction in which she had been heading before taking a detour into police work.

"Liz Falla! What can I do for you?"

Gord Collenette was a big man and his generous proportions overflowed the narrow space between the desk and the doors. His dark hair and eyes reflected his

Norman roots and, although outgoing by nature and relaxed of personality, he had a reputation as a sharp businessman.

"Hi, Gord. I want to have a word about a possible customer last night."

"Hang on, I'll get the reservations list. It was busy — silver wedding anniversary party."

"You won't need it — if she was here, you'd remember. Lady Fellowes."

"She was here, and you're right, I don't need any list to remember. As my Sally said, 'All heads turned when that outfit walked in.' According to my daughter, Gail, who was on the desk, when she was told we were booked solid she said she'd be quite happy to sit at the bar. Which she did, drinking Manhattans."

"Do you know what time she arrived?"

"Late-ish, after ten. Looked at her watch a lot. Everyone thought she was nervous and already tipsy, to use my wife's word."

"Who is everyone?"

"Me, for a start. Sally the waitress, Gail, Steve the barman — he's married to Gail."

"Do you know when she left?"

"Around midnight, I think, but I'll ask Steve. He's off-duty at the moment, but he'd have a better idea."

"Was this the first time she'd been in?"

"No, but it was unusual. She used to come with her husband, Sir Ronald Fellowes. War hero, I was told. But she's been in rarely since he died."

Gord Collenette gave one of those apologetic half-laughs that, in Liz Falla's experience, some males made when they were about to make an uncharacteristically intuitive or sentimental observation.

"He was a nice man, crazy about her, you could see it in the way he looked at her. I'm not one for fanciful stuff, but Sally once said it was like he still saw her the way she was, when she was a star."

"Interesting," said Liz Falla, amused to hear herself use Moretti's default response in similar situations. "When it comes to fanciful stuff, you must hear a lot of it in your business. Did you ever hear any gossip, anything at all out-of-the-way about the Fellowes?"

Gord Collenette thought a moment. "Well, I was told by a couple of people that Sir Ronald lost a heap of money at one time. 'Been taken' was the expression used, I recall."

"Really? Did anyone ever say who did the taking?"

"No. It was more like island gossip. You never know how these things get started."

Gord Collenette seemed suddenly evasive. With his particular clientele it did not pay to give credence to rumour and gossip, even if — and especially if — it might be true. Discretion and secrecy were as much a part of his life as that of the brokers and bankers who used the Landsend, sometimes almost as an extension of their offices. His dark eyes turned away from the policewoman.

"Is there anything else? I've got to get back to the kitchen."

"That'll do for the moment — oh, did you happen to notice if Lady Fellowes was carrying a handbag, or a bag of any kind?"

Gord Collenette grinned. "Not my thing, Liz, noticing handbags. But she paid cash for her Manhattans, I remember. I'll ask Sally and Gail."

"Great, thanks. We may have to talk to some of the other staff, some of the silver wedding party, but that's it for now."

"So, Liz —" the restaurateur's eyes turned back in her direction "— what's Lady Fellowes been up to? She's doolally, but she looks a bit frail to me to be up to anything."

"Can't tell you, Gord, if she's been up to anything. But as you can see, there's an investigation going on at the moment, and we are talking to anyone who was seen around this area yesterday evening."

"On the CCTV cameras, I imagine. This is about whatever is going on over at that luxury yacht?"

"Right."

As she turned to leave, Gord Collenette held the door open for her.

"Oh, by the way — that doorman of yours. What do you know about him?"

Gord Collenette looked surprised. "Why do you ask?"

"Just curious. That's quite an attitude he's got."

"Isn't it, though?" said Collenette proudly. "His name is Vittorio DeBiase and he came with excellent references. Don't ask me why, but élite diners expect to be treated like he's stomping on them."

Outside the Landsend a brisk wind was blowing the potted palm trees and flapping the awning over the entrance.

"Liz! Hey, Liz Falla, fancy bumping into you!"

Liz Falla closed her eyes. Maybe if she called on her necromantic ancestors, Denny Bras-de-Fer would be whisked off in a cloud of fire and brimstone. She opened her eyes.

No such luck. There he stood, long blond hair blowing in the wind, long body, long legs, languorous smile. Bedroom eyes. Where was her Becquet witch blood when she needed it?

"Hey, Denny. I don't fancy bumping into you."

She had once. Fancied bumping into him, that is. In one insanely stupid moment of weakness she had allowed those bedroom eyes to persuade her into bed with him, and, after a night of remarkable physical abandonment with a complete lack of commonsense and intelligent objectivity, she had opened her eyes the next morning and known she had done something very, very silly.

Denny Bras-de-Fer was a fraud. Not a criminal — not quite — but even his name was recently acquired. It was now about two years since Englishman Dennis Bradford and his fiddle landed in Jersey to play for the tourists wherever he could get a job. With his good looks, his charm, and a touch of larceny, he did very nicely for a few months, writing the occasional article for the *Jersey Evening Post* and appearing on Channel Television, until his somewhat slanderous account of the love life of a local celebrity hit the air waves and, rechristened Denny Bras-de-Fer, he took flight with Aurigny Airways to Guernsey. He played in bars, restaurants, took up his writing career once more with the *Guernsey Press*, and slept with anyone he thought might be useful to him. If they would let him, and there were few who said no.

Liz Falla was one of them.

"Hey, no fair. You dumped me. When are you going to invite me to play with Jenemie?"

Here was the problem. You could throw Denny out of your bed, but it was difficult to throw him out of your life.

"Never, Denny. I already told you."

This was the other problem with Denny Bras-de-Fer. He was brilliant in bed, not bad with the pen, but not very good with the fiddle.

"Worth a try. So, Liz, what's going on with the luxury yacht? Some American been murdered? What are the divers looking for? A gun is what I hear. Right?"

"Come off it, Denny. None of your business."

"But it's your business, isn't it? For old times' sake, give me a scoop, darlin'."

"Get lost, Denny. I'm on duty."

Denny Bras-de-Fer hunched his shoulders and gave one of his carefully crafted wry smiles that crinkled up his eyes. "Sorry you feel that way, Liz. See you around."

With a wave of his hand he sauntered off down the pier, leaving Liz with the uneasy feeling she had, somehow, told him too much.

As she got back into the car, her mobile rang. It was Moretti.

"I'm on my way back to the station. Leave the customs people for later, Falla. I want to look at the

CCTV tape, and I want you along when we go to Lady Fellowes's place."

Even at night, Lady Coralie Fellowes stood out on the Albert Pier CCTV camera like an orchid in a field of crabgrass. She was wearing a long, flowing dress topped with what looked like a feather boa, and a pair of very high heels.

But what was most striking about the image on the screen was the furtive way she moved, body slinking almost theatrically into the eye of the camera, with lowered head and tiny, tottering steps. Clearly the woman was fragile, a wraith on the screen, but this was more than frailty; this was fear.

"Run it again, Falla. Hell, she's close to the edge, isn't she? For a moment, I thought she was going right in — look. What's she doing?"

"Throwing something away was what I thought. I'll freeze it and try the zoom."

"There — right there. Hold it."

Time and Lady Coralie Fellowes stood still.

"She's throwing something in the water, Guv — she took it from her bag. It's a bit hidden by the boat, but let's see — I think it's a gun." Liz Falla's deep voice rose an octave.

"So do I."

So, was it going to be that simple? Something personal? Sex, and not money, after all? And yet, Coralie Fellowes had to be well over eighty years old and, from the sound of things, the murder victim liked them young.

"Okay, Falla, get on to the harbour master's office and arrange for divers. I want the area covered by the camera and around the yacht searched. Tell them they're looking for a weapon, most likely a gun. I want a word with PC Brouard, and then we'll head out."

Moretti found PC Brouard at the desk in the entrance lobby, chatting with the duty sergeant. The discussion seemed to be about football, and was stirring up intense emotions in both men. The young constable turned around, his face the colour of a Manchester United jersey.

"Jerseys, PC Brouard."

"Jerseys, sir?"

With a cynical curl of the lip, the desk sergeant resumed his paperwork.

"Yes, jerseys. I want you to check up on something for me, and the jersey in this case is almost sure to be American and a sports sweater of some kind — football, basketball, I don't know. It's grey, but there could possibly be other colours. It has the word *Panthers* above the face of a snarling panther, complete with paws and claws. Also, check out a series of children's books about Warren and Wilma Woodchuck by Sandra Goldstein, illustrated by Julia King."

PC Brouard had returned to his normal colour. "Woodchucks?" he queried incredulously, scribbling in his notebook.

"Right, woodchucks. Anything you find, bring it directly to me." Moretti spelled the names of both woodchucks and both women for the constable and went outside. Liz Falla was already waiting with the car.

"The divers will get started this afternoon, Guv. That should give us time to be there, if they bring anything up."

"Good. You know where we're going?"

"I checked. St. Andrew's Parish, near the Chemin du Roi."

The parish of St. Andrew is south of St. Peter Port. Even before the island was divided up into parishes it was separated into fiefs, holdovers from the ancient feudal system. Tenants owed allegiance to the local seigneur, but were able to rule themselves reasonably democratically through the feudal courts. Most of the ancient customs were, however, long gone.

Moretti and Falla's route took them past one of the smaller fiefdoms, the Manor of Ste. Hélène, now in private hands, and St. Andrew's Church, carefully restored to its twelfth-century self, after eighteenth-century changes had weakened its structure. In an island this size, the past and present were often juxtaposed with jolting speed. Once past the squat spire and constellations of the old church they crossed the Candie Road, close to the site of the vast German Underground Hospital, relic of the Nazi occupation, now a tourist attraction. They then turned into a narrow lane near the borders of the parishes of Forest and St. Martin.

As they jolted along, Moretti thought of his visit to La Veile.

"I went to see Gwen Ferbrache's tenants this morning. There's something, I don't know what, but I don't think the child is in danger, and I don't think Gwen is either. PC Brouard is checking some stuff on the Internet for me."

"Then you can set Miss Ferbrache's mind at rest — oh, isn't this a pretty place."

Ahead of them, Lady Fellowes's home was bathed in sunshine. It was a typical two-storey Guernsey farmhouse in ivy-covered granite, a curved stone archway around the front entrance, and an extension built at right angles to the main structure. Ivy, moss, and pennywort covered the crumbling stone wall through which the car passed into a small, cobbled courtyard.

"Lots of upkeep," observed Liz Falla, bringing the car to a halt, "but lots been done. New windows, new roof. Tiles instead of thatch. But the witches' seat is still up there, near the chimney. Only it's not really a witches' seat, my dad says, it held up the edge of the thatch. I prefer to believe my dad. You know how I feel about the whole witch thing."

"Right," Moretti responded.

He knew how Falla felt. She had an aunt who chose to believe the maternal line was descended from one of the premier providers of witches in Guernsey dim and distant past.

"There's a face in the window."

There was. A pale circle, a flash of something

bright, then it was gone. Next to Moretti, Liz Falla suddenly shuddered and sneezed.

Moretti looked at her, eyebrows raised, but she said nothing.

"Anyway, witches or no witches, if your thumbs prick, let me know, because I plan to leave most of the talking to you."

The front door opened, and Coralie Fellowes stood there.

"I am so glad to see you. Do come in," she greeted them, the perfect hostess. She was in full maquillage, kohl-rimmed eyes set in a nicotine-raddled face beneath black, close-cropped hair, cheek curls sprayed into position. Her dress was an extraordinary rainbow of colours, salmon pink, orange, scarlet, and powder blue. Had she been expecting them? Was the Guernsey grapevine *that* good? Moretti took out his ID.

"Lady Fellowes, I am Detective Inspector Moretti, and this is Detective Sergeant Falla. We —"

Coralie Fellowes held out a thin, scarlet-taloned hand, burdened with rings, drooping wearily from an insubstantial, skeletal wrist.

"There's always a catch, isn't there? A price to pay for pleasure, don't you think?"

Her voice was still seductive, husky with nicotine and age, the accent beguiling. Moretti took the proffered hand in his. Her skin was cold, cold, cold.

"This is an official visit, if that's what you mean, Lady Fellowes. May we come in?"

"I have already invited you."

She stood to one side and smiled at Moretti, hardly glancing at his partner.

"Do you live alone, Lady Fellowes?" Liz Falla asked, as she and Moretti squeezed themselves into the narrow entrance hall.

"Yes. If it's any of your business."

There was no smile for Liz Falla. Coralie Fellowes made no attempt to hide her hostility toward the younger woman, and Moretti saw he might have to change his plan of attack. Clearly, the former star of the Folies Bergère still looked on other women as rivals.

"You invited us in before checking who we were. That's risky."

"Far more risky things in life than letting a stranger in your door, wouldn't you agree?"

This was directed at Moretti with what once must have been a coquettish look from under pencilled eyebrows. *Very Clara Bow,* he thought, *thank God I brought Falla with me.*

"Such as, Lady Fellowes?"

"I'll tell you when you tell me what you're doing here."

She waved her hand in their direction and tottered ahead of them toward a room off the narrow hall. A blast of perfume drifted toward them, heavy with musk and rose. She had very long legs.

The room they entered was a symphony of pinks, apricots, and reds, not a cool colour in sight. Paris boudoir with a touch of the *soukh*. Berber carpets underfoot, a cornucopia of tasselled cushions covered in pink and gold silk. English-style armchairs upholstered in what looked like old Persian rugs, a chaise lounge draped in a huge, crimson, fringed shawl. The smell of Sobranies hung heavy in the air.

"Do sit down. A drink? No? Of course, you are on official business."

"These are — remarkable." Moretti gestured around him.

Photographs in silver frames, mahogany frames, gilded frames. Paintings and portraits and miniatures. A small bronze statue. Coralie Chancho in silver lamé, Coralie Chancho in black chiffon, Coralie Chancho in countless strings of pearls, Coralie Chancho in ostrich feathers almost as tall as she was. Coralie Chancho in nothing at all.

"But of course. They are me. You like them?"

"They are beautiful," said Liz Falla, and was rewarded with a smile in her direction.

"I was beautiful." The pink-shaded lamps that lit the room softened the lines on Coralie Fellowes's face. "But just as important, I played my cards right. Not all of them did, you know."

Lady Fellowes arranged herself à la Bernhardt on the chaise, and Moretti and Falla sat opposite her on matching gilt chairs. Like an audience.

"I'm sure," Falla responded.

Moretti added, "Not all of them would have been clever enough."

This time Coralie Fellowes directed her response toward Liz Falla. "Ah, to tell a beautiful woman she is intelligent! So irresistible."

"Right."

Falla smiled and pulled out her notebook in what she hoped was a non-threatening manner, and pressed on. "We are making enquiries, Lady Fellowes, into an incident last night on a yacht in Victoria Marina. The owner, a Mr. Bernard Masterson, was killed some time during the night. We are checking on anyone who was in the area at the time."

"Killed? Murder? Men fought over me, you know. But that was long ago. Why would a dead man on a yacht be of any interest to me? I live a quiet life, here in my little hideaway."

Her voice trailed off into a whisper and she turned her face away from them, her long red nails digging into the brocade-covered arm of the chaise.

"But last night, Lady Fellowes, you went to St. Peter Port, and you were at the harbour, late at night."

"Who told you this?" She seemed shaken, as much as angry, leaning toward Liz Falla as she spoke.

"There is a closed-circuit television camera in the area and you are on it. There is no mistaking you."

"There wouldn't be, would there?" Suddenly, she was all vivacity, smiling widely, showing a mouth of yellowed teeth.

"Why were you there?"

"What was I wearing?"

Prevarication? *Or is it?* thought Moretti. Leaning close to Falla, she seemed eager to hear the answer.

"A long dress, looked like chiffon to me," Liz Falla replied. "And a wrap — marabou, was it?"

"You are right. My Poiret, I remember now. I gave myself a night on the town. No crime, I think. So, I was on camera?" Coralie Chancho seemed delighted to hear of her CCTV appearance.

"Yes. Where did you spend the evening?"

"At the *boîte* at the end of the pier. I have been there before."

"The Landsend Restaurant."

"My husband used to take me."

Coralie Fellowes put her hand over the edge of the chaise and picked up a photograph from the table alongside it. A good-looking middle-aged man smiled back at her. Even in the photograph the eyes were warm, loving. She put a finger to her lips, kissed it, and then put it on his face.

"I went for old times' sake."

"How did you get there?"

"By taxi."

"And you were not picked up at the restaurant?"

"The camera does not lie, they say."

She's playing games, Liz Falla thought. "No, it doesn't," she agreed. "In that case, what did you throw into the water?"

Coralie Fellowes' hostility returned. "I had a cigarette and I threw an empty packet into the water."

"You are not smoking on the camera, Lady Fellowes," Moretti interjected.

A shrug of the shoulders, a little moue of the mouth. "My memory is not what it was. Why — what did it look like?"

The kohl-rimmed eyes challenged Moretti, all seduction gone from them. Physically frail she may be, but she's tough as old boots, he told himself.

"A gun, Lady Fellowes."

She did not flinch, or avoid his gaze, and he was reminded of Masterson's housekeeper.

"I think not, Inspector," she said.

"We have divers searching the area. You wouldn't like to reconsider your reply?"

"I would not." A fringe of heavily mascaraed eyelashes now hid her eyes from Moretti. "If a gun killed this man, then you may find one, *n'est-ce pas?* Proves nothing, does it? *Mon dieu, que vous êtes beau.*"

The sudden switch was as disconcerting as she intended it to be. Moretti recoiled as if she had touched him physically. Liz Falla blinked, looked at Moretti, and hastily back at her notebook. Coralie Fellowes laughed.

"Handsome is as handsome does, say you English, and I always preferred the handsome ones doing it, Inspector."

She laughed again, raucously. Scratch the surface and there she was, the streetwise chorine, the tough little girl who had survived and prospered to become a tough old woman, capable of killing. No doubt about that. But why?

Moretti got to his feet. "That will do for now, Lady Fellowes, but we shall have to ask you to come to the station, and I suggest you get in touch with your lawyer first. If you think of anything else, here is the number to call." He took out one of his cards and handed it to her.

"Long time since a man gave me his number. But I never phoned them, you know. They always phoned me." She peered at the card, her eyes disappearing from view between heavy black fringes. "Moretti, I think? Not an island name."

"No."

"The dress —" Liz Falla put her notebook away "— you said the one on camera was a Poiret. What about the one you are wearing now?"

"Ah, my coat of many colours." Coralie Chancho's voice took on a crooning sound as she stroked the fabric. "Sonia Delaunay. Delicious." The crooning sound became a quavering, faltering singing, and the song was "La Vie en Rose."

Quand il me prend dans ses bras, qu'il me parle tout bas, je vois la vie en rose.

In the pink-lit museum of her past life, Coralie Chancho was back performing on some long-gone stage. Gently, quietly, Liz Falla started to sing with her.

Il me dit des mots d'amour, des mots de tous les jours, et ça me fait quelque chose.

It was the first time Moretti had heard his partner sing. It was surreal. The setting and the song blended, and the liquid flow of Liz Falla's voice against the cracked-bell sound of Coralie Chancho's smoke-shattered vocal chords shivered through his veins and the length of his spine.

"Pretty, isn't it? Look at that engraving on the barrel, all those leaves and scrolls and whatever. Never thought you could say that about a gun, but this one's like an ornament, right?"

Liz Falla shivered and pulled her raincoat collar up around her neck.

A chilly wind blew across the marina, and a light rain had started to fall. A small group consisting of Moretti, Falla, the harbour master, two divers, and a constable from the uniformed branch were gathered around the tiny object on a tarpaulin spread on the ground. Nearby stood a melancholy group of seagulls, hoping for a chance at any leftovers that might remain. The diver who had brought up the gun touched the handle, which still gleamed through the sludge from the bottom of the harbour.

"Looks like mother-of-pearl. My granny had some cutlery with this stuff on it."

"It is," said Moretti. "And the trigger's gold-plated from the look of it. It's a Browning Baby — lady pistol, pocket pistol, various names. Some versions of it became the American Saturday-Night Special."

Moretti looked down at the constable, who was still crouched over the small pistol. "Le Marchant, I'm leaving this with you. Get it to the SOC lab."

Le Marchant eased the tiny object into a plastic bag.

"So that's the murder weapon," said the harbour master, who'd come along for the ride, murder not being a common occurrence in his fiefdom.

"No," said Moretti. "That's not what killed him. There's no way that gun shot the bullet that was in Masterson's head. No way."

"You mean there are *two* guns?"

The diver stood up and swore, unzipping the front

of his wetsuit. "Shit! I thought we'd got the weapon sewn up with this baby. If you don't mind me saying, Ed, isn't that unlikely? With the yacht moored right here, and the fact we don't get that many guns laying around — hell, this isn't New York."

"Don't get me wrong," Moretti stood up, thrusting his hands deep into his jacket pocket, encountering his lighter talisman as he did so, "I didn't say it has nothing to do with Masterson's murder. I said it was not the gun that killed him."

"Holy shit," said both divers in unison

"My feelings exactly," said Moretti.

Sometimes he had a glass or two of wine at the Grand Saracen, but mostly he didn't, unless there was someone like Ludo Ross in the club. "Not a chance," he'd said to Ludo, and now he regretted it. After he'd written his reports for Chief Officer Hanley he didn't feel like returning home, so he'd eaten in town, and then shown up at the club.

The Grand Saracen was named for a legendary Guernsey pirate and operated out of one of the great vaulted cellars of an eighteenth-century house that faced the harbour. Above it was the restaurant once owned by his father, and named after him: Emidio's. Moretti still retained a part interest in both businesses, but the restaurant was run by a distant relation of his mother's, and the club by a tough and efficient local woman, Deb Duchemin.

Tonight he saw no one he knew well, so the pleasure was in the playing. The audience was small, but they were in the pocket tonight — he and Lonnie Dwyer, Garth Machin, and Dwight Ellis on drums. Garth was his usual scatological self, peppering his remarks with oaths, insults, and cuss words, but his playing was bittersweet — the one not unconnected with the other, in Moretti's opinion.

In the immortal words of Charlie Parker, if you don't live it, it won't come out of the horn. Garth would never give up his Fort George mansion for a garret in town. But the angst produced by his poor-little-rich-boy lifestyle enhanced the sound of his alto-saxophone. Behind Moretti's own playing lay the echo of Falla and Coralie Fellowes's voices and, from time to time, he found himself "going out," leaving the music's harmony and rhythm behind, returning to meet the others again. Playing Bud Powell's "Tempus Fugit," the smooth sound of Miles Davis's trumpet in his head blending with Garth's sax, remembering Coralie Fellowes's final words, directed at Falla.

Jeune fille en fleur. Young girl in bloom.

A scattering of applause as the set ended, and Moretti automatically reached up to find his unfinished cigarette waiting for him. But there was no welcoming curl of smoke against the dim light and he groaned out loud.

"Want one?"

Dwight Ellis took a pack out of his shirt pocket and shook it in Moretti's direction. Above his drums, Dwight's skin gleamed like lovingly burnished cherrywood, hand rubbed by a hundred willing handmaidens — which, given Dwight's success with women, probably had been. There was something about Dwight's cheery insouciance and tender smile that awoke a maternal response in females. That, and the raw energy of his playing, often led to the bedroom.

"Get thee behind me, Dwight."

"Okay, man. Chill out."

Dwight grinned, shrugged his shoulders, and shook loose a cigarette for himself.

Moretti turned away. Beyond the lights he could hear a familiar bray of a laugh, a savage bray, teetering on the edges of intoxication. Nichol Watt was in the audience.

He was sitting near the front, and he was not alone. Nichol was rarely alone. Slumped against him was a young woman of about twenty, who looked not unlike Liz Falla, so presumably this was the idiot cousin. She had his partner's dark hair, and a similarly shaped face, but there the resemblance ended. Her hair was worn in some exceedingly untidy style Moretti vaguely recognized as currently chic, and a ghoulishly dark lipstick on her full lips. As far as Moretti could see above the level of the table, she appeared to be wearing virtually nothing, but given club rules he presumed this was not the case.

"Ed! Over here!"

Reluctantly, Moretti left the tiny platform and went over to the table. The girl smiled up at him, dreamily, drunkenly.

"You know Toni?"

Nichol Watt was a middle-aged man whose success with women had more to do with his income and veneer of well-travelled worldliness than any other obvious qualities. He was rangily built and seemed loosely put together, as if his limbs might detach at any time. His puffy eyelids and reddened skin showed the ravages of too much booze and too many babes, and he was fast acquiring jowls beneath a fleshy chin. He was, however, intelligent and highly experienced in his field, and Moretti never made the mistake of underestimating him.

"No. Hello."

"You're Liz's boss."

"Partner."

"Liz was right."

The girl stood up, leaning against the table, and Moretti saw she was just about clothed in a white tube top and a minuscule black leather skirt.

Moretti did not particularly want to hear what Falla was right about, and fortunately neither did Nichol Watt, who required the undivided attention of any member of his harem.

"Come on, Toni. Let's get you out of here while you're still ambulatory." Nicol stood up, steadying himself by grasping the girl under the armpits, his fingers sliding inside her top.

"Amatory, you mean." The girl giggled. "I'm always amatory." She looked up adoringly at Nichol.

The girl's profile reminded Moretti of Falla.

"You're not driving, are you, Nichol?"

"Once a policeman, always a policeman, eh, Ed?"

"Are you?"

Jeune fille en fleur. How in the name of all that's precious and lovely and ephemeral could this particular young girl in bloom waste her sweetness on the likes of Nichol Watt?

"No, officer. We'll mosey along to my little watercraft."

As they started to move away, the girl called out. "That's what Liz said — she said, 'always a policeman,' she said. 'Always a policeman.'"

Just as Nichol and the girl were about to go up the stairs leading to the ground level, Moretti saw Garth Machin go up to them and take Nichol by the arm. A few words were exchanged, and from the look on Nichol's face those few words were not mere pleasantries or idle chatter. The surgeon's face darkened, and his reply was short and sharp. He jerked his arm away from Garth's grasp and pulled the girl against him, half-carrying her up the stairs. Moretti could not see Garth's face immediately, but when he turned back and headed toward the stage, he appeared shaken. His normally pale skin was flushed, and his strong, full-lipped mouth was trembling. He ran one hand over his short-cropped fair hair so that what was left of it stood up on end.

"I didn't know you knew Nichol Watt," Moretti remarked, as his horn player bent down to take the instrument out of its case.

"In my line of business you need to know anyone who is anyone, Ed, and Nichol Watt is someone. A piece of slime, granted, but nevertheless he's someone on this blessed bloody plot set in a shitty silver sea."

Which really didn't answer his question, of course. Perhaps it was about the girl, but Garth had never shown the faintest signs of chivalry and, as far as Moretti knew, had a stable and conventional home life. He had met Melissa Machin only once or twice at the few obligatory formal occasions he could not duck out of, and she seemed pleasant, looked pretty, and made all the right noises for the wife of a successful money man.

The Esplanade was deserted when Moretti left the club. He could see the lights near the yacht, where they were keeping the incident van, a police car, and a watch on the *Just Desserts*.

Just deserts, as in revenge taken? Unlikely. More likely to be about silence, the removal of a witness, of someone who knew too much. Hopefully by tomorrow they would have the reports in from the Canadian RCMP, giving them some more background on Bernard Masterson and Adèle Letourneau.

He thought about what Nichol had said. *My little watercraft*. That's right, he'd forgotten that Nichol kept a boat in the marina. He thought about what Ludo had said. *He has experience in America, hasn't he ... I've always wondered what made him leave.*

Should he throw Nichol into the mix? Had Watt examined the body of the man he had — Christ almighty, he was getting paranoid himself.

Still. Instead of going straight to his car, Moretti headed south a short distance on the Esplanade. He

could see the three decks of lights of the *Just Desserts*
floating like a great white shark, and he was painfully
aware of how inadequate their precautions were. The
yacht was approachable — easily approachable —
from the water, and although the police launch was
now making regular trips to ensure the security of the
crime scene, it was probably a case of closing the stable
door after the horse had bolted.

Not only getting paranoid, but now misapplying
metaphors.

Nichol Watt's boat was not as impressive as
a Vento Teso, but it was a very nice cabin cruiser,
a 2052 Capri LS, with an enclosed forward cabin
and all mod cons — well, a portable toilet. Which,
given the amount drunk by the two occupants, they
would be needing — one way or the other. Moretti
knew roughly where it was moored, but he doubted
he would see anything useful. Ironic that he'd mused
about getting a boat for himself, things being quiet.
He needed one now. If he used the police launch he'd
be spotted a mile off.

Pointless. Peering into the darkness, he could
just about make out the Capri, beyond a smart new
Chaparral and Garth Machin's cherished 1959 Alan
Pape wooden motor yacht.

Had the killer come by water? Quite possibly.
Moretti remembered the damp wetsuit. So possibly not
directly by boat. The murder weapon was presumably
already on board, and perhaps Masterson's nemesis
could swim like a merman.

Or mermaid.

Moretti went back to his Triumph and made for home, heading north on the Esplanade to the Grange, up past the eighteenth-century mansions of the privateers who had made their fortune on the high seas, coming back to build these splendid monuments to their wealth. Guernsey has always been run by money, from those professional pirates, their skills harnessed by the sovereign to fill the nation's coffers as well as their own, to the present-day financiers with their far-flung fortunes in cyber-coffers, their castles in Marbella, and Monaco, and Miami.

Ten minutes later he turned into the lane leading to the cottage he had inherited from his parents, driving between the stone gateposts that were all that remained of the great house that had once stood there. He had done little to alter the cottage's interior, and had now lived there long enough to feel it his own, and not to expect his father to walk in the door.

Not his mother. She had died when he was fifteen, and he and his father had lived with her ghost a very long time.

The thought of the unaltered interior of his place reminded him of Lady Fellowes's sitting room. He grinned as he brought the Triumph to a halt on the cobblestones outside his front door, mentally comparing Coralie Chancho's lush and louche chaise lounge with the clean, hard lines of Ludo Ross's Italian-designed chaise with its sweep of matte red fabric and steel. *And yet,* he thought, *I'd lay money on la Chancho being as tough as Ludo.*

La vie en rose, my eye. I think she sees life exactly as it is.

PART TWO

Improvised Counterpoint

Chapter Five

Day Three

The incident room was crowded for the early morning meeting. A handful of officers stood around looking at the information Liz Falla had started to put up on the incident board when she arrived that morning, and another group were listening to PC Le Marchant describe for the umpteenth time the discovery of the Browning Baby. Moretti and Chief Officer Hanley arrived outside the door at the same moment.

"DI Moretti, a quick word with you before we go in."

The head of the Guernsey Police Force was not an islander. He had been brought in a few years earlier to help with the reorganization and expansion of the force due to the burgeoning offshore business and a tightening up of regulations. He was a man of lugubrious countenance and mournful disposition — Buster Keaton without the laughs — who always expected the worst and, in his line of work, was rarely disappointed. He had quickly learned about the various power bases on the island — local, international, and financial — and had been distressingly swift, in Moretti's opinion, in trimming his professional sails to the prevailing winds.

"Good morning, sir." Moretti waited. He had an idea of what the quick word might be.

"Lady Fellowes. I gather you paid her a visit yesterday."

Got it in one. "Yes, sir."

"Was it necessary? I mean, as far as I can see, she was only one of many on the CCTV cameras, wasn't she?"

"Yes, sir, but she was the only one throwing a gun into the harbour."

"Good God!"

"Precisely. After you, sir."

The excited buzz in the room died down as the two men came in. Moretti stood back and allowed Chief Officer Hanley to take centre stage, from where he swept the room with a look that spoke of the loneliness of command.

"This is a serious matter, I need hardly say. Murder, an uncommon crime on Guernsey, using a gun, an uncommon weapon on the island. Have we got the gun yet, DI Moretti?"

"Not the murder weapon, sir. But we have a gun."

Briefly, Moretti described the Browning Baby. Looking at his superior officer he added, "For the moment I want to leave the circumstances surrounding that particular gun and concentrate on the gun that was the likely murder weapon, and most probably the victim's gun. Give us what you've found, PC Brouard."

PC Brouard stood up. A gullible giant in his twenties, he had once allowed himself to be misled by trusting one of Moretti's suspects, and had redeemed himself with his knowledge of computers and his ability to keep his mouth shut.

"The gun owned by the victim is a Glock 17. In one piece it looks like this —" he turned and pointed at one of the photographs on the board "— but you can do this to it." He pointed to another image that showed the frame detached from the barrel, with two other pieces lying beside it. "It's made of plastic — at least, most of it is. Makes it lighter, cheaper, and easier to fire, because the plastic absorbs most of the recoil. The trigger and the magazine are also made of plastic, but the guide rails are steel. The barrel, the frame, the recoil spring, and the guide rail all come apart."

"Is it American?" Hanley asked.

"No, Austrian, sir. Used by the Austrian army."

"So you see the problem." Moretti pointed at the pieces of the gun. "It could have been disposed of all over the island, or in the harbour, or out at sea."

Next to him, Chief Officer Hanley shifted and sighed. Things were turning out just as badly as he expected.

"However," Moretti continued, "if it was disassembled, whoever did it knew how. It's unlikely they'd stand around checking the manual. Let's move on." He turned to Liz Falla. "DS Falla has the information that just came in from the Mounties. Go ahead, DS Falla."

"The RCMP know the murder victim well."

Moretti thought Falla sounded good, even reading out this stuff.

His partner glanced at her notes and continued. "He first came to their attention five years ago over problems with a business he'd inherited from his father, Bernard Le Maître — possible Guernsey connection here. The father was legit, in the fur business in Montreal, and passed on a going concern to his son, and the son used the money from the business to buy up other businesses on the fritz and turn them around. So far so good, on the surface. But the RCMP suspected Masterson was using his various businesses to launder money for criminal organizations, specifically the Italian and Russian mafias. They seem to have stumbled on to him by accident, when they were carrying out a major sting operation, trying to trace the movement of money between Montreal, the Caribbean, and Europe. They had him in for questioning and, since then, the trail has gone cold. They think he's moved in another direction."

"Do they know which direction?" Hanley asked.

"Not exactly," Liz Falla replied, confirming yet again her superior's belief in the worst of all possible worlds. "But they believe his above-board role as an intermediary in arms sales is a cover for a dirtier business as a mover of cash for underworld arms dealers who supply, for instance, Russian arms to countries like Iran."

"So," Hanley asked, searching for a bright spot in the midst of gloom, "this murder may have nothing at all to do with Guernsey?"

"I don't know, sir," Liz Falla replied. "The Mounties are very interested in the fact that it happened here, but have no idea why. It *could* mean we have a new criminal element moving in on the island, according to them," she added, thus spreading further gloom and instantly dissipating any chance of bright spots.

"Let's move on," said Moretti, forestalling the prolonged and unfocussed discussions that made him impatient. He turned to Jimmy Le Poidevin, head of SOCO. Jimmy Le Poidevin, full of pomp and circumference, also made him impatient. "Jimmy, could you go over what you and your team found on the yacht, if anything."

"If anything?" The head of SOCO gave a short, sharp laugh. "Even nothing can be something, Moretti, as you know."

The expression on Chief Officer Hanley's face suggested he would not appreciate further philosophical observations and the usual verbal sparring, and Le Poidevin pressed on. "The yacht is a big bugger, and we still have a team on board. We have taken fingerprints from the crew, and will continue to match them with the ones we have already found. The two items of interest so far are a tipped-over magazine rack in the main bedroom, and a lipstick-stained glass in the main stateroom. Neither has produced anything of interest. The rack has only two sets of prints, those of the victim and the housekeeper, and the glass has none. But we are sending a sample from the lipstick to the mainland for DNA testing, and also to see if the lipstick can be identified."

"Entry?" Hanley enquired. "How did the killer get on board?"

"There are no signs of a break-in, sir," Le Poidevin replied.

"So he or she was known to the victim."

Moretti interjected. "Perhaps. There is also the possibility that Masterson was set up, left the yacht unsecured because he was expecting one person, and found himself facing another."

"Such as who? Do we have any evidence to support this?" Hanley asked.

Jimmy Le Poidevin's lip curled and he crossed his arms over the convenient shelf of his belly.

"None, but we have little evidence of anything at this stage," Moretti replied. "However, according to his housekeeper, he — I quote — 'liked his babes.'"

There was a burst of laughter in the room.

"Did the CCTV cameras show any babes getting on the yacht?" someone asked.

Liz Falla responded. "I have a list of names I'm going to hand out to be checked. They are all people identified from the cameras. Find out why they were there. Most of them probably came from the party at the Landsend, and we can cross-check them from the booking list, but not everyone is named on it. The restaurant just needed the numbers."

Jimmy Le Poidevin continued. "As to the murder itself, Dr. Watt says it occurred between about eleven p.m. and midnight, probably closer to midnight, death was instant, and the bullet was a hollow-point."

At this point in the proceedings, Moretti was grateful for Hanley's presence. Otherwise, Jimmy would be spewing theories like an out-of-control slot

machine, and Moretti would have moved from impatience to outright and outspoken irritation. "That's all
for now," he said. "DS Falla will hand out the names
to be checked. Any questions?"

"Did we check with customs and the Harbour
Authority?" PC Le Marchant's tone of voice suggested
otherwise.

Liz smiled. Being part of the investigation was making PC Le Marchant uppity, it appeared. Uppitiness
was something she was used to, particularly since her
promotion to sergeant.

"We checked. The harbour master checked. There
was nothing out of the ordinary in their arrival, which
was around five p.m. They filled in all the forms,
answered all the questions. The only thing of interest
was that they were keen to get moorings here and not
at Beaucette Marina."

"What about the crew, Moretti?" Hanley asked. "I
understand they're under guard at the Esplanade Hotel,
but how about suspects among them? Any joy there?"

Joy would reign unconfined, Moretti knew, if he
could nail a non-islander for the murder.

"Some, sir. Not one of them has an alibi that
would stand up to scrutiny. We're checking if any of
them has a record, and I think it's possible we'll find
Masterson's bodyguard has one."

"Good God, the bodyguard!"

"Yes, sir. He says he handed over the gun to
Masterson, but there's no proof he did so. I've interviewed the crew, and we're getting written statements
from all of them."

"Anything else?" Chief Officer Hanley threw the question to the room. Liz Falla took another look at the fax sheet she had in her hand.

"There is something else, something that came from the RCMP. Masterson had a nickname, and so did his father. Masterson senior was known in Montreal as '*Boule à mite*.'"

This got a mixed reaction, depending on who spoke French and who did not. Most didn't.

"Mothball. The French for mothball. Came from the fur business. Masterson senior always smelled of mothballs, and the victim was known as '*Bébé boule à mite*.'"

"Baby Mothball?" Laughter.

Hanley quelled the hilarity with a look and turned to leave. "You will, of course, keep me informed, DI Moretti."

"Of course, sir."

Moretti waited until the chief officer had left the room and beckoned to PC Brouard. "Got that other stuff for me? Okay, we'll go to my office. You too, Falla."

Once in his office, the door closed, Moretti turned to his partner. "PC Brouard was checking some background for me on the La Veile tenants. Go ahead, Brouard, let's hear what you've got."

PC Brouard lowered his husky frame into a chair, and pulled out a sizeable wedge of papers from his jacket pocket. "That panther jersey first, Guv. It's not football or basketball. It's an ice-hockey uniform. They sell all kinds of stuff with the logo, besides the sweater. The colours change depending on whether the team is home or away — well, it becomes more red or more white, but the logo stays the same. The team's called the Florida Panthers." He handed one of the sheets of paper to Moretti. "Here's a picture of it. Is that the one?"

"Yes," said Moretti. "What about the wood-chucks?"

"Big sellers as far as I can see, got their own web-page. Titles like *Warren and Wilma See Their Shadow, Warren and Wilma's Babies, Warren and Wilma and their Porcupine Pal*. Really interesting, Guv, the wood-chuck. Also called a groundhog. Great fighter, but not a great mover, mostly they get away by diving into bur-rows. There's one book called *Warren and Wilma Move Burrows*. Amazing, really, the burrow's set up so there's a separate toilet — well, not an actual toilet, but —" PC Brouard was warming to his topic.

"Thanks." Moretti was reminded of the small child's book report: "This book told me more about penguins than I wanted to know."

"What about the author and the illustrator? Anything about them?"

"Quite a bit about the author, Sandra Goldstein. Degree from Yale, that kind of thing. Lives in Florida. Explains the sweater, doesn't it. Her local team."

"Right." Moretti and Falla looked at each other. "What about the illustrator?"

"Not as much about her, something about her art training. And the name's different."

"Not Julia King?"

"Julia's the same. But the last name is Meraldo. Julia Meraldo."

"Meraldo." Moretti thought of the child's colouring and Gwen's comment. "Great, Brouard, good work. And I've got another job for you."

PC Brouard beamed and sat up straighter in his chair, like a friendly Labrador puppy, eager to cooperate.

"The computers from the yacht, are they still with us?"

"Yes, Guv. I was told not to touch them."

"That's what I want you to do. Tell Jimmy I said so. The problem will be the password."

"Yes, and if they've been erased. Not that it's that easy to delete anything from the hard drive."

"Then we may have to send them away, but give it a try."

PC Brouard beamed again. "Any suggestions for the password, Guv?"

"Nicknames are important to people. Personal. Start off with variations on *Boule à mite*." Moretti picked up a scrap of paper and wrote out a few versions of the name. "I wouldn't worry about the accent, and I'd try combining the words into one. And you might add this to the combination."

"Two letter *B*s?" PC Brouard peered doubtfully at what Moretti had written

"In French, the letter *B* in the alphabet is pronounced exactly the same way as *bébé*. Baby. Babe."

"I get it!"

Liz Falla watched an elated PC Brouard leave the room. "Connecticut's nowhere near Florida, is it, Guv?"

"Nowhere near. Interesting that there was so little on the website about Julia King-Meraldo. I'd guess the information was there originally, and then removed."

"So it's the child and the mother who are probably in hiding — at least, that is what it looks like. That they're hiding out from something or somebody."

"Most likely a husband or ex. To someone from Florida, Guernsey must seem like the ends of the earth."

"Safe as houses." Liz Falla looked at her boss, who appeared to be doodling a woodchuck on one of the sheets of paper. "What are you going to do, Guv?"

"I'll see Gwen and tell her what we think the situation is, and then I'm going to leave them alone."

"Want me to check on whether there's a warrant out?"

"Not right now, we've too much on our plate." He pulled a tiny fragment of paper from his pocket. "I want you to get on to the RCMP, and see if they have anything about this Offshore Haven business. Nothing came through on our initial enquiry?"

"No, but I didn't specifically ask. Did you get anything from your contact about guns, wheeler dealers, and million-dollar deals?"

"General stuff, but this was pointed out to me —" Moretti handed over the scrap of paper to Liz Falla. "Limited partnership. He thinks this is about something different from just selling someone a yacht. I'm going to get hold of a friend in the financial business to see if we can dig anything up about Masterson. He didn't just turn up here to visit his money. He was here to see someone about something, and that something got him murdered."

"By the way," Liz Falla stood up and closed her notebook, "Gord Collenette says he seems to remember something about Lady Fellowes's husband — 'being taken' was the expression he used. But either he couldn't or wouldn't be specific. You might ask Don Taylor about that while you're at it." She grinned at Moretti and turned to leave.

"You're one sharp cookie, Falla."

Moretti's voice was sombre and she wondered for a moment if she'd overstepped some boundary. Then he added, "You've just given me another reason to worry about Coralie Fellowes."

"Lady Fellowes, Guv?"

"Hasn't it occurred to you with whom she might have had that glass of champagne?"

By the pricking of my thumbs. Liz Falla remembered the visit to Lady Fellowes, the witches' seat, shuddering, sneezing. At the time she had hoped, or had chosen to believe, that it was an allergic reaction to her aunt's superstitious beliefs rather than a manifestation of what her aunt called "the gift."

"The murderer. Whoever killed Bernard Masterson had champagne with Lady Fellowes."

"As I said, you're a smart cookie, Falla."

Money is the root of all evil. Of course, the aphorism was always quoted incorrectly. *The love of money is the root of all evil*, according to Saint Paul, a converted bad boy who saw many human emotions as sinful.

Money. Moretti was reasonably sure that the money boys in the Commercial Branch and the Financial Investigations Unit wouldn't move in unless there appeared to be some real connection between Masterson's death and his financial dealings. And that was fine by him. The body on the boat was by far the most interesting island crime in a long while, and he hoped to be left to investigate it, but he needed some specialized help. Which was why he was putting in a call to Don Taylor, his contact on the Guernsey Financial Services Commission, known simply as The Commission.

The Commission had a different mandate from the Financial Investigations Unit. It acted as a watchdog and inspection body, and was therefore involved in the financial scene on the island in general, and not necessarily as a result of a criminal investigation. Moretti had worked with Don when he was looking into the operations of so-called "captives," the subsidiaries set up by insurance companies to cover the risk of their own financial dealings.

Don Taylor screened and taped every call, so Moretti listened to the brief message, and began. "Don, it's Ed Moretti. I need to talk to you."

Almost before he finished the sentence there was a click and the sound of Don's voice. "So I hear. A body with a bullet in the head, a Porsche in the belly of the boat, and a fortune in Euros in the bed-head."

"Do you have a direct line to Hospital Lane?"

"Word spreads, need I tell you. A contact in the harbour master's office rang me about something else, and he'd heard about the body and the boodle from the driver of the police car. I could come over in an hour or so."

"Meet me at my place."

The only really significant addition Moretti had made to the contents of his family home was the sound system he had installed to carry the music so essential to him. It was a vintage quad tube system that drove a set of ESL speakers. The large speaker panel gave an incredibly smooth, sweet sound that had never, in Moretti's opinion, been bettered. He had not had to add a piano. He still had the one that had belonged to his mother.

The sound of Oscar Peterson filled the cottage, upstairs and downstairs, above the sound of the rain that had started to fall as Moretti drove up Les Gravées. He made himself a sandwich and put on coffee for himself and Don Taylor. As he did so, he heard Don's motorbike outside in the courtyard and went to the door.

"Christ, these things are slippery, Ed! Nearly lost my balance."

Don Taylor was a small, wiry man of about forty, whose chief regret about working on Guernsey was the lack of space for his favourite hobby, running marathons. His other pet hobby was his ancient Rudge motorbike, which, when he was not riding it, he was either under or alongside working on it.

"That's cobblestones for you. Covered with the slick and moss of two centuries. Come in."

Don shook off his oilskins under the overhang by the door, then hung them and his helmet over one of the hallstand hooks and sniffed the air appreciatively.

"Oscar and freshly ground coffee beans, what could be better. You were on form last night."

"You were at the club? I didn't see you."

"Tucked away at the back. I saw the yacht when I came out — spectacular, if you like that sort of thing."

"Don't you?"

Moretti brought two mugs of coffee from the kitchen and put them down on the flat-topped oak chest that served as a coffee table. He turned a knob on the stereo and the sound of Duke Ellington's "Love You Madly" faded away.

"You ask that of a man with a pre-war motorbike, no car, and a penchant for running over twenty miles at a time. Not particularly."

"I should ask you first, I suppose, if you saw anything unusual when you left. When *did* you leave?"

"Eleven, or just after."

"Did you see Nichol Watt arrive, by any chance?"

"Indeed I did. Plus the usual floozy."

Moretti felt a twinge of protectiveness toward Falla's cousin, but decided to ignore it. "What time did he get there?"

"You had just started on 'Night and Day.' Hated to leave when you were all in the groove, but I had some paperwork to do. Not a thing, to answer your question about anything unusual, and I've given it some thought since I heard about the shooting. Okay, what do you want from me?"

Don's eyes behind the wire-framed spectacles he always wore glinted intelligently at Moretti over his mug of coffee.

"Are you working on, or do you know anything about a Canadian called Bernard Masterson?"

"The body, eh? Nothing comes immediately to mind. Are the Financial boys in on this?"

"Not yet. At the moment there's no evidence of financial finagling. I am assuming if they had anything on Masterson they'd let me know. One can but hope."

Don Taylor grinned. "Life's a sight more complex for the island bobby since the era of just tourism and tomatoes passed into the history books. Anything more you can tell me about him?"

"Here." Moretti handed over a copy of the RCMP information. "This is what we have so far."

Don read through the notes, sometimes going back and rereading an earlier page. This he did two or three times.

"Something's caught your attention," said Moretti.

"Yes." Don looked up. "It's this nickname of his. Funnily enough it reminds me of —" he tapped his head. "It's in there somewhere, but I can't access it at the moment. I'm sure you too have asked yourself why in the hell a bloke like Mr. International Montrealer was here at all. Who's this Adèle Letourneau?"

"Also of Montreal. His housekeeper, so she says."

"Interesting what the Mounties have to say about her." Don read from the paper in his hand: "Masterson's personal assistant, Adèle Letourneau, is involved in all his dealings. No question, she's the one with the smarts, but we've never been able to get anything on her."

"Having met her, I can see why. Cool as a cucumber, speaks perfect English, but I'd say French was her first language. They were once what she called 'an item,' but love had changed to a business arrangement, according to her. He needed someone he could trust."

"*Jealousy* —" Don sang the word softly. "Yet another possible motive, right?"

"Which is why, if you can find out anything about his finances, it might be helpful narrowing them down."

"Of course," said Don, reaching for his mug, "he could have all kinds of financial arrangements on the island, and his name would not appear in connection with any of them."

"I know. One other thing —" Moretti held out the scrap of paper he'd been carrying around. "What do you make of this?"

Don peered at the tiny fragment and then up at Moretti. "Looks like Masterson was thinking of buying another yacht. Why?"

"That's what Letourneau says. But I've spoken to one other person outside the investigation, Ludo Ross, and he pointed out the 'limited partnership' phrase. Said it didn't sound like a straightforward yacht sale to him."

"You talked to Ludo?" Don pulled his glasses down on his bony nose and looked at Moretti over the tops of the wire frames.

"Yes. Why, do you think that was a mistake?"

"God, I don't know." Don laughed and flicked his glasses back into place. "It's just that — the man is an enigma, Ed. What the hell is he doing, sitting here in that fortress of his, as if the enemy might come around the corner any second? The war was a long, long time ago, and most of those who hated his guts are long gone, I should think."

"Paranoia, perhaps. He once told me you never get over the fear of discovery, or betrayal."

"Maybe. And maybe Ludo has new fears to add to old ones."

"Such as?" Moretti felt his own paranoia rising from the pit of his stomach to somewhere in his chest, where it tightened like a steel strap across his sternum.

Don shrugged his shoulders. "Don't get me wrong, Ed, I really like the guy. This paper you showed me —" Don changed the subject "— could be legit, could be swampland in Florida. Not much here to go on, but if it's swampland, two possibilities come to mind. That this is being touted as a tax dodge and you'll end up paying the taxman anyway. And the other is that there are no yachts at all — remember the film *The Sting*? Could be all smoke and mirrors."

"Would a sophisticated investor get caught by such a scam?"

"They do, every day, my son, every day. Greed strikes the smartest operators blind."

"Thanks, Don. I'd rather you didn't mention any of this to anyone. I've already made that mistake."

Don stood up, draining the last drop of coffee from his mug. "I'm sure it's not a mistake, Ed. I was just voicing some thoughts of my own about Ludo Ross, that's all."

Outside the rain was coming down steadily, occasionally sweeping in gusts across the courtyard. Don looked even smaller than usual, enveloped in his bulky oilskins and cumbrous helmet.

"Spring has sprung," he shouted over the revving of his bike. "Dark as night and twice as nasty."

Moretti watched the slight figure cautiously wheeling his Rudge over the slippery cobbles. Thinking he should grab something quick to eat, he went back into the house. The phone was ringing. Not Falla. She'd phone his mobile.

"Edward? It was Gwen Ferbrache.

"Gwen. I was just about to phone you with some information on your tenants."

"That's why I'm ringing you. One of them is here — Miss Goldstein, that is — and she says you came to see her, and she'd like to talk to both of us."

"Here being your place?"

"Yes. I didn't think I'd find you at home."

"I'll be right over."

It took about fifteen minutes to reach Clos du Laurier, and on the way he put in a call to Liz Falla. She sounded tense.

"I'll be at Hospital Lane in about an hour, Falla. Anything I should know meanwhile?"

"No prints on the Browning Baby, Guv, as you might expect. The divers are down again, looking for the murder weapon. And there was a call from Gord

Collenette. His wife and daughter say Lady Fellowes was carrying a small silver bag. She was also wearing long satin gloves, and she kept them on the whole time."

"She wasn't wearing them on the CCTV tapes, was she?"

"No. I've passed that on to SOCO in case they turn up on the yacht. I'm going through the statements that have come in so far from people identified on the tapes. Nothing of interest and nobody saw anything or anybody."

"Frustrating, Falla."

"Yes."

Maybe that was what he heard in her voice. Frustration. "I'm on my way to see Gwen Ferbrache, just to say hello. Sandra Goldstein is there and wants to speak to me. Phone me if anything comes up."

Back at police headquarters in Hospital Lane, Liz Falla put down her mobile and stared again in disbelief at the copy of the *Guernsey Press* that had been delivered to her attention at the station. Across the front page ran a headline, the inch-high letters standing out in stark relief against the white background.

EX-FOLIES STAR, JUST DESERTS, AND MURDER

Beneath, in smaller print, the "Special correspondent to the *Press*" trumpeted:

Inside sources at Hospital Lane confirm the presence of glamorous Coralie Fellowes on

the marina at midnight when multi-millionaire
Bernard Masterson was murdered on his yacht.
Staff at the Landsend Restaurant on Albert
Marina revealed that her visit to the fashionable
watering hole is of great interest to the police.
Detective Inspector Ed Moretti is leading the
investigation, assisted by Detective Sergeant Liz
Falla. For further details, see page 10.

Liz Falla turned to page ten. Apart from some
details about an earlier murder case of Moretti's there
was little of substance, but the *Press*'s special correspondent had spun quite a yarn out of very little. He
did not name his inside sources, but it was clear who
they were.

They were DS Liz Falla.

"I'm on duty," was all she had said, but he'd seen
her leave the restaurant and taken it from there.

The special correspondent of the *Guernsey Press*
was, of course, Denny Bras-de-Fer.

Chapter Six

There was no sign of a bicycle outside the Clos du Laurier, so Sandra Goldstein must have come by taxi, or walked down the lane and taken the bus. Moretti parked the Triumph inside the gate and walked up to the house. As he reached the front step, Gwen Ferbrache opened the door. She gave him a welcoming smile, but her face was grim.

"This is good of you, Edward. Come in."

Books, books, books, that was one of his earliest childhood memories of this house. Books in bookcases, on tables, lying open on chairs. Her tiny hallway was lined with books, and there were a couple lying on the side of the stairs.

"Miss Goldstein is in the sitting room. Go on through. I'm making tea."

Sandra Goldstein was sitting in a chair near the French window overlooking Gwen's garden. She was rubbing her hair with a towel and she was very wet. A pair of trainers stood by the window, and her brown nail-polished feet were bare. There were patches of damp on the knees of her grey sweatpants. She looked up as Moretti came in and smiled apologetically.

"I'm sorry about this, but it was my only chance."

"Why didn't you use the number I gave you?"

"I didn't want to leave a message on a machine. Besides, Julia doesn't know I'm doing this. I'm supposed to be at the store, picking up groceries."

"Can I ask why you decided to do — whatever this is?"

"Because you are a bright guy, and I didn't want you making enquiries and jumping to the wrong conclusions."

"Would a bright guy do that?" Moretti sat down opposite her.

She laughed and gave her hair a final rub before putting the towel down on her knees. "Touché. I guess I decided we needed someone else in the know. I've told Miss Ferbrache, and she told me she had already spoken to you."

"About the gun, you mean."

Moretti watched her face carefully.

"The gun." Sandra Goldstein leaned back in the chair, closed her eyes, and laughed again, but this time there was no humour in it. "It's a replica, a fake. A good one, but no more use to us if things got ugly than a stage prop."

"How did you get something like that through customs?"

"I didn't. I picked it up at the tattoo parlour in town — The Art o' Torture. I know places like that sometimes carry this kind of merchandise."

At this point, Gwen came into the room carrying a tea tray. Making a mental note to check out the tattoo parlour, Moretti got up to take it from her.

"Thank you, Edward. Put it down there." Gwen indicated a table near the wing chair in which she usually sat. "I'll pour the tea and let Miss Goldstein tell her story."

"It's really Julia's story," said Sandra Goldstein. "I imagine you've already guessed it's about Ellie's father."

"Guessed, yes, but I'm going to drink my tea and listen."

Moretti took the flowered china teacup from Gwen, and one of her cupcakes. They were another childhood memory, his memory-madeleine, his mother and Gwen sitting together, laughing together in this room.

Sandra Goldstein put her cup and saucer on her lap, and began. "Julia and I have known each other since we were children. We had started collaborating on the books well before Julia met and married Sam Meraldo. I never liked him, but Julia was crazy about him. From the beginning he tried to isolate her, put distance between her and family and friends. He disparaged her talent, jeered at our friendship, said I was a lesbian and jealous of him. Then Ellie was born, and things went from bad to worse. He started hitting her, threatened to take Ellie away from her, even kill them both. You cannot imagine some of the things that happened, but I'll cut to the chase." Sandra Goldstein's voice shook. "Julia got a court order, came to me, and stayed with me through the divorce. Ellie was only a few months old when Julia got away from him, and the three of us had to go into hiding. That was when things got *really* scary."

"Things got worse?" Moretti took another cupcake, remembering his missed lunch.

"Yes. We moved, no one knew where we were, except our editor and our lawyer." Sandra Goldstein leaned forward in her chair, her long damp hair swinging around her face. "But he always found us. Always, always. We moved again, and he found us — oh, not in the flesh, but he kept sending us these *things*. Dolls with ropes around their necks, X-rated videos and DVDs, articles cut out of newspapers and magazines about violent death or torture with the worst details highlighted, that kind of thing. The persecution went on and we could never understand how he found us — heck, we even started suspecting our own families, and at one point Julia even started suspecting me. It was our lawyer who finally said what we didn't want to hear: that in this cyber age he could always find us. Or hire someone to find us. We were vulnerable to anyone who had access to our name and social security number, we were exposed any time we used a cellphone or a bank card, any time we made an appointment with a dentist or a manicurist we were vulnerable."

"Did you think of changing your names?" Moretti asked.

"A long process to do it legally, which would have meant exposing ourselves again and therefore would have been pointless in the end."

Sandra Goldstein put down her cup, got up, and walked over to the window. "But the real problem was the books." When she turned back to look at Moretti she was smiling. "No woodchucks out there, right? We're miles away from woodchucks, but they keep us here. Financially, I mean. Warren and Wilma keep us very comfortably, Julia and me. In the States, Goldstein and King are as well-known as, oh, A.A. Milne. And Sam Meraldo knows that. He has said as much. *I'll follow the woodchuck trail*." The American woman sang the line quietly to the theme from *The Wizard of Oz*. "He'd sing that to us over the phone. It was — chilling."

"So you came here." Gwen took Sandra Goldstein's cup from her and refilled it.

"After the photographs."

"Photographs?"

"They started arriving, every week, sometimes every day — Julia at the doctor's office, me at the grocery store, Ellie and Julia and me at the park. And every time they arrived the phone would ring and there'd be no one there. Call untraceable. He knew where we were every hour of the day. *That's* why we're here."

"Why Guernsey?" Moretti asked.

"Some of what we told you was true. We'd seen a video owned by an American friend with Guernsey roots a few years ago, before Julia met Sam, so we felt he'd not be able to work out where we are. I had to keep my name, because I've always been Goldstein, but Julia had kept some of her accounts and so on in her maiden name, so she went back to King. The only reason she changed her professional name was to appease Sam."

Moretti felt a wave of depression sweep him up and deposit him in an unpleasant trough of sadness and disgust. "What a bastard," he said. "Sorry, Gwen. What do you want me to do?"

"Nothing. In fact, that's why I am here, to beg you to do nothing. No enquiries, no checking up on Sam Meraldo, nothing that might lead some pursuer in cyberspace to us. See how paranoid we are?"

Sandra Goldstein stood up. "I must go. I still have to get the groceries. I'm so grateful to you, Miss Ferbrache, for —" She stopped.

"Tea and sympathy?" Gwen spoke briskly. Having suppressed her own feelings of loss for half a century, she was not partial to emotional breakdowns of any kind, and for a moment it seemed as if the American woman was about to lose control. She had no desire to revisit distant anguish, and the unsuppressed pain of others often did that to her.

"Come on, Edward, take Miss Goldstein to do her shopping."

"I'm just fine — you don't have to —"

"It's not a problem," said Moretti. There had been no phone call from the station, so he presumed there was no emergency — apart from investigating a murder, that is. "Where were you planning on doing your shopping?"

"If you're heading into town, that'd be fine. Julia is in the midst of a new painting, and she's feeling pretty good today."

As Sandra Goldstein started to put on her trainers, Moretti picked up the tea tray and carried it through to the kitchen, followed by Gwen.

"Edward," she said, closing the kitchen door, "they have no phone, and Miss Goldstein won't get what she calls a cellphone, because she's afraid it can be traced."

"I'll see to it," Moretti said. "DS Falla or I can buy one in our name, and Miss Goldstein can reimburse us."

"Unbelievable," said Gwen as she started to take things off the tray.

"I wish it were," said Moretti, "I only wish it were."

"Gwen tells me your mother was a Guernsey girl, but your father was Italian. A prisoner of war on the island."

A teenage slave labourer, his father, dragging trucks of rubble as they dug out the underground hospital.

"Yes, he was. He was a partisan, and was captured toward the end of the war."

"She saved his life, your mother. That's so romantic."

"She smuggled food to him, yes. He came back after the war, found her, and married her." Moretti turned and looked at his passenger. She smelled faintly of rainwater on cotton fleece. "I would have thought life had made you cynical about romance."

"Crazy, aren't I?" Sandra Goldstein turned and laughed. She had a mole like a beauty spot, he noticed, on her cheek. "May I ask whether you *did* check on us? You understand why."

"I checked on the sweater you were wearing and your website."

"Sweater? Oh, my hockey sweater."

"Florida Panthers. So Connecticut was a fabrication."

"Yes, sorry. We muddied the waters a tad."

Moretti turned the Triumph on to the Esplanade and past the Guernsey Brewery with the old dray in the forecourt, painted in the brewery's traditional blue and white. He could barely see Castle Cornet through the mist and rain. As they passed the bus terminal Sandra Goldstein said, "You can drop me here, Edward — can I call you Edward? After all, I'm not a case of yours, am I? I'm Sandy, by the way."

"I'll call you Sandy if you call me Ed. Only Gwen calls me Edward, which is not actually correct. I was christened Eduardo."

Moretti pulled in under the trees by the line of bus stops and leaned across to open the door.

"Thanks, Ed. I know you're tied up with a murder case. I appreciate it."

"You're welcome." She had hazel eyes, he noticed, like topazes against the pale tan of her skin. "I'm going to arrange a mobile for you — what you call a cellphone. It will not be traceable to you or to Ms. King."

"You are kind." Her voice wavered. "If you come to the cottage, just sound your horn as you approach, okay? Then you'll not be greeted by Julia and her fake firearm."

She touched his arm again, and then let herself out of the car, slamming the door behind her. Moretti watched her run across the road toward the town, her long hair bouncing on her shoulders. She was going to need a towel again. Then his eyes were drawn to a *Guernsey Press* billboard by one of the bus stops

EX-FOLIES STAR, JUST DESERTS, AND MURDER

Even at this distance he could read it quite clearly. The mobile in his jacket pocket began to ring.

"Inside sources, Falla?"

Liz Falla stood on the other side of Moretti's desk. She was feeling nauseous, sick to her stomach. Not that it showed.

"Le Marchant? Brouard? Who?" Moretti slapped the newspaper down on his desk. "Christ, Falla, we laugh about the grapevine, but this is beyond a joke. This could compromise the investigation, or the safety of a witness, and I tell you — this time I'm out for blood. Who tipped off this creep?"

"I think it was me, sir."

His partner's face was white. She swallowed hard, her jaw clenched.

"You?"

Moretti stared at her in disbelief. In the months they had been partners, Liz Falla's love life had not been a major topic of conversation, but enough had been said for him to grasp she had an approach his mother's generation would have considered flighty at their most charitable, and "no better than she should be" the more likely verdict. Not that he had given it much thought, but his own evaluation was more along the lines of foot loose and fancy free.

"Don't tell me you've had anything to do with this clown."

"Not anymore, and I'd rather not discuss it, if you don't mind. Could I stick to what I think happened?" She didn't seem chastened so much as defiant, looking him straight in the eye, chin held high.

"With pleasure. Go ahead."

"I ran into Denny when I came out of the Landsend. He was hanging about the yacht. He asked for information, and I told him to get lost."

"That's it?"

"Not quite. I told him I was on duty, and he'd seen me coming out of the restaurant. After I left he went into the Landsend and asked what I'd been doing there, and someone — I think it was probably Gail Collenette — told him I'd asked about Lady Fellowes. I checked with Gord, and he confirms Denny was there, denied saying anything, but said something like 'You know how he is with the ladies.'"

"You told him nothing?"

"Nothing. Denny could always make a silk purse out of a sodding sow's ear, and that's what he's done."

"Has Hanley seen this yet? I'll answer that — no, or you and I would be on the proverbial mat."

"He's in a meeting. Only a matter of time."

"Then why are we hanging about here?"

Moretti got out of his chair. He still felt angry with his partner, although he wasn't quite sure why. Except she'd been critical enough of her cousin, so why the hell did she herself make such a lousy choice of lover?

"You don't believe me, do you?"

"It doesn't matter whether I believe you or not. It's whether Hanley does. But I wonder if you obeyed the rules of procedure, or whether you let something slip."

"Obeyed the rules of procedure?" Beneath the jagged wisps of her bangs Liz Falla's dark eyes flared into laughter. "Like you did, Guv, when Jimmy Le Poidevin said there was nothing of interest in that magazine rack?" Her laughter disappeared as soon as it had come and, for the first time, she looked contrite. "Sorry. I shouldn't have said that."

"You counterpunched. Fair enough. Let's get out of here."

"Speaking of magazine racks, did you hear anything yet from the RCMP about Offshore Haven Cred, or whatever it is?"

It was the first words they had exchanged since leaving the office. Standing on the other side of the car in the Hospital Lane courtyard, Liz Falla replied, "No, Guv. I got an email off to them late yesterday, about midday their time. Hopefully there'll be a reply by this afternoon." She opened the car door. "Where do you want to go? Lady Fellowes?"

"Later. For the time being I've sent PC Le Marchant out there to keep an eye on her. It'll be good for him. She'll flirt and embarrass the hell out of him." Moretti got into the passenger seat. "I want to have another go at the crew members at the Esplanade Hotel. There was a message from Betty Kerr saying they were having problems with the *petit salaud*. I want to lean on him a little, threaten possible confinement unless we get cooperation."

"He's got a record." Liz Falla started the BMW and turned to exit under the high stone arch of the old wall.

"So I gather. Chucked out of the forces, GBH, and other misdemeanours. I'll use that. But he also won awards for marksmanship at Bisley, so Martin Smith is not just a pretty face."

"You think the little shit did it, Guv?"

"At the moment, I think any of them could have done it, including Masterson's ex, but that doesn't explain why he was here in the first place. And I think someone on the crew knows why Masterson came to Guernsey."

They were now passing the taxi rank on St. Julian's Avenue, where North Esplanade turns into Glategny Esplanade. To their right lay St. Julian's Pier and White Rock Pier. The rain was clearing, and Moretti could see Herm in the distance. He thought of Peter Walker, paddling about among the rock pools, happy as a clam.

"Taxis, Guv."

"Taxis, Falla?"

"I forgot, what with those headlines and all. PC Brouard found the taxi driver who drove Lady Fellowes. Pick-up was at nine forty-five, which tallies with the time she arrived at the Landsend."

"And?"

"That's it, Guv. There's no record of anyone taking her home at or after one fifteen a.m. And *that* pick-up would have to be prearranged. Not many drivers hanging about at that hour of the night, unless she bribed some driver to keep quiet."

"Unlikely. Word would have got around. I think we can guess who took her home."

"Champagne Charlie, whoever he was." Liz Falla suddenly stepped on the brake, jolting them both forward. "Oh, Brutus!"

Confused, Moretti looked in the direction his partner was pointing. A large striped cat was skidding to a halt on the pavement that edged the eighteenth-century terraced houses that curved around Glategny Esplanade across from the seawall.

"He'll do that once too often, he will."

"Of course, you live here. He's your cat?"

"After a fashion. I think he's his own cat myself. Must have been owned by someone once. He's fixed, and he's well-fed. But he shares my bed from time to time, when the weather's rough — a foul-weather friend, you might say."

So the ex-flatmate, Len, had been replaced by a tabby. Where did Denny Bras-de-Fer fit in this picture, Moretti wondered. Not his problem, and he didn't want to know.

"Ludo Ross says there's a word for a collection of cats. A clowder. Myself, I don't think Brutus has ever belonged to a clowder."

"You know Ludo Ross? He said he'd heard you sing."

Beside him in the driver's seat, Falla chuckled. "Does anyone know that man? Yes, he heard me sing at the Dunes Restaurant at La Fosse, and afterward came up and introduced himself. We met a couple of times after that. I had a drink at his place."

"That's it?"

Why hadn't Ludo mentioned this? After his earlier conversation with Don Taylor, this sudden revelation that Ludo had not just seen and heard her, but had invited Liz Falla into his home, struck Moretti like a mini-bombshell.

His partner turned sharply toward him, then looked back at the road. "Don't know what you mean by 'that's it,' Guv, but I went and had a drink at his place in St. Martin's. I guessed he was your expert in million-dollar deals, but I didn't think I needed to say I'd been there. You know him better than I do."

"Do I?"

Christ, what was the matter with him, rabbiting on like this. Ludo couldn't have been trying to get information, because this meeting took place before the murder investigation, and certainly nothing too earth-shattering in the way of crimes had been committed in the winter. Break-ins and domestics were hardly in Ludo's line.

Liz Falla had brought the BMW to a halt in front of the main entrance to the hotel. The sun had come out. It gleamed wetly on the leaves of the hydrangeas and fuchsias and dripped off the sword-shaped leaves of the cabbage palms. A wet palm tree, Moretti decided, is a depressing sight.

"You're right there, Guv — does *anyone* know Ludo Ross. There's someone who's never been part of a clowder either, I'd say. We talked about music mostly, so we talked about you and your music. He says you're in the wrong profession, but that most people are."

Liz Falla didn't look at him, and Moretti felt she was not so much avoiding his eyes as revisiting another scene. "What's comic is I went to his house because he was old enough to be my grandfather. Don't get me wrong, he was a perfect gentleman and there you have it. There you have it," she repeated. Moretti wondered what exactly she was saying, but certainly a perfect gentleman of breeding, even though of advanced years, was a damn sight more appealing than the Lens and Dennys of this world, not to mention neutered tabbies.

"How do we know the crew will be here, Guv?"

Falla had moved on to other things. Truth was, she was feeling muddled about Ludo Ross and preferred not to explore her confusion. Here she was, worrying that her attraction to this septuagenarian meant that she was in need of some serious therapy. Normally you didn't have to examine whether you wanted to sleep with a man. Normally. You knew or, at least, she did.

"Because I told Betty Kerr to let them know this morning we might be returning their passports."

"Not seriously?"

"Not seriously."

Betty Kerr was hovering in the lobby, and she positively sprinted to greet them. "DI Moretti, thank goodness you're here. We have an emergency on our hands."

Betty Kerr held her hands out in front of her, as if urging them to visualize the weight of the crisis.

"In the next few weeks I am fully booked, and I cannot possibly keep these people in four of my best rooms. They will have to go."

"I thought," said Moretti, "the emergency was to do with Mr. Smith's behaviour."

"Well, it's quietened down in the past little while."

As she spoke, Moretti saw Adèle Letourneau appear at the far end of the carpeted corridor that led out of the lobby. She was flanked by the two Germans, with the chef bobbing along behind them, and they advanced in measured fashion toward the lobby as if taking part in some formal procession. Watching them, Moretti had the feeling of watching something rehearsed, lacking in spontaneity.

"Inspector, thank God you're here." The house-keeper's opening speech was delivered *sotto voce*. She rested her hands on the arms of her escorts and gave a ragged sob.

"Why is Mr. Smith not with you?" Moretti asked.

It was Hans Ulbricht who answered. "Because he has disappeared, Inspector. We have not seen him for hours."

"No wonder he's quietened down," said Berry Kerr, no irony intended. "We've had a terrible time with him. These two gentlemen got him settled down finally."

"How long has he been missing?"

"It's difficult to say," Adèle Letourneau responded.

Masterson's housekeeper's emotions were not under perfect control, but her appearance was. She was dressed in a black and white striped sweater and black pants, hair and makeup immaculate.

"What happened was he came in to see me, and he'd already been drinking."

"That early?" asked Liz Falla. "Was that unusual?"

"No." The four answered in unison, and Werner Baumgarten took up the story. He had had the least to say of all the crew members since the murder, and Moretti was interested to see how the others turned to him, as if he were their leader in some way.

"He got rough with Madame Letourneau and I heard her call out. When I went in he was tearing at her clothing. Madame was fighting tooth and nail, but he's very strong, as you know. I pulled him off, I hit him, Hans came in, and then Miss Kerr. We got him to his room, and we locked him in, and took the key."

The German gave his account coolly, in even tones, without any overt emotion crossing the strong planes of his face.

Betty Kerr added, "I thought of contacting you, but we've had enough police in this hotel, and these gentlemen said they could manage him."

"So how," Moretti asked, "did he get out of a locked room? Is it on the ground floor?"

"No. He broke the lock." Betty Kerr looked thunderous. "One of our waiters, Shane Durand, saw him leave by the door in the dining room. Shane says he was laughing. He said to Shane, 'I'm going to see a man about a yacht.'"

"The waiter's sure that's what he said?"

"Perfectly."

"What time would this be?" Liz Falla asked.

"Shane isn't sure."

"If Shane Durand saw him leave," Liz Falla asked, "why is it difficult to say when he left?"

Moretti looked at the hotel manager. Her face was flushed and she avoided his eyes.

"DS Falla, get on to Hospital Lane about Mr. Smith, will you, and then continue this with Ms. Kerr in her office." Moretti indicated the empty hotel lounge to one side of the lobby. "We'll use this, Ms. Letourneau. I have some more questions I need answered. And gentlemen —" he looked at the two Germans "— if you could stay in the hotel for the time being?" The tone of voice made it clear this was not a request.

The hotel lounge was a small room at the front of the hotel, filled with flowery chintzes and flower paintings. There were no games and no television, just a small writing desk and a telephone. Moretti pulled out an upright chair from the desk, and turned one of the armchairs around to face it.

"Bear with me, Ms. Letourneau." He smiled at the housekeeper.

Adèle Letourneau said nothing. She leaned back in the chair, hands resting on the padded arms, face expressionless. *Equilibrium regained,* Moretti thought. *Let's see what we can do about that.*

He took out his mobile. "PC Brouard? That report come in? Good. Give me the gist." He listened to the constable's voice, watched the housekeeper's face. Her eyes met his, cool and unflinching.

"Thanks. Have you had any joy with that password? Great. And —?"

At "password" the merest flicker of something moved through those disconcertingly pale eyes.

He put his mobile away. "So, Ms. Letourneau, the Mounties believe you are the brains of the business — for sake of a more accurate word to describe whatever it was that you and Mr. Masterson did."

"*Cochons.*" Her anger seemed to Moretti to be displaced, directed against something other than her true concern. "Shouldn't you be doing something about Martin Smith? Doesn't it look as if the little bastard may be the one you want? We've only his word for it he didn't get the gun back from Bernard, right?"

"Right. And since he's an expert on firearms, the likelihood is that he's scattered it, if not to the four corners of the island, then possibly to the four corners of the bottom of the harbour. So, Ms. Letourneau, tell me this — if you're the brains, why did your deceased boss download virtually everything he could find about the *hawala* financial system on the net?"

"*Hawala?*" The housekeeper's brow knotted in apparent confusion. "You've lost me, Inspector."

"I doubt that. I'm sure you know it's a way of moving money from one country to another based on trust, used for centuries in countries like Pakistan, India, and the Middle East."

"Oh." The knotted brows now unfurrowed. "Bernard was an international entrepreneur. What could be more natural than an interest in how others managed their money? What is so surprising about that?"

"His area of interest. Much of the information he was looking at dealt with the uncovering of illegally obtained funds from racketeering of various kinds, transferred by *hawala*. Cigarette smuggling, credit card forgery, cheque fraud."

Adèle Letourneau looked earnest. "You have to be so careful in Bernard's line of work, not to get caught in such schemes. He always made sure he had up-to-date information about such things."

I'll bet, thought Moretti.

He continued. "There were also a series of numbers on one of his files. Just numbers. Might they be bank accounts?"

"I don't think so." Adèle Letourneau looked amused now. "Bernard was not a whiz on the computer, but even he knew about hackers, that the Internet is not entirely safe. He loved to gamble, and often used the same combination of numbers. Perhaps that is what they are."

"Perhaps. We will, of course, check them out."

"Of course."

Whatever had bothered her when she heard the word *password* was now under control, or what she had heard so far had put her mind at rest. They would have to send the computer away, to see if anything had been erased.

Moretti stood up. "Thank you, Ms. Letourneau. That'll be all for now."

"The hotel manager said something about us getting our passports back."

She was lounging back, relaxed against the cushions of the chair, her smile now almost contemptuous.

"Not now, I'm afraid. The disappearance of Mr. Smith changes all that."

Moretti watched with some satisfaction as Adèle Letourneau's long, square-tipped nails clenched against the arms of the chair.

"What did the amorous Ms. Kerr have to say for herself?"

Liz Falla looked away from the road and grinned.

"Well, they were in the sack all right, and she managed to pin down the time as somewhere around six o'clock this morning. Mind you, she mightn't want anyone to know she was carrying on during office hours. I said we'd send someone to get a statement from Shane. And Hospital Lane has sent over two constables who will stay at the hotel. No sign of Martin Smith on or around the yacht."

"That is no surprise. Martin Smith the firearms expert is a loose cannon. I have a feeling he has miscalculated, and runs the risk of meeting his nemesis."

"Goddess of retribution, right? Don't look so surprised, Guv. You said that once before on our first case, and I looked it up. I always liked those Greek gods and goddesses myself. Sometimes I felt they were a lot more likely a bunch than an almighty single deity that stood on the sidelines and allowed war, famine, and pestilence to carry on regardless. Once shocked my mother to the core by saying that out loud on a Sunday."

As they approached Glategny Esplanade, Liz Falla slowed the car.

"Looking for Brutus?" Moretti asked.

"No, actually. I was going to suggest we stopped off at my place for a sandwich or something before we get to headquarters and meet *our* nemesis. You know who I mean."

Moretti hesitated before replying. Accepting the invitation crossed a line, a line he had put in place at the beginning of a partnership not of his choosing, or hers. He saw a flicker of a smile cross her face, and took it as a challenge.

"Good idea. My lunch was a couple of cupcakes. It'll give me a chance to go over what Brouard told me on the phone."

Liz Falla pulled the BMW alongside the crescent of houses.

"Here we are, Guv. This one's mine." She pointed to an olive-green door.

Falla's flat was on the second floor up a narrow flight of stairs. She unlocked the door that led into a small living room with a large window overlooking the Esplanade, with a kitchen alcove tucked into one corner. Presumably the other doors opposite the window led to bedroom and bathroom. While she put the kettle on and got rolls, cooked meats, and cheese out of the fridge, Moretti looked around.

Presumably the room reflected its owner, although he knew virtually nothing about his partner's private life. Aside from it including the likes of Denny Bras-de-Fer, and Ludo Ross, perhaps. He thought it was eclectic. That was what the magazines who specialized in such things as interior decorating might call it. None of the furniture matched and yet it did. The sofa was covered in a leafy print in various greens, and two armchairs were in a plain bronze fabric with a slight nacreous sheen. There was a large, kilim-covered cushion on the floor by the window on top of a square wooden frame, and a low circular brass-topped table. A high-quality sound system stood in one corner, with CD-stacked towers on each side.

Liz Falla's guitar lay alongside its case on a narrow table against the wall near the kitchen area. It was a beauty, a Martin, with a mahogany body from the look of it, and a rosewood headplate. Moretti bent down to take a look at some of the CD titles. Much folk, some jazz, some classical, little pop. The classical, he noticed, was mostly piano.

"In case you're wondering," Liz Falla put down mugs and plates of food on the low table, "I do read. My bookshelves are all in the bedroom. It's how I get to sleep at night, reading."

"Beautiful guitar. A Martin."

"Of course, you'd know something about guitar. I always think of you as — well, not as a pianist, if you see what I mean. My precious baby, that guitar, my one and only. Sweet as honey, a resonance to die for. Heaven. Help yourself."

Liz went back to the kitchen and returned with a teapot.

"I like this." Moretti pointed at one of the pictures on the wall nearest him.

It was of a woman in a white Victorian dress and broad-brimmed hat, standing in a verdant tropical landscape. Behind her, huge peach-like fruits hung in the trees, and pink disks centred the spidery flowers that rose behind towering ferns on each side of her, threatening to engulf the slender figure. Yet she seemed, somehow, in control, confident in her jungle setting. The signature in the corner was easily read, the artist's identity unmistakeable.

"Rousseau. This is new to me."

"A school friend of mine who went to the States sent it to me. It's in some collection there. It's called *Woman Walking in an Exotic Forest.* I love it."

"You see some reflection of yourself perhaps."

"Perhaps." She changed the subject. "What did PC Brouard have to say?"

"The Mounties got back to us about the Offshore Haven Credit Corporation. Bernard Masterson's name appears on the letterheads of the outfit as principal financial advisor. It's a tax shelter for the very wealthy — or, at least that's what it's supposed to be, only Revenue Canada won't play along. At the moment it looks as if a few hundred investors stand to lose millions of dollars instead of being able to write them off on a fleet of floating palaces, none of which actually appear to exist."

"Were there big names involved?" Liz Falla cut herself another chunk of cheese. "I really like this stuff. It's called *Chaume.* I looked it up. It means 'humble abode.' Perfect, I thought."

"Thanks." Moretti took the piece Falla handed to him from the tip of the knife. "Yes, very big names, and some of them are dangerous customers, and all of them are very, very cross."

"Hmm. We'd better check recent arrivals by air and by sea, hadn't we."

"I'll get Brouard to do it, although if this was a professional hit man he may well have arrived on someone's private Trilander. Hanley will be tickled pink if this is an outside job, which is what it looks like."

"Appearances," said his partner sagely, "can be deceiving."

As she spoke, Moretti's mobile rang.

"PC Brouard, speak of the devil — he is? Where? We'll go straight over."

Closing the mobile, Moretti picked up the rest of his roll.

"Grab your lunch, Falla —"

Before he could finish his sentence, his mobile rang again.

"Ah, Chief Officer Hanley — yes, most unfortunate, I agree — yes, I might indeed put it more strongly myself, sir, but we have other priorities at the moment. The body of Martin Smith has just been found — yes, sir, the bodyguard — and it's certainly not an accidental death. Looks like he's been shot with the same gun as his boss."

On the other side of the brass-topped table, his partner's brown eyes were as large as saucers.

"Nemesis, Guv," she said, as he put his mobile back in his pocket. "You were right."

Moretti stood up and took a last mouthful of *Chaume*.

"Well, Falla, you've been saved for now from Hanley's wrath by the death of the little shit. From your point of view you could say that nothing so became *le petit salaud* in his sordid little life as the leaving of it."

Chapter Seven

"What a place for a toe-rag like this to end his days."

Moretti looked around him.

Martin Smith lay flat on his back in a flower bed of pink geraniums. Beneath the bullet hole in the centre of his forehead, his unseeing eyes seemed as nonplussed as Moretti at finding himself on the front lawn of one of the multi-million-pound homes in the exclusive enclave known as Fort George.

In Guernsey all residential properties are either "local" or "open" market, with tight restrictions on who can own what. When the offshore financial business started to boom in the eighties, a solution was found to the problem of housing those who administered it by building an enclave of lavish homes within the walls of the old seventeenth-century fort, constructed to protect the island during the Napoleonic Wars.

Even a casual visitor coming in through the gate
of the old fort, or approaching by the Fermain Road
entrance off Val des Terres, the steep, winding road
that leads to St. Peter Port from the south, would
sense its apartness from the outside island world. The
speed limit is twenty miles an hour, all dogs have to be
leashed, there is no street parking, no vans allowed on
properties. For manicuring the lawns surrounding each
bastion a gardener is a requirement, not an option.
Not a child in sight, not a sign of life.

At least the lifeless body of the little shit did not
disturb that particular norm, lying there in track pants
and hooded jacket, which lay partly open to reveal a
T-shirt with the word *Bruiser* writ large across his barrel chest.

"Whose property is this? Do we know?" Moretti
asked PC Brouard, who was standing on the path leading to the front door of the house. The constable must
have upset the entire neighbourhood when he arrived
in a police van with Jimmy Le Poidevin and his team,
and parked it on the street, thus breaking two bylaws.

"A Mrs. Amsterdam, Guv. She phoned us when she
found him. She'd come outside to pick flowers, she said,
and there he was. She's in the house with PC Priaulx.
I brought her with me when I heard where it was and
that it was a female calling, if you see what I mean."

"Good thinking, Brouard. No sign of the weapon,
I suppose."

"Not so far, but it's a big property. The back
garden stretches down as far as the cliff path above
Soldier's Bay."

"How is the lady of the house taking it?" Liz Falla asked, standing up and brushing off her skirt. The impact of the bodyguard's fall had displaced some of the soft, weedless soil of the flowerbed, sprinkling the enamelled green of the grass with small chunks of earth.

"Shocked. Embarrassed."

"Embarrassed?" Moretti and Falla said in unison.

"That's what it sounded like to me — you know, what will the neighbours say?"

Moretti was aware of a curtain across the road moving, but no one appeared outside the walls of his or her personal fort to question their presence on Mrs. Amsterdam's lawn.

"Do you mind? I'm assuming you are as interested in footprints as I am, and we're losing the light," Jimmy Le Poidevin shouted in their direction. He and an assistant were unrolling SOC tape around the front lawn. "Nichol Watt's on his way."

"See how he fell?" Moretti said to Liz Falla, pointing at the body. "Right across the length of the bed. Whoever shot him came toward him from the direction of the house next to this one. He's facing the other property. Brouard, check if there's anyone home and, if not, find out who lives there."

PC Brouard moved his hefty body with athletic alacrity out of the way of a constable banging a supporting pole into the pristine grass, and made his way next door.

Moretti and Falla crossed to the front door, which was locked in spite of the presence of a policewoman on the premises. The constable opened it when he rang the bell. Moretti took in the spy hole in the centre of the door, and what looked like a speaking device of some kind on a side wall. Behind the front door stretched a reception hall into which you could have dropped the whole of Falla's humble abode. Moretti wondered if she was thinking that also.

"Sir, PC Priaulx, sir. She's — Mrs. Amsterdam — is in here."

"Here" was a smallish sitting room at the end of the hall, looking out on to the garden behind the house through a wall of glass. It was expensively furnished, upholstered, and decorated, yet managed at the same time to be impersonal, like a five-crown hotel suite. As they approached, Mrs. Amsterdam stood up, slowly and shakily, from a satin-covered sofa, glass in hand. Brandy, from the look of it.

"Are you in charge?" It was said in the tone of one used to being in charge herself.

Mrs. Amsterdam was a woman small in stature, but generously proportioned. She was fair-skinned, but the high colour in her cheeks suggested not only present emotion, but a tendency to tipple even when not confronted by violent death on her front lawn. Her hair was of an even tint not unlike the gold satin of the sofa from which she had risen. She was dressed quite formally for the time of day in a paisley-patterned silk dress and she teetered ever so slightly on her very high heels before regaining control of her balance.

"I am Detective Inspector Moretti, Mrs. Amsterdam, and this is Detective Sergeant Falla. You have had a shock."

"I most certainly have. Sit down, Detective Inspector. I'll sit down myself. What a dreadful sight!"

Not her kind of corpse, thought Liz Falla, and then silently reproached herself. At least Mrs. Amsterdam was not hysterical, which she might reasonably have been in the circumstances.

"Can I get you medical help, Mrs. Amsterdam?" she asked. "Phone your doctor?"

"No, but you could pour me another brandy. The decanter's over there."

Liz Falla fetched the heavy cut-glass decanter from a side table, where it stood on a massive silver tray with a stoppered sherry decanter and a bottle of single malt whisky. She poured a generous dollop into Mrs. Amsterdam's glass and handed it to her. Not having been invited to sit down, she stood where she could watch Mrs. Amsterdam's face as she answered Moretti.

"Tell me how you found him."

"Well —" Mrs. Amsterdam fortified herself with a gulp of brandy "— I have people coming in to dinner tonight, and I'm going with the rose and gold Spode, so I wanted the pink geraniums for my Chelsea Bird."

"Your —?"

"The china pattern, Inspector. Around a hundred pounds a plate if someone is butterfingered, but there you are. I like to do the flower arrangements myself, because we have an excellent cook who can ice a cake and cut a perfect pastry flower for a pie, but is hopeless with table decorations. One flower in a vase with one stalk of something or other is not my idea of adornment. I'm a bit rococo, and Fritz is all for minimalism, you see,

so out I went with my secateurs, and there was this —
person, looking straight up at me." Mrs. Amsterdam's
voice shook, and she fortified herself some more.

"Did you see anyone? A car? Anything at all?"

"Well, no, I didn't exactly stay to look around. I
picked up my secateurs — I'd dropped them, you see,
the shock — and then ran, literally *ran*, back into the
house, locked myself in, and phoned for you people."
She closed her eyes briefly, then continued. "My husband always says don't rock the boat and not to over-
react, it attracts attention, but what else could I do?"

"Should we phone your husband for you?" Liz
Falla asked. "Is he at the office?"

"No, as a matter of fact, he's not. He's in the hospital, having his gall bladder removed. I didn't like to
bother him with *this*."

*Don't bother the man with the death of a little
nobody,* thought Moretti. "Is the dead man known to
you?" he asked.

"Good God, Inspector, no! I have never seen him
before, and he is the most unlikely person to end up
here, in one's flowerbed, don't you think? I was going
to ask you the same question — is he known to the
police?"

"We know who he is." Moretti chose his words
carefully. "He is a recent visitor, arrived on a yacht."

"A yacht! Not his, I presume."

"No. He was the owner's bodyguard."

"Bodyguard! Dressed like that! Oh, Gareth will be
so upset!"

"Your husband?"

At the corpse's lack of dress sense? At the body's choice of profession? Liz Falla wondered.

"Yes, my husband. I assumed the man was a drifter, who'd got into bad company, that sort of thing."

Moretti stood up. "I think we can fairly say he got into bad company, Mrs. Amsterdam, but no, he was not a drifter. We shall have to bring in more police, go over your garden. It extends as far as the cliff path, I believe?"

"Yes, but there's a high wall, with broken glass along the top. I really don't think anyone could have got in that way. Gareth has been talking about enclosing the front garden and installing a gate with electronic security, but he put it off because of his gall bladder."

"Why was he planning to increase your security? Have you had any problems?"

"Oh no, but you can never be too careful, Inspector. Gareth is with Crédit Genève and safety is their middle name, so of course we made it ours. Surely this is just a random shooting, Inspector, and this man ended up by chance on our property."

"We cannot answer that yet, Mrs. Amsterdam. By the way, who lives next door, to the left of your house, near the flower bed?"

Mrs. Amsterdam looked surprised. "I have no idea. Someone like us, I imagine."

As they left the room, Mrs. Amsterdam finished the last of her brandy and rose to replenish her glass.

* * *

"So, Falla, what are your gut feelings about Mrs. Amsterdam?"

Liz Falla glanced briefly at Moretti, and then redirected her attention to Val des Terre's hairpin bends.

"Lives in a bubble, doesn't even know the someone-like-us next door. Why was she having a dinner party when her husband was in hospital, Guv? Was it a hen party? Didn't sound like it to me, but perhaps a girls' night out — or in — for this crowd does require the best china. She'll have to change her colour scheme, won't she, because Martin Smith has pretty well flattened her pelargoniums. We'll have to talk to the staff, since they probably know who was coming."

"Especially the minimalistic cook who's no good with flowers. Something else, Falla. About the corpse. About his face."

"It was a neat, expert job, wasn't it?"

"Yes, like the death of his employer. Now, think about Ms. Letourneau's story. She had to fight him off, she said, tooth and nail. Did you see the length of her nails?"

"Her nails!" The BMW took a twist in the road with extra velocity. "There wasn't a mark or a scratch on him, except for the hole in the middle of his forehead."

"Exactly. Now, maybe the little shit was a quick healer —"

"— or maybe Ms. Letourneau was lying through those teeth she supposedly fought him off with."

"And if so, why? That's the interesting question, Falla. Why would she lie about fighting him off?"

"Because there wasn't a real fight in the first place, and maybe it was staged for Betty Kerr's benefit — and ours — and maybe he wasn't supposed to have said what he said to Shane. 'I'm going to see a man about a yacht.' That's what he said to him, right?"

"Right. And what better place to go than Fort George if you are looking for a well-heeled somebody who might be involved with floating palaces. I doubt he arrived on foot, so we'll have to do a door to door enquiry about vehicles, etc."

"That'll go down like a lead balloon, I imagine. The sound of the gun, Guv. Surely someone in that particular neighbourhood would react to a gunshot."

"They must have used a silencer — I assume one can be used on a Glock. I think we can call off the divers, because clearly this gun is not on the harbour bottom, and I don't think we have a third weapon."

"Time of death?"

"Nichol will be able to tell us. Whether it was a crime of opportunity, or carefully planned, it took nerve on the Amsterdams' front lawn in broad daylight."

Moretti's mobile rang. It was Brouard, sounding animated. "I found out who lives next door, Guv. Friend of yours."

"A friend of mine in Fort George? I think not, Brouard."

"He's in your band, Guv. Garth Machin. I just spoke to his wife."

The music always played in Moretti's head. Snippets of Cole Porter while looking at the dead body of Martin Smith, snatches of Dizzy Gillespie when talking to Mrs. Amsterdam, segments of "An American in Paris," played on the piano by Gershwin, whenever Sandy Goldstein crossed his mind, which was happening from time to time.

Pieces coming together, like fragments of music, into some sort of coherence, or semi-coherence. Garth, Gareth, Gareth, Garth. Coincidence? Or confusion because the names were so alike. Had Martin Smith meant to end up at the Machins'? Masterson's insistence on being in Victoria Marina, where his Vento Teso was close to Garth's boat. Not to forget Nicol's Capri, and the scene in the club between the two men.

The music still played, but the soundtrack had changed. Still Gershwin, but now it was "Rhapsody in Blue," and the wail of Garth's horn that rang through Moretti's head.

Garth Machin worked for a company called Northland Private Banking, whose offices were in a small enclave of similar businesses quite close to the police station and Government House Hotel, one of the premier hotels on the island. All the buildings in the area were new, but designed to blend in with St. Peter Port's traditional architecture. Behind a false front of becomingly aged stone in pale ochres, greys, and creams, the bank discreetly announced its presence on a small brass plate to the right of the main entrance, alongside two other similar plaques for banks in the same building. From the corners of the structure CCTV cameras looked down on all who left or arrived, like angular, featureless gargoyles.

As far as Moretti could recall, Northland was an offshoot of one of the major British banks, specifically set up to handle financial planning for clients with an international asset base. It was one of many such offshore banks, which unabashedly proclaimed themselves as operating solely for "high-net" clients with assets in the millions, and whose own assets were in the billions. High on the list of attributes touted in their brochures or on Internet sites, right up there with the depth of their assets or the breadth of their services, was the quality of discretion. Facts would not be difficult to come by, if all Moretti wanted to know was the name of any of the funds administered, or types of accounts available, but if he wanted to know the names of any of the people whose funds or accounts those were, he would be stonewalled, shown the door, or simply laughed at.

He was surprised at the instant response when he identified himself to the disembodied female voice on the intercom. "Yes," said the voice, and there was the sound of the lock releasing on the glass and metal door.

Melissa Machin must have phoned, he realized. He was glad he had sent Falla on to the station to call off the divers and see how Le Marchant was doing. There was the possibility that Garth might be more open with him if he were on his own. That is, if there was something to be open about.

As she dropped him off, Falla asked, "Why did you send Le Marchant out there in the first place? Why not send a policewoman to look after her and keep an eye out for trouble?"

"Because if she is gaga — and I am not at all sure that she is — she is much more likely to spill the beans in an unguarded moment to a man than to a woman. Le Marchant is young, wet behind the ears, and not as cool as he likes to think he is, and I have a feeling La Chancho likes dominating the male of the species."

Falla's laugh echoed around the square as she pulled away from the curb. Moretti could still hear it as the BMW turned into Hospital Lane.

Garth's office was on the second floor, according to the list by the stairs, and according to the young woman in the lobby.

"He's expecting you."

So Melissa had phoned. Damn.

As Moretti came around the corner at the top of the stairs, Garth was coming toward him. In his navy blue suit and crisply knotted tie he was quite unlike the sax player whose usual dress was casual to the point of dereliction, but the tie made a statement of some sort. Against a black background a well-endowed and cheerful woman rode what looked like a unicorn across its shiny silken surface.

"What the hell's going on, Ed?" Garth's voice was in a higher register than usual, betraying an anxiety he was unable to hide.

"I'm here to ask you the same question, Garth," Moretti replied. "Let's talk in your office."

Garth's office was a room of modest proportions whose outstanding feature was a complete lack of any individual touches. There was a large desk, a host of filing cabinets, a computer, printer, fax, all the usual office equipment. The two windows were screened by white vertical blinds, and an oatmeal-coloured carpet covered the floor. Moretti could not see a single family photograph, one piece of anything that reflected the married man or the musical man, no evidence that here was a human being with a life that gave him any pleasure. There were two photographs on the wall opposite the door, one of the bank's London headquarters, the other of St. Peter Port Harbour. Neither was an interesting piece of photography — not that it mattered much, since both were tucked away beyond a cabinet and therefore unviewable from the desk.

"For God's sake, Ed, the next-door neighbour has a fucking corpse in her fuchsias and one of your lot gives Melissa the third degree. She was in a state when she phoned me, and she's not the hysterical sort, Melissa."

Garth took himself round to the far side of the desk, but he remained standing. Moretti had the impression of someone gathering control by putting distance between himself and an adversary.

Moretti pulled out the chair nearest the desk and sat down. He watched as Garth sat down pulling out a pack of cigarettes from a desk drawer, and cursed himself for quitting. It might have given them a blokes-together moment if he hadn't.

"Why not you, damnit, instead of one of your heavy-footed minions?"

"Brouard's a big lad, it's true, but he's a kindly soul. Not me, because I'm here." As Garth lit up, Moretti leaned across the desk into the enticing fragrance of Benson & Hedges. "As you said to me, Garth — what the hell's going on? Or — *is* anything going on? The dead man was the personal bodyguard of the murder victim on the yacht in Victoria Marina, and I am wondering if he was trying to see you. He was certainly trying to see *someone* in that neck of the woods."

"The next-door neighbour from the look of it, whom I wouldn't know from a hole in the ground. Would anyone in his right mind try to get hold of me at home on a working day? I'm always here, God help me, even at this God-forsaken hour." Garth swept an arm around the sterile confines of his workplace.

"This particular victim was not that well-informed about how your sort live. Also, there's a possibility he was trying to see your wife, Garth."

"Melissa? Why in the hell would he want to see Melissa?"

"Blackmail." Moretti paused a moment to let the word sink in. "I think he may have hoped to blackmail either one of you. Preferably you, perhaps, but your wife could be more easily intimidated. Intimidation was very much this fellow's forte."

Moretti watched as the muscles in Garth's face tightened. The underdressed lady on the unicorn galloped merrily along on the undulations of his accelerated breathing, and the cigarette in his hand shook as he put it to his mouth, scattering ash on the dark surface of his suit. Before he could respond, Moretti said, "I don't think you are going to tell me anything, are you? So let me guess this is somehow linked to whatever passed between you and Nichol at the club the other night."

It was a wild shot in the dark, but it found its target. Garth dropped the half-smoked cigarette in the ashtray on the desk and rubbed his hands over his face. When he looked up at Moretti he seemed almost on the verge of tears.

"Leave it, Ed. You're way off base. That was something else altogether. Nichol Watt is an arsehole, as well you know, and he made a pass at Melissa. He's a bastard, that's all. A bastard," he repeated.

"No argument here." Moretti stood up. "No point, is there, in continuing this, so I'll be off. Just remember, Garth — I'll do whatever I can to help you and to protect your wife, if that's necessary. I can't speak to your financial or fiduciary skills, but you're far too good a musician to lose."

"As I've already told you, I don't know what the hell you're talking about."

"So you have. Will you be at the club tonight?"

"If I'm not hauled away to the calaboose." Garth gave a feeble attempt at a laugh that caught in his throat and died.

"I'll see myself out."

"Do that." He was pulling out his cigarettes again before Moretti got to the door.

It was a short walk to the station, and Moretti had just reached the courtyard when his mobile rang. It was Don Taylor, sounding triumphant.

"Ed, I've got it. Why his nickname rang a bell. Something that happened about fifteen years ago, to do with deregistering a deposit taker."

"Great news, Don. I'm tied up at the moment — but I'll be at the club tonight, so why don't you come over to my place afterward."

He and Don had done this before, going back and continuing the evening with jazz, and more jazz, until dawn. Less tiring than with Ludo, because he didn't drink as much in Don's company.

A break maybe. God knew they could do with one. Because if this case involved the kind of people and the kind of money he suspected it did, he would have to have it all laid out in black and white, cut and dried, everything dotted and crossed and beyond the slightest suggestion of a shadow of a doubt. Whoever had seen to it that Masterson died with a bullet in the brain was a very big gun indeed.

He was playing "Angel Eyes" when Sandy Goldstein walked into the club that night. He must have hesitated or changed the beat in some way, because Dwight Ellis followed the direction of his glance, raised one eyebrow, grinned, and gave a soundless whistle.

She was on her own. She looked around a moment, then sat down at a table near the back. Moretti turned his attention back to the piano, and watched Garth Machin stand up and start to play. The navy-suited banker with the shaking hands earlier in the evening was nowhere in sight. This Garth Machin was a cool and collected cat, full of confidence and cuss words, very much his usual silver-tongued Fénion self. It was quite a performance, any sign of weakness gone.

Ah well. *Here's hoping Don has something useful,* thought Moretti, as the sublime tone of Garth's horn floated across the smoky room toward the table where Sandy Goldstein sat. She looked up to thank the girl who brought her a glass of wine, then back to the stage, raising the wineglass and smiling at him. Then she mouthed something at him, but Moretti could not read her lips.

He sometimes felt bliss when Garth was in full flight. Add to that a beautiful woman smiling at him, and he felt no pain. He saw Dwight grin at him again and he grinned back. One more number, then the set would be over, and he could find out how she managed to spring herself loose from La Veile and Julia King.

A piano solo for him, with some soft bass accompaniment from Lonnie. Johnny Mercer's "Laura." Applause, acknowledged with a wave of the hand. He still had to stop himself from reaching up for a cigarette from the ashtray on top of the piano.

He had just stood up when he saw Don Taylor arrive and stop to talk to Deb Duchemin, who had taken a break from restaurant duties upstairs and, with a feeling that was far from blissful, he remembered their arrangement.

In theatre and in politics, timing is everything, so they say. He crossed the room to Sandy Goldstein's table.

"Hi. I'm glad you made it, but how did you make it?"

Sandy Goldstein laughed. She was wearing neutral colours again, black this time, with a pair of striking turquoise and silver earrings, and her hair was caught up in a loose chignon held by a large silver clip.

"Julia is working on a series of pictures for the new book, so I left her in peace. I took a cab — Gwen recommended someone reliable, and the path's not that wet at the moment. I'm glad I made it. You're good."

"You sound surprised."

"Yankee superiority. We invented the stuff, after all."

"Not Yankees, if I remember my history."

"True."

Moretti pulled out a chair and sat down. He didn't know what perfume she was wearing, but it definitely wasn't damp fleece. He called the server over and ordered a Scotch and another glass of wine for Sandy Goldstein.

"I have a phone for you, a mobile. Or, rather, my partner has. It's in her name, so there shouldn't be any problem. I was going to bring it to you yesterday, but we had new developments in the case I'm working on. It's at the office."

"Thank you so much. Perhaps I could pick it up tomorrow? Unless, that is, if it's not too late — we could get it after this?"

More tiger eyes than angel eyes, looking right at him and making it quite clear that this was an opening he could walk right into, if he wanted. The drinks arrived.

"I wish. But I have a —" he hesitated, and then said "— a previous arrangement. I'll get it to you tomorrow, without fail."

"I see." Her voice was cool. A previous arrangement, what a brilliant choice of phrase. He wouldn't have blamed her if she'd taken the glass of wine and poured it over his head. But he wanted no one, not even Sandy Goldstein, to know he was meeting with Don Taylor.

She was gone before the end of the last set, and he didn't see her leave. But it was a relief not to walk out of the club on his own in front of her, leaving her there.

Don moved out of the shadows where he was waiting near Moretti's car. As he got in he said, "I liked the way you played 'I Don't Stand a Ghost of a Chance.' *Con fuoco*. Did the stunning woman in black and silver give you the old heave-ho?"

"Something like that." Moretti resisted an impulse to clip Don around the ear, and accelerated away from the curb. This, after all, was his idea, not Don's. "Tell me about deregistering, tell me you've got something for me. Tell me you're not wasting my time."

"Your time?" Don sounded aggrieved. "How about mine? I'm getting a bit old for this wee small hours of the morning shit."

"I had to turn down the stunning woman in black and silver if you must know, because I had a date with you, and I couldn't tell her I had a date with you."

Don laughed with unrestrained and heartless glee. "Happens to me all the time — brush-offs, I mean — but I know you don't spend so much time hanging out with Captain Heartbreak as I do."

"Captain Heartbreak? God, Don, where'd you get him from? The back of a cornflakes box?"

They drove in silence the rest of the way, while Don hummed "Just a Gigolo" under his breath, and Moretti thought about Val and his broken mainland relationship. Appearances can be deceiving. He too had hung out with Captain Heartbreak, more than once. Then there was timing, and all that stars-are-against-me shit.

The night was indeed starless, presaging more rain. Moretti's Triumph squeaked between the old gateposts to the cottage, and he brought it to a halt on the cobblestones. As Don got out, he leaned over the low roof of the car and grinned. "Cheer up, honey, I'll make this date worthwhile for you, I promise. It's all in the name, Ed, all in the name."

"Come in, you idiot."

Don refused coffee, but settled for Glenmorangie instead, and Moretti joined him. He put some Branford Marsalis on the player, something with a clean, astringent quality, appealing to the intellect rather than the senses. Marsalis was wonderful, but he did not touch Moretti's heart.

"Okay, what have you got?"

"Remember I said that nickname rang a bell? Well, about fifteen years ago, I think it was, the Advisory and Finance Committee refused to renew the registration of a deposit taker — the reason being that the outfit was on the verge of bankruptcy. In fact, it went into liquidation a year or so later."

"That's happened more than once," Moretti responded. "The committee did its job."

"Ah, but on this occasion what they *didn't* do was tell anyone they had deregistered the company. It was assumed the outfit would take no more deposits, and the legal wallahs told the committee they were under no obligation to publish the withdrawal. So, a heap of people went on handing over their money which the company — surprise, surprise — went on taking and, of course, they lost it. Moreover, if the Advisory and Finance Committee *had* published their decision in the first place, the outfit would have immediately gone into liquidation and the depositors would have got a bigger dividend."

"So a lot of people got angry."

"One did more than get angry. He sued and won. That set the cat among the pigeons for the States. All hell broke loose, and they were inundated with summonses from other depositors. So they did what you'd expect them to do."

"They set up a Committee of Enquiry."

"Got it in one. It dragged on for about two years and the judgement they handed down was a beaut: that the depositors should not be recompensed in full because — listen to this — it was never the intention of the States that there should be any kind of guarantee to depositors their deposits should be repaid. Besides, anyone using this particular outfit should have accepted it was a lot more risky than placing their money with a well-established subsidiary of a well-established clearing bank."

"In other words, *caveat emptor*." Moretti held up the bottle, and Don held out his glass for a refill. "So, how does this tie in with my corpse?"

"The name. That's what came back to me, so I checked some of the details. Of course, it may be just a strange coincidence —"

"— I don't believe in coincidence."

"Bulmit. The name of the deposit-taker was Bulmit Finance Limited."

"*Boule à mite*. Bulmit."

"Said I'd make it worth your while," Don said cheerfully, holding up his glass. "Happy hunting, Detective Inspector. By the way, did you know that witches only wear silver — and that black is their favourite colour?"

After Don left, Moretti went over his plan of action for the next day. It was a plan already decided on before Don's visit, and the Bulmit story made little difference. There were a lot of loose ends to tie up, he would have to leave many of them in Falla's hands, and this just made one more. From a desk drawer he took out his personal mobile phone, and placed it near the door so he would not forget it in the morning. Then he turned off the record player, and went over to the shelf where he kept his collection of videos and DVDs. He knew exactly what he wanted, and it took him only a moment to find it.

Casablanca.

Ingrid Bergman and Humphrey Bogart.

Of all the star-crossed lovers, those two were right up there with Romeo and Juliet, in his book.

Chapter Eight

Day Four

"Loose ends, Guv. It's all loose ends at the moment, isn't it?"

Liz Falla was feeling a bit like a loose end herself. Frazzled and frayed. She had been hauled over the coals by Hanley when, as far as she could see, the problem was the decrepit, pistol-packing vamp he was trying to shield, and not anything she herself had done. Or not done.

"Right. So I want to sort out priorities. We can forget about such minutiae as the lipstick, for instance. We'll not get the results back for a while yet, and we know whose it was without asking for the lady's DNA. Tell the crew they can go back on the yacht, but we are keeping their passports. We'll keep a watch on them — I'll set that up — but it might be useful to see what, if anything, develops. Martin Smith's murder makes me a lot more interested in those two Germans.

I've called the divers off, because there's no point in keeping them on a lookout for a silver handbag and a pair of satin gloves. She could have burned or buried them by now."

"Why isn't she under arrest?"

"Come on, Falla, you know the answer to that one. What's ironic is that my chief worry is *her* safety rather than the safety of others because of her. It's very possible that Ronald Fellowes was taken, to use Gord Collenette's word, and that gives Lady Fellowes a motive for killling Masterson. But it also gives others a good reason to kill her, and I doubt she charmed Le Marchant into driving her down to Fort George so she could put a bullet through Martin Smith's brain. Someone else did that."

"More likely the same person did both, and she stood in the doorway of Masterson's bedroom and cheered him on, first time around."

"That's the most likely scenario and it means that La Chancho knows who killed Martin Smith. I have Nichol's preliminary report on Smith, and there's nothing extraordinary there — almost certainly the same weapon, around midday, and there's not a single scratch on his body or face from frenzied female attacks. No claw marks. Also, Jimmy says from the trajectory of the bullet, whoever shot Smith was standing on the Machins' front lawn." Moretti looked up from the notes on his desk. "Falla, could you run a check on our pathologist for me? Don't farm this one out, do it yourself. See if there's anything we should know about Nichol's time in the States."

Liz Falla looked surprised, but all she said was, "Okay, Guv, will do."

"And if you could drop in on Miss Ferbrache's lodgers at La Veile with this in the next day or so —" Moretti took out the mobile and handed it over. "It's in your name, tell them."

Liz Falla took it and asked, "Any message? Anything you want me to say, or to look for?"

"Not that I can think of. I'm doing this as much for Miss Ferbrache as for any other reason."

Liar, he thought. This has become a peace offering, laid at the lady's feet. See what a nice guy I really am, Sandy Goldstein.

"What about the Glock, Guv? Do you think the killer still has it?"

"I do. The door-to-door enquiries turned up nothing, because nobody set foot outside their front doors."

"Except Mrs. Amsterdam and her secateurs. Any footprints?"

"Quite a few. The ground was soft, and Jimmy says he's got one set that isn't either the Amsterdams' or their gardener. Probably the killer, definitely a man from the size, and trainers rather than dress shoes."

"Mightn't they be someone from the Machins' place?"

"Could be, although there seems to be little coming and going across those front gardens. But tomorrow I want you to go and talk to Melissa Machin. Do it in office hours, so you get her on her own."

"Okay. Any hints as to how to go about it? You know her, right?"

Moretti shrugged his shoulders. "Only met her a couple of times, and never at the club. Struck me as inoffensive, say the right thing type of woman. A bit of a Stepford wife, know what I mean?"

"Not a hair and not a comment out of place. Got it." Liz Falla looked up from the pad in which she was taking notes. "Those numbers on Masterson's computer — Brouard wonders if they're post office box numbers. He's checking on that."

"Interesting. It'll take time because, if they are, they're more likely to be American."

"Why would Masterson keep a list of post office box numbers in the first place?"

They were in Moretti's office. The starless night had turned into a rainy day, and the lights were on. Liz Falla could see from her superior's face he had not slept much the previous night, or had drunk too much — or whatever. In the fluorescent overhead glow he looked pale and drawn, and his eyes were sunk in their sockets. Pale — but interesting, to use one of his favourite words.

"Presumably because they had something to do with one of his schemes. If there's one thing clear about Bernard Masterson, he had any numbers of irons in the fire, Falla. But there's one aspect of this above all that puzzles the hell out of me."

"Just one, Guv? Sorry, bad joke in the circumstances."

Moretti didn't seem to have heard what she said and made no comment. He went on. "One thing, Falla, just one frigging thing that still doesn't make sense. Why was he here at all?"

Before Liz Falla could attempt an answer, Moretti added, "Here's my guess at the most likely reason. He came here to meet someone, possibly more than one person. I cannot believe he came all this way for a rendezvous with Lady Fellowes, although it's a mystery how she knew him, and how she knew he was here. So that leads to one big, gigantic, overarching question."

"If not Lady Fellowes, who?"

"Exactly, Falla. Who the hell was Bernard Masterson here to meet?"

Moretti got up and walked over to the window. Turning back to his partner he said, "I'm going to Herm today, to talk to someone, and I may have to go to London."

"So you'll be away a day or two?" Liz Falla smiled. "Will I have to cover for you, Guv? Is this something a bit unscheduled, as you might say?" She had covered for him before, when he took off to Italy on their last murder investigation, their first case together.

Moretti smiled. "I don't think it'll be necessary this time. If Hanley wants us to leave La Chancho alone, then I think he'll fall in with my plans."

"Which are —?"

Moretti came back to the desk, sat down, and explained.

"The fulmars are nesting on the cliffs near Caquorobert, and I am actually beginning to believe that God's in his heaven, as I once did in the good old days, when

I was eight years old. And you want me to return to the real world?"

Moretti found Peter Walker eating lunch at the White House Hotel. It was a quiet day on the tiny island because of the weather, and they were virtually alone in the dining room. He ordered grilled trout and coffee, and waited until the waiter had left the table before replying. "Only in your mind. Lend me a half hour or so of your expertise, Peter."

Walker sighed and put down his glass of beer. "So much for 'I won't ask you to help with the villains.' Fill me in, Ed. It'll be the murder on the yacht, I assume. Yes, we've even heard about it over here."

Peter Walker listened without comment as Moretti went over the events of the past few days. He had just finished when the waiter returned with his meal, and he paused while Peter Walker ordered another beer.

"Go on."

"I'm done. That's it," Moretti said, taking up his knife and fork.

"No, you're not. You have a theory about why Masterson was here. I can hazard a guess at your theory, and you're probably right."

"So tell me what I'm right about."

"Come on, Ed. Don't get coy with me. I am not going to put words into your mouth."

"Okay, here it is." Moretti took another mouthful of fish, and put down his knife and fork. "I think Masterson was here because there was some sort of meeting set up between a handful of individuals about some sort of scheme, almost certainly international in scope, and the significant thing about Guernsey was that it was off the beaten track. I suspect whatever funds are involved are here too, but what brought them together here was the comparative anonymity the island could afford one or two high-profile people. The scrutiny at the airport is low-key and low-tech compared to that in most countries. As to why, there are all kinds of possibilities, and terrorism certainly comes to mind. However, there's a problem with that one."

"I agree. This Masterson was not the kind of operator who put himself on the line up front, and he wouldn't need to. He would hide behind his far-flung bank accounts."

"Exactly. That's what I keep coming back to, like a frigging dead end. So that means — what?"

"That whatever this is, it's very, very big. That it required the movers and shakers meeting the money man face to face for some reason or other. That scrap of paper about yachts could provide a clue. You say that, from what the RCMP told you, it's a scam that backfired. It could be that Masterson had various schemes underway to provide funds for this group, and the failure of one of his schemes — which attracted unwanted attention — gave them cold feet. He could also have been cheating them, or they thought he was cheating them, and he had to reassure them he was not. Apparently, that didn't work, and he paid the price."

Peter's beer arrived. Moretti drank his coffee and waited for the question he knew was coming.

"But you didn't just come here to disturb my holiday with a brainstorming session over lunch, did you,

Ed?" Peter Walker looked at Moretti over the top of his half-empty glass. "Tell me what you want me to do."

"You still have high-level contacts at Scotland Yard — with the Fraud Squad, among others, and in MI6. At the level I require for information on this case, this is a game of contacts, and I want you to put me in touch with the kind of people who would know if there is some kind of major operation in the wind. Forget terrorism. I know there is no way you or anyone could get me information about that, so what I want is to talk to someone who might give me something useful about international operations that might involve fraud on a massive scale."

"Investigative work at the level you're talking about, Ed, is a competitive sport, just like professional football. And just as cutthroat. Do you really think that anyone working on something like that will give you a helping hand?"

"I think there's a chance they might, in exchange for some fresh info. Such as a list of post office box numbers in the States."

Let's jump to conclusions, thought Moretti, *and pray that Brouard's idea holds water.* He added, "And you know the other reason, Peter?"

"I know why *I'll* be doing this, but the fact that you're a nice person who plays great jazz piano will butter no parsnips with anyone else."

Moretti grinned. "Thanks. The other reason is that I'm only a copper from a little, unimportant channel island and not a wannabe mainland hotshot detective climbing up the same greasy pole."

"You could be right." Peter Walker stood up, draining the last of his beer. "But the only way anyone will listen to this unimportant little copper is with a personal introduction. Arriving letter in hand at the portals of New Scotland Yard will not be enough, not for what you need. Come on, Ed. We've both got some packing to do and a plane to catch."

It was fortunate Moretti had already done his packing. The alacrity with which Peter Walker rose from his chair and bounced across the room suggested that the charms of bladderweed and butterfish had started to pale. Men of action do not find it easy to go gently into their golden years. Except, perhaps, for Ludo Ross. Maybe he was an exception.

Liz Falla eased the police Vauxhall along Verte Rue, the mobile bouncing about on the seat beside her, the car sliding on the mud-filled ruts at one moment, stalling in the troughs between them the next. She wouldn't want to take any car of hers down here, not that she had a car of her own.

She was quite happy to run this errand for Moretti, because she was curious to see the two American women for herself. She was somewhat surprised at the ease with which her boss had accepted the story he was told, and was keen to see if her theory as to why was correct. Of course, the murder enquiry took top priority, but Liz Falla was of the opinion that was only part of the reason.

As she approached the house, she saw one of the blinds in a downstairs window flick open, then close again. She rolled down the window of the car, and waved at whoever was watching her arrival. Hopefully they would see it was a woman's hand, and give her a chance to explain. After all, they only had the word of one woman that the gun was a replica, and it had never been produced as evidence. She turned the car so that it drew up alongside the house, with her face in full view.

"Hello!" Picking up the mobile from the car seat she waved it out of the window. A moment later, a tall dark-haired woman with a slender, long-legged build came out of the house, closing the door behind her.

So, her theory was correct. Ed Moretti's motives had as much to do with hormones as the milk of human kindness. This one was a looker all right.

"Hi. Are you Ed's sergeant?"

So he was Ed now, was he? As the woman came to the side of the car, Liz saw that the slenderness was misleading. The sleeves of her sweater were pushed up, and her forearms were muscled, her hands strong.

"That's me, Liz Falla. You are —?"

"Sandra Goldstein."

Sandra Goldstein's eyes were watchful, something almost animal about them. Liz smiled in what she hoped was a warm and reassuring manner. "DI Moretti asked me to give you this, and to check everything is in order."

Not that he had asked her to do that, strangely enough, in the circumstances. She handed over the mobile.

"We're fine. Ed couldn't make it himself?"

"No. He's off the island at the moment, on police business."

"Oh."

That was all she said, but Liz Falla felt a wave of something very much like hostility from Sandra Goldstein. Not fear, and that she might have expected, given the story they had been told, but a feeling it was she, and not some distant ex-husband, who was the enemy.

"The phone's got all the bells and whistles. DI Moretti thought you'd need them — overseas calls and suchlike. I will be billed for the phone, and DI Moretti will submit it to Miss Ferbrache, who will add it to your rent. Okay?"

"Okay. Thanks."

If she had hoped to be asked in for a cuppa or whatever, it clearly wasn't going to happen. Liz peered beyond Sandra Goldstein's shoulder at the house, but there was no sign of the other two occupants, no sound of a child. There was something sinister about the little house, standing there in the midst of nowhere, rain dripping noiselessly from a downspout at the side of the building. It seemed less like a haven than a hideaway. Which was what it was also supposed to be, Liz reminded herself. Hideaways are not only for outlaws and escapees.

"You'd better go in," she said. "You're getting wet, standing there in the rain. So, if everything's in order, I'll be off then."

The rain glistened on Sandra Goldstein's long dark hair and dampened the sleeves of her sweater, on the front of which the Florida panther snarled menacingly into Liz Falla's face.

"Everything's in order."

"Goodbye then."

The car swerved as Liz turned around on the soggy rough grass in front of the house, sloshing Sandra Goldstein's jeans with muddy rainwater. She swore under her breath and jumped back, glaring at Liz as though she had done it deliberately. Maybe she hadn't been as careful as she might have been, had the lady shown any gratitude.

In her rear-view mirror she saw Sandra Goldstein still standing and watching until the police car had disappeared out of sight.

It was only later it occurred to Liz that the animosity she had sensed was connected with her answer to the question about Ed Moretti: that he was away on police business. While she was checking out Nichol Watt she'd take another look at Sandra Goldstein.

It wasn't far to her next port of call, and she was in the right frame of mind for it. It was a relief to be out of the muddy morass of Verte Rue and on paved road again. Liz gunned the engine and cut the corner, narrowly avoiding a small van whose driver honked protestingly at this enforcer of law and order breaking the rules. It took only about ten minutes to reach the strange circular construction of Ludo Ross's house and to turn down the short, steep lane to the open entrance to the courtyard. Within seconds she heard the barking of the two ridgebacks, who ran out to meet the car, teeth bared. She turned off the engine and waited for Ludo to appear before she got out of the car. A moment later, there he was.

"Liz Falla — what a sight for sore eyes! Benz, Mercedes, here."

He said something else to the two dogs that she could not catch, and she remembered him doing the same thing on her first visit to the house.

Pissed off though she was with him, after her last reception it was nice to be appreciated.

"Are you here in your official capacity? Please say no."

"No."

"So why then are you looking at me as though this is a bad thing, instead of a good thing?"

"Look, I just had a less than wonderful conversation through the window of this car, and I am in no mood for a second one. Can you call off your hounds so I can get out?"

"I already have."

He was laughing at her and at her tetchy response, but with such apparent delight at her arrival that she found herself laughing back at him. As she got out of the car he took her by the elbow, and she felt the current of electricity she had felt before when he touched her. Both dogs were now wagging their tails, and seeming as pleased to see her as their master. The female pushed her muzzle into Liz's hand.

"Are they as dangerous as they look?"

"Yes. Come in and tell me why you're here — my God, where have you been with this vehicle?"

"To the back of beyond, about five minutes from here. Did DI Moretti tell you about his sort-of aunt's lodgers?"

"No, he didn't. Sounds intriguing. That'd be Gwen Ferbrache, would it?"

They were in the house now and, as Ludo closed the door behind him, the dogs moved ahead of them into the living room.

"Yes. You know her?"

"Knew her before I met Ed. She introduced us, and then I went and heard him play."

"I still haven't done that."

"How strange. So, if you're not on duty, can I offer you a glass of wine?"

"I'd love a beer. Annoyance makes me thirsty."

Ludo Ross said nothing in response. He disappeared in the direction of the kitchen, leaving Liz with the two dogs, who appeared relaxed, but who reacted slightly to her every move. They watched as she walked around the room, looking at books on the shelves, examining a small bronze sculpture of a horse, hooves pawing the air, mane flying, petrified in space.

When he came back with the beer, Liz was holding one of the books in her hands.

"Most of your library is in French."

"I don't know about most, but a lot, sure. It's a language I love."

"And the language of love." She took her beer from him, and her fingers buzzed at the contact.

Hold on, she told herself, *you are angry, remember.*

"I thought that was Italian." He was laughing at her again, the lines around his eyes crinkling into deeper folds.

"DI Moretti would know more about that than I would. At least, I imagine he would, but he's a difficult man to read, my boss. But he'd be an open book, I think, if he knew how much you hadn't told him — especially as he came to see you about Masterson. Didn't he?"

"He did."

No laugh lines now. Ludo Ross's face was expressionless, still. He turned away from her for a moment, and she wondered if he was removing himself from the force field between them, or whether she alone felt it and he was merely composing both his features and his story. She sat down on his elegant red sofa with its glacial lines, and waited for his reply.

When he turned back again he said, in a voice as lacking in inflection and emotion, as if he were giving directions to a stranger on the road, "I suppose you know I want to go to bed with you."

Disconcerted, thrown off course as she was intended to be, she spluttered peevishly, "That's not fair, that's not what I want to talk about, that's not why I'm here."

Ludo Ross sat down on the far end of the chaise, not touching her, letting his eyes do the touching for him. "Look. You tell me you're not here on official business, you talk about the language of love, and then you're knocked sideways when I say what is on my mind — well, my mind is not exactly where it's on, but let's not play word games. Why are you here in a tizzy because Ed Moretti came to see me about your case?"

Had she expected to be wooed? Yes, she had. His declaration was a strategy to throw her off, and it had succeeded. He was counterpunching, she recognized, as one who could play that game herself.

"Yes, I know you fancy me. And this is not an official visit because my boss doesn't know I'm here. He was quite surprised, in fact, to find out we had met. I got the impression he thought you had just heard me sing, that's all."

"So you want me to brag about my conquest? Well, my semi-conquest, I suppose you'd call it. One kiss, a lot of heat, and a few sleepless nights."

"So what? Big deal, you're an insomniac, so you tell me. Am I supposed to feel sorry for you?"

"God no. I don't want your pity, Liz. I want your —"

"Knock it off, Ludo. The element of surprise has gone now." Liz put down her glass on the blue stretch of carpet, pushing his hand away when he tried to pick it up. "Leave it. I don't want another, and I like it there, mussing things up a bit. Why didn't you tell him about Garth Machin and you?"

"You make that sound like a *relationship*. Dear girl, what the hell do you mean?"

The Ludo Ross who challenged her now was not the elegant, charming, patrician gentleman of their earlier meetings. A remote and chilly stranger looked down at her, standing very close, dominating her with his height and physical presence. The only electricity she felt now was a tremor of actual fear. But she had come this far and there was no point in stopping. She pressed on.

"That you and Garth Machin have some sort of something going — and before you make that infantile joke again, no, I don't think it's sexual. I think it's —" she searched for the right word "— conspiratorial."

Suddenly Ludo Ross was sitting beside her, and she had to stop herself pulling away against the curved back of the chaise. But his voice now was tender, caressing. "You came here one day and Machin was here, that's true. He was in such an emotional state he couldn't conceal it. He's got problems that, sadly, I cannot help him with as he hoped I could. Why in the hell should you extrapolate from that some sort of conspiracy that Ed should know about, and that I have deliberately kept quiet about? Just because Machin is in the Fénions does not mean I have to inform Ed, does it?"

"Ludo, why is it that you have never mentioned your friendship with Garth Machin to my boss? He's in the group, you go to hear them play, and yet DI Moretti doesn't have any idea you are on close terms. It's the silence, Ludo. It's suspect, especially now, and while the DI's away, I want to get it straight."

"Especially now?" Ludo Ross bent toward her. "Why especially now?"

Without going into details, Liz told him about the body on the Amsterdams' lawn, close to the Machins' house. It would all be in the paper soon anyway, and some of the mainland press were already sniffing around.

Ludo listened in silence, and when she had finished he bent down, picked up the empty glass, and put it on a nearby table. She thought it was as if controlling his physical environment gave him control over situations. And emotions. On her previous visit she had watched him straighten pens on a table, lining them up side by side, flick down a wayward strand of the fringe of the Kirman, slightly alter the angle of a chair.

"Would it be of any use to tell you that my — I prefer to call it acquaintanceship — with Machin has absolutely nothing to do with these killings? Garth's personal problems have nothing to do with your enquiry."

He stood up abruptly, startling the two ridgebacks who rose to their feet and came over to him. Three pairs of hostile eyes surveyed her, reminding Liz of Sandra Goldstein and her snarling panther. They were all concealing something, even those two damn dogs, but challenging him would be pointless, so she'd change course, like he did. She'd thrown a mobile at one, so why not throw this one a bone and see what she got in return.

"Hope you're right, because it's a minefield already, without adding Garth Machin. You probably saw from the *Guernsey Press* that we have another island celebrity involved?"

"I don't get the local paper." He looked her straight in the eyes with what she thought was too much apparent candour for such an insignificant comment. He was lying.

"Lady Fellowes." Liz laughed and drew her feet up under her on the sofa. "God, Ludo, you should have seen her on the CCTV cameras, and when we interviewed her. What a dog's dinner! All tarted up like she was about to do her act — whatever that was, back in the Dark Ages."

"Jesus Christ, what a little bitch you are." Ludo Ross walked away from her, turning his back. No eye contact now.

The vehemence of his outburst jolted her. She had imagined he'd become curious, ask questions, perhaps even begin to say something about what had passed between him and Machin. He took a moment to pick up his pipe from the desk by the window, and as he pulled the tobacco pouch from the pocket of his jacket he continued, the words cutting and stinging, but his tone as detached and casual as if he were discussing the weather. "Just how special do you think you are, Detective Sergeant Falla? She was a star, that woman, with lovers and worshippers enough to fill the Guernsey telephone book. You, on the other hand, are a little girl of little talent, playing in a little group on a little island. And in between you are second banana to Ed Moretti. You are not in the same league, and will never be."

Liz Falla got to her feet, her legs shaking beneath her. What had released this verbal torrent of invective, spewed in her direction like molten lava? Her ego was sorely shaken and bruised, but this was not about rejection — besides, she hadn't actually done that. This was something beyond her, beyond whatever it was that had happened, or not happened, between them.

"I don't know you at all, do I?"

Stay cool, she told herself, *cool as he is*. Although, of course, he isn't.

"No." Beyond the pipe-curls of smoke, his face showed little, but there was contempt in his voice. "I still want to sleep with you. Notwithstanding."

"Tell you what, Ludo, if you're going to scrape the bottom of the barrel, it won't be with this little girl. Notwithstanding. Call off your hounds, would you?"

"They won't touch you."

"Good. That makes three of you."

She got up and left, seeing herself out, three sets of angry eyes burning a hole in her back.

What happened there? Her hands on the steering wheel were shaking. What in the hell happened there? *Shape-shifter*, she thought, *that's what happened there*. He's one thing, then the other, and then another. After years of changing face, why be surprised if he no longer knows who he is.

She knew she was being naïve. *She* didn't know who he was, but Ludo Ross knew exactly who he was.

In the midst of uncertainties, one thing was certain. She should find out more about Coralie Chancho. She must talk to Le Marchant, see if his gauche young charms had shaken anything loose. Getting Lady Fellowes to reveal the identity of Champagne Charlie had now taken on an added dimension for Detective Sergeant Liz Falla.

Chapter Nine

But first there was Melissa Machin.

During office hours, Moretti had said, and it was still early afternoon. Both her previous interviews had lasted no more than half an hour, since both her interviewees had sent her packing. She appeared to be on a roll, so she might as well add Melissa Machin to her list and be done with rejection and contempt on the same day. Liz stopped for something to eat at a small café near Saint's Bay, then continued on to Fort George.

As she drove down the steep upper slope of Val de Terres, a gleam of sun broke through the heavy cloud over the distant bay, like a hand parting a curtain. *I'll take it as a sign,* she thought, except things usually happen in threes, according to her mother. In which case, she was in the right frame of mind to take on one of Fort George's look-down-your-nose denizens.

Angrier than a wet hen. A spurned second banana of a wet hen of little talent.

The woman who opened the door of the Machins' house to Liz Falla had very little of the haughty householder about her, and far more of the damsel in distress. She had obviously been crying, and she made little effort to conceal the fact from her visitor.

"Mrs. Machin, I'm Detective Sergeant Falla of the —"

From somewhere in the house came the sound of music, a violin playing something disjointed. At least, to her ears.

"Yes, I know. Well, not you specifically, but I recognized the police car. We're getting used to them around here, aren't we?" Melissa Machin gave a ragged laugh and added, "I wondered when you'd be around again."

"I'm sorry to disturb you, but there are a few more details I'd like to ask you. Perhaps it would be better if I came in?" Liz gestured in the direction of the sequestered, shuttered mansions in their secretive gardens.

"If you mean because of the neighbours, I don't give a tinker's damn about any of them, but come in anyway."

Having blown Ed Moretti's character assessment out of the water in about one minute flat, Melissa Machin stood back and motioned to Liz Falla to come through. She was a taller than average woman, about forty years old, perhaps late thirties, with the pale skin, dark hair, and eyes of someone of Irish descent. The black track suit she was wearing emphasized her translucent skin tone, and her only pieces of jewellery were her wedding and engagement ring, the latter a colossal sapphire surrounded by diamonds, almost as spectacular as the ring worn by a late, lamented princess. Liz noted that her earlobes were pierced, but she had not bothered to put on earrings — as if, when she got out of bed that morning, the track suit had been close at hand, and the rings already on her fingers.

"Come on through. I'm having a coffee, so please don't say you don't even drink coffee on duty. I could do with some company."

"I'd love a coffee. You've had a difficult twenty-four hours, I know."

The interior of the Machins' house bore no resemblance to that of their neighbours, the Amsterdams. There was no gilt, no gewgaws, not a frou-frou in sight. Not that it was spare, like Ludo Ross's. The rooms opened into each other, warm with panelling of various woods in golden-brown tones, and the paintings on the walls were extraordinary. Abstracts, all of them, the colours so vivid they could kick-start a comatose camel, as dissonant and startling as the music.

"God, would that it were twenty-four hours! It's not so much having a shoulder to cry on I need, officer. Or to lean on for that matter. I've done a hell of a lot of leaning over the past little while, and I'm sick to death of it. I have, as you can see with your sharp policewoman's eyes, been on a crying jag without benefit of shoulder, and it's the best thing I could have done. Here we are."

They were in the kitchen of the house. Melissa Machin went over to a small and expensive-looking piece of stereo equipment on one of the counters and switched it off.

"Sit down, Sergeant. I hope you like your coffee strong."

"That's just how I like it. Thanks."

Liz watched as Melissa Machin poured coffee from a vacuum jug into an earthenware mug and handed it to her. The kitchen was just the kind of kitchen she would have chosen, if her husband were a high-powered banker. There was a huge window overlooking the back garden, terracotta floor, an open hearth around a massive fireplace, dark-veined marble countertops, a long table of what looked like pine, on it a splendid pottery bowl in oranges and reds splintered with deep blue.

"What was the music you were playing? I didn't recognize it."

"Stravinsky, the Violin Concerto in D Major."

"Beyond me, I think. Difficult to understand."

"Not really, not when you listen to it a few times. Then it lets you in."

"That's interesting."

Careful, Liz thought, *you are feeling sympathetic because she's been crying and because you like her taste in decoration. Disarming you with coffee and tears could be just as effective as Ludo's shock tactics. Don't let your guard down.*

Which reminded Liz Falla of the little shit.

"Forgive me if I ask you questions you have already answered, but did you know the deceased?"

"Bruiser? That's what his shirt said, wasn't it? No, never seen him before, and he's not someone you'd forget in a hurry, is he? Was he, I suppose I should say." Melissa Machin changed direction abruptly. "I felt sorry for the officer yesterday. I lost it."

"Hardly surprising in the circumstances, Mrs. Machin. The victim was not a pretty sight at the best of times."

"Oh." Melissa Machin's reddened eyes looked sharply at Liz. "So you had spoken to him already?"

There you go, thought Liz Falla, *who's interviewing who here?* "We had spoken to him in the course of our enquiries about the murder on the yacht. He was an employee of the murder victim."

"God."

Liz waited to see if Melissa Machin would add anything to her call on the divinity, of either invective or invocation, but she simply closed her eyes and took a mouthful of coffee.

"When I said you'd had a difficult twenty-four hours, Mrs. Machin, you said it had been longer than that. What did you mean?"

In response, Melissa Machin asked another question of her own. "Do you know Ed Moretti?"

Of course. Liz remembered that she hadn't seen them together or been interviewed by either of them. "Yes, I do. He's my superior officer, I work with him. He'd be doing this interview himself, but the case has taken him away for the moment. He asked me to speak to you."

In my second banana capacity, thought Liz.

"I have begged Garth, pleaded with him, to talk to Ed — the band, you know, the Fénions?"

"Yes. They play in it together, I understand. You mean, before the incident yesterday?"

"Yes, oh, for a few months now." Melissa Machin put down her coffee mug and wrapped her arms around her body, rocking on the high stool. She might be denying she needed a shoulder to cry on, but her body language said something quite different. "Ed came to see him at the office yesterday, Garth told me that."

"Yes. Your husband was unable to help in any way. He says this has nothing to do with you, or with him."

"I wish I could be sure of that."

The rocking had stopped and, her arms still hugging her rigid body, Melissa Machin sat quite motionless.

So did Liz Falla. Quietly, as if talking someone down from a parapet high above a busy street, she asked, "Are you saying that your husband knows something that might help us in our enquiries?"

"That's just it, I don't know. But something has been bothering Garth for a while now, something new. See —" Melissa Machin swung round on the stool and looked directly at Liz "— are you married, officer, or do you have a partner, a significant other in your life?"

Just as she thought she was getting somewhere …

"Mrs. Machin, I don't see what —" she began.

"Sorry, what I meant was do you know the feeling when something's changed?"

"Oh," said Liz, "that I can answer. That feeling I know well."

Did she ever.

"Then you'll understand what I mean. I am married to a man who should never have been a banker, and that's a constant in our life together. I have begged him to throw it all over, but he likes the good life too much. We're not always here, you see, we have other homes, back in London and in France. Being what he doesn't want to be is the price Garth pays for them. Me, I'd be happy with a brush and some paints and a nice piece of canvas."

"Are those your paintings — the abstracts?" Liz reached across for the jug and poured herself some more coffee. She couldn't wait to tell first banana how wrong he had got Melissa Machin. "I love your colours, even though I don't understand what you are doing with them."

This brought a warm, deep-throated laugh from the Stepford wife. "Thank you, Sergeant. That's really a great compliment, because I'm not sure I want you to read them too easily. But, like the Stravinsky, they would eventually let you in."

"So —" Liz drank some of her coffee, taking her time "— you're saying that whatever is bothering your husband is not the usual."

"Exactly. I know the signs when he's fed up to the back teeth with Northlands and all it represents, but over the past few months there's been something else going on."

"Is this just the feeling you talked about, or has anything specific happened to make you uneasy?"

Melissa Machin got down from the stool and crossed to the window. She pointed toward the garden beyond it. "See that? A sanctuary it is, or should be, although I'm not so sure sanctuaries should be protected by a wall like something out of a gulag. About a couple of months ago, last autumn, I came back to the island after taking my two children to their boarding schools." She looked toward two framed photographs on one of the counters, of a boy and a girl around ten and twelve years old. "I came back earlier than Garth expected, because I curtailed my shopping expedition in London. I hate parting with the children, and I just wasn't in the mood. On a whim, I decided to surprise him, and to cheer myself up. I knew Garth would be home, because it was the weekend."

Suddenly, Melissa Machin looked embarrassed. "It's — it's a turn-on for Garth and me, you see, the stranger walking in the door. It's a game we play." For a moment, her expression lightened and she giggled.

Liz Falla grinned. "Okay. Just tell me what happened next."

"Well, I have a key to the gate at the bottom of the garden on my keychain. It opens on to the cliff path above Soldiers Bay, as do the other properties. I left my luggage in the left-luggage office on Albert Pier, put on my track shoes, and walked from the harbour, taking the cliff path. It's a bit of a distance, but I'm in good shape and I needed the exercise after sitting in the plane. I let myself in the gate, which was surprisingly easy — that was the first unusual thing. The hinges had obviously been oiled recently. As I came up to the house, I saw through this window that there was someone in the kitchen. Damn, I thought, he's got company. Then I heard raised voices."

Melissa Machin was crying quietly again, the tears rolling down her cheeks. Liz Falla hesitated, not wanting to break the mood, or the frame of mind that had led this woman to open up to her.

"Raised voices," she repeated. "Could you hear what they were saying?"

"Some of it. It was a warm day, the window was open, but I knew if they saw me they'd stop, and I felt sure that, whatever this was, it had something to do with the change in Garth. I could only get so near because, as you can see, there's a patio outside the window with no trees or shrubs, so I kept close to the wall on one side. I could see Garth quite clearly, he was closest to the window, but the people he was speaking to —"

"People?" Liz Falla interrupted. "How many were there?"

"Three, I think. Garth and one man were doing most of the talking, but someone else was interrupting from time to time. A man definitely, but I couldn't see him. He was speaking softly, as if he was nervous, or as if he was threatening Garth. I really wasn't sure which it was, because I couldn't hear what he was saying."

"What about the other man? Did you see him? Was he anyone you knew, or recognized?"

"I saw him, but no, I'd never seen him before. He was impressive. In his mid-forties I'd say, spoke in an almost stagy manner — like someone used to speaking in public was what struck me. Powerfully built. Black."

"Black as in West Indian, or African? Or American? Did he speak with an accent?" Liz asked. She was beginning to wish she'd taken out her notebook earlier on, but she didn't want to risk interrupting Melissa Machin's confidences.

"Oh, he certainly spoke with an accent. One that I couldn't place. They were speaking in French."

"French?"

Melissa Machin nodded. "Yes, French. Both Garth and I speak fairly fluently. I studied in Paris, and Garth's father was in the diplomatic service, so he spoke French as a child."

"Could the accent have been French Canadian? Or from, say, French-speaking Africa?"

"Definitely not French Canadian. And if he was a French-speaking African, he must have spent considerable time in France, and probably Paris. I am told that, when I speak French, I have a Parisian accent, and so did this man. But it was still different, although his French was elegant, and his vocabulary was that of an educated man. Sorry, I'm not being very precise."

"Actually, that's just what you are being. You say you heard some of the conversation?"

"Yes. It was about the need for a meeting before things got underway — 'get underway' was what the hidden man actually said at one point. That, I heard. The man I could see, the African — if that's what he was — apparently agreed with this, and Garth did not. 'It's too risky,' he was saying, over and over. And the man I could see said, 'Nothing ventured, Garth, this will cut you loose forever.' Then the third man said something I didn't catch, but whatever it was frightened the hell out of my husband. I saw his face." Melissa Machin's knuckles against her coffee mug were white. "I wanted to rush in and scream at them, stop them, anything, but I knew I might trigger something more terrible."

"Such as?"

"I thought they might kill both Garth and me." Melissa Machin gave a deep sigh.

"What did you do next?"

"I went back the way I came, picked up my luggage, took a taxi, and came in the front door. By that time Garth was on his own, but he couldn't hide what he was feeling. He said it was Northlands, I said I don't believe you, he walked out, and came home in the small hours. I presumed he was at the club."

Now she had to use not just her sharp policewoman's eyes, but her copper's nose, or the pricking of her thumbs. Use that witch blood of yours, as Moretti once said to her. Should she tell her, or not tell her, about the scene she walked in on at Ludo's house?

Nothing ventured, like the man said.

"Mrs. Machin, do you know a man called Ludovic Ross?"

If Melissa Machin was surprised by the change in direction she didn't show it. She smiled and answered, "Well, I've met Ludo Ross, but he was more a friend of Garth's than mine. He's a jazz lover, and he's what we used to call 'a man's man.' Do people say that much anymore?"

Her assessment of Ludo Ross's character took Liz by surprise.

"Anyway, why do you ask?" She seemed mildly curious rather than anything else, certainly not like a woman who was concealing some dark secret.

"Because I know him, a bit." Tame, but true. "Once when I went to his house in St. Martin your husband was there. He appeared to be having a serious discussion of some sort with Ludovic Ross and seemed quite disturbed. He left when I arrived. This would be about last autumn, as a matter of fact."

"Perhaps that's where he went that day. Given Ludo Ross's past history, that makes me even more sure that Garth has got himself mixed up in something, God knows what."

"With the murder victim's past record, we wondered if he might have been coming here to try blackmail. Perhaps there is something in your husband's past —"

"Sergeant," Melissa Machin's tone was peremptory, her irritation barely concealed, "don't you see? Don't you understand what makes Garth vulnerable to a risky, get-rich-quick scheme of some kind? As the man said, something, anything, that will cut him loose? It's not my husband's past that's responsible for — whatever this is. It's his present."

The atmosphere in the room had changed. It didn't take a pricking thumb or a copper's nose to sense that all confidences were now over and that, for some reason, Melissa Machin had moved in a moment from vulnerability to something close to hostility. Liz Falla gave the woman her extension at Hospital Lane, and her mobile number, and made her exit.

She was still in the car when her mobile rang. It was Melissa Machin.

"Sergeant Falla, I've remembered something else I overheard. The man I could see said something like, 'We have to because we cannot trust the bastard.' Perhaps he meant the man on Mrs. Amsterdam's lawn, the bruiser."

"Perhaps. Thank you, Mrs. Machin."

Perhaps. But it was far more likely he meant the Baby Mothball.

Boule à mite. Petit salaud. A roomful of books, in French. Montreal French, African French, Paris French.

Merde, *but there was a lot of French in this case*, thought Liz Falla as she headed back to Hospital Lane. But the sun had indeed gleamed, just for a moment.

Day Five

"Ask me anything, any question you want to know about the sodding Folies Bergère and I can give you the answer. Want to know the depth of the stage? Twenty feet. Want to know how many seats? Sixteen hundred. Want to know how many people it takes to feather a costume —?" A fed-up, worn-out PC Le Marchant sat slumped in the chair opposite Liz Falla and groaned loudly, lengthily.

"I want to know everything." Liz Falla broke into his noisy exhalations. "Stop bleating, Le Marchant. You've been hanging out with a star, and you are just a person of little talent, did you know that?"

"That's what she said, but I didn't expect to hear it from you, Sergeant Falla."

"Don't feel bad. You're a nobody, and I'm just a second banana."

"That what she called you?" PC Le Marchant cheered up. "Mind you, the food was good. Pity about the booze — having to say no, I mean."

"The food? Who cooks for her?"

"She's got a service that brings stuff in, and a cleaning lady comes in every day. Mrs. Evans."

"Did the cleaning lady have anything interesting to say?"

"Not a sausage. She says she tuned out years ago, she's been coming since the husband was around. She's going to stay overnight with Lady Fellowes for the next while. It's been on the cards, she says, and she gets a good laugh. Some of the stories she tells — well, talk about spicy. She could write a book, Mrs. Evans says."

"I thought you said she tuned out. Sounds like she stays awake for the naughty bits, doesn't it."

PC Brouard put his head around the office door. Liz had moved into Moretti's office while he was away. "You wanted to know about the do at the Amsterdams'."

"Right. Come in, Jeff. Who was going to eat off the pink Spode?"

"Eat off the what? Oh. Well, the cook told me it was her Scrabble club."

"Her Scrabble club?" Liz Falla and PC Le Marchant responded in chorus.

"Yes. It's a regular get-together. Not quite like it sounds, apparently. It can become quite rowdy, according to the cook, with extra points for, you know, certain words — like, rude ones — and they always have their meetings when Mr. Amsterdam is away on business."

"Or in hospital, having his gall bladder removed. Do we know who these rowdy Scrabble players are?"

"I've got a list." PC Brouard pulled his notebook from his pocket. "The regulars are the wife of the president of Crédit Genève, the wives of two local bank managers, and — get this — the ex-wife and the ex-girlfriend of Dr. Watt. Dorothy Watt and Crystal Plummer. The cook says some of their stories about Dr. Watt and his, er, little ways in the sack get the biggest laughs of the evening."

"Combined in mutual hatred. Hell hath no fury like two women scorned," observed Liz. "Is that everyone?"

"Not quite. The other regular is Anthony Bonamy — he's an interior decorator. All girls together, as you might say. The cook says he's the one that gets them going when they're really sauced. There's even been the odd striptease."

"Very odd striptease, I'd say," a highly diverted PC Le Marchant remarked. "Mrs. Evans could add that to her naughty book."

"Well, well," said Liz. Life in Fort George sounded a lot less buttoned-down than outward appearances might suggest. "Thanks, fellers, that'll do. I don't think we need worry Mrs. Amsterdam's Scrabblers."

As soon as the two constables left the office, Liz picked up the phone and checked. Yes, Dorothy Watt and Crystal Plummer were listed. At the back of her mind something she could not grasp slithered in and out, like a name you cannot quite remember. It was something Melissa Machin had said, something that stuck and would not compute, or tuck neatly away in an orderly fashion.

Whatever in the heck it was she had no idea, but remember it she must. Because it just didn't add up.

"You want to talk to me about —?" Dorothy Watt sounded weary. Her words were slurred, as though she had just woken up.

"Dr. Watt. Specifically, Mrs. Watt, your time in America. And I want to keep this confidential."

She was, of course, taking a risk. If it got back to Nichol Watt, there would be hell to pay, both from him and from Moretti, let alone Hanley. It would make the brouhaha over Denny look like a tinkle in an egg cup. But she was banking on Dorothy Watt's apparent taste for scapegoating her ex.

"Our time in America? Is this about the MRI machines?"

Well, well, well, as the first banana liked to say.

"I'd rather not say over the phone, Mrs. Watt. When would it be convenient to speak to you?"

"I'll be here all day. I had rather a late night at Mona Amsterdam's. I imagine you know about her upsetting experience."

"Yes. I should be there in an hour."

Liz replaced the receiver, thinking that perhaps she ought to contact Moretti before she did this.

Perhaps she should, but she wasn't going to. Without a doubt he would say no, wait until I get back. After all, he had asked her to check into Nichol Watt's time in America, which was exactly what she was about to do.

Chapter Ten

Day Five

Peter Walker lived in Kensington, just off Kensington High Street. He owned a flat in one of the tall, narrow houses that line a quiet road not far from Holland Park, and he had been there for many years, not choosing to move after either retirement, or the death of his wife. Ed Moretti had only met her once or twice, but his memory was of a warm, good-looking woman who matched her husband in intelligence and wit. Even in the rather louche surroundings of the jazz club she gave off an impression of old money, and the ease of manner such a background brings with it.

But the arbitrary nature of life being what it is, the silver spoon she was born with did not protect her from the drunk driver who knocked her down only a few yards from her doorstep. Moretti had flown back to England for the funeral, and in so doing had strengthened what had become a distant and occasional contact with his old friend.

After they took the Tube from Heathrow into town, Walker showed Moretti the room he would be using and said, "I'm going to make some phone calls. If I can get hold of this person I have in mind, we'll probably be in business. Just pray she's in town?"

"She?"

"Yes. She. Make yourself at home, pour yourself a drink if you feel like it. With any luck I'll be taking the lady out to a late lunch."

The phone call was made behind the closed doors of his office, and then he bustled off after a brief, "Wish me luck, Ed."

"Luck, so they say, Peter, is a lady. Sometimes."

"She's a bitch most of the time. I'm going to twist the rather attractive arm of this particular lady." Peter Walker grinned and closed the front door behind him.

Interesting. Either Peter knew where a few bodies were buried, or he had been at some point closely acquainted with this particular lady. Moretti went into the kitchen, poured himself a beer, made a sandwich, and took them through into the sitting room that overlooked a small square of trees and shrubs. The rain had stopped, and a tentative sun touched the iron railings around the area with a soft, oily gleam. He drank some beer, took out his mobile, and phoned Falla.

"Falla, Moretti. I'm in London now. Any developments?"

"Some."

"Fill me in."

"The Stepford wife isn't."

"Isn't?"

Moretti listened attentively to Falla's account of her interview with Melissa Machin.

"My, I had her pegged wrong! She plays Mrs. Offshore Banker's Wife to the manner born. What she told you confirms a few things, even if we don't know what those few things are. At least we seem to be on the right track. Anything else? A Scrabble club — good God! How is our chantoozie? — I suppose Mrs. Evans is better than nothing — oh, did you get that phone out to La Veile? Good. Anything yet on Nichol Watt? No? Get in touch if anything else comes up, okay?"

"Okay. Good luck, Guv."

"Thanks, Falla. I'll need it." He sat on one of the leather chairs in Peter Walker's sitting room, opened his briefcase, and took out his notes.

Two hours later, Peter Walker returned looking, Moretti thought, almost boyish. The word *radiant* came to mind.

"Peter, you look like you just won the lottery."

"I have, my boy, I have. Let me just grab a beer for you and for me."

There in his sitting room, beneath a splendid series of Gillrays, Peter Walker told Ed Moretti a love story.

"Bear with me, Ed. This goes back to my early days at the Yard. I was an ambitious young sod, pushy, prepared to cut a few throats if it meant a quicker path to the top. Prepared to do anything if it got me ahead of the pack. I was working on a fraud case involving two of the biggest names in the London underworld at that time. We wanted them for dozens of other more heinous offences, but our best bet was to get them this way, rather than for murder or torture or any of their other hideous crimes. One of the officers on the case was a woman, working undercover in one of the bastards' bars, chosen not only because she was smart as a whip, but a looker."

Walker paused, shaking his head, the thatch of white hair falling over his face. "God, what a beautiful girl she was. I fell for her, so heavily you could have heard the crash clear across London and the Home Counties. And, by some miracle, she fell for me. Christ, I died a thousand deaths every night she was in that bloody bar. So, to cut a long story short, we caught the two bad lads on fraud charges, the lovely lady and I got promotions and —" he paused.

"And —?"

"I married Anita. Her father was in the cabinet at the time, the PM's right-hand man."

"You broke the lovely lady's heart. Possibly your own?"

"Ambition doth make cold-hearted codfish of, well, some of us. Including the lovely lady."

Moretti raised his eyebrows. "She married the son of a cabinet minister?"

"Wrong. She didn't marry at all. It would have interfered with her goals, she told me. She informed me she'd never have married me, in any case. Mind you, it wasn't as easy as that. There was a lot of screaming, and we went a few rounds. Never get on the wrong side of an expert in various forms of self-defence. I still bear the marks."

Moretti looked at his old friend. How little he knew about this man, who had changed the direction of his life.

"Let me jump to conclusions. This is the lady you had lunch with?"

Walker laughed. "A brilliant deduction, Detective Inspector. Yes. You see, my career may have gone well, either because of my own ability or my wife's connections, or a combination of the two. But this woman went right to the top, the very top, and not of the Met, but another, even more prestigious organization, some would say. And she did it on her own, no husband, and no sleeping around with the right people. That much is true, because you can be sure I'd know otherwise. I'm sure she had affairs, relationships, but there was no sexual stairway to the stars. That kind of trajectory cannot be swept under the organizational rug."

"This is Janice Melville, first woman to head MI5."

"This is. She just retired."

"Good God." Moretti hesitated, then asked, "And you're still talking?"

"We are now, thanks to you. I've been looking for an excuse, a reason to contact her, something more than just 'let's get together for old times' sake,' and you gave me one."

"So I'm your cupid?"

"Don't need one, Ed. I was hit by that arrow a long time ago. What you are is my cover story."

"And there I was, thinking this was all for my sake."

Above Peter Walker's head, the lilac-jacketed gentleman in Gillray's *Delicious Weather* treated himself to a pinch of snuff as he sat on a bench surrounded by flowers, shaded by leafy trees, a picture of contentment and bliss.

"How soon can I talk to her, or is she putting me in touch with someone?"

"Not sure about that yet. So let's go take in some jazz, only we won't be playing."

"What's good?"

"A little bar in Battersea High Street called CaffConc. Has an extraordinary young guitarist who plays Gypsy jazz."

Moretti groaned. "God, Peter, how your tastes have changed. Not jazz *manouche*, please. My Django Reinhardt period ended over a decade ago."

Walker leaned forward and tapped Moretti on the knee, hard. "The lady in question is an aficionado. Or is it aficionada? Anyway, that's where we're meeting her. So rediscover your boyish enthusiasm, Ed. Fast."

They took the Tube to Battersea High Street. As always on his return trips to London, Moretti was struck by the changes since his university days. In one of the most ethnically and culturally complex cities in the world the word *cosmopolitan* seemed inadequate to describe the range of race, creed, and colour that filled the streets and the shops. Certainly it had not been a white little, tight little town when he was there, but the diversity now was mind-blowing. Whole neighbourhoods were given over to being Beirut or Bangladesh or Bahrein in miniature, and there was probably a transplanted Guernsey somewhere. And it seemed to him that, since the arrival of suicide bombers in the heart of the city, the ease with which passersby brushed shoulders with each other had changed into a wary watchfulness, as the citizenry looked out for dynamite-lined jackets or loaded backpacks.

In spite of Dwight's dark face in the Fénions, Moretti realized he spent most of his life in a now uncharacteristically almost-white society, and CaffConc confirmed that impression. Early though it was in the evening, it was already busy, and the crowd spanned a wide age group, as mixed racially as the wardrobe its clientele wore. The club itself was self-consciously Left Bank in style, its décor and furnishings a cross between Art Nouveau boudoir and Empire salon chic, with a touch of the bordello thrown in. It was not an ornamental conjunction Moretti was fond of, and he felt despondency settle on his shoulders like sodden gabardine. Somewhere across the dimly lit room he could hear, not the sound of a guitar, but the sound of a piano. A middle-aged man with a fez on his head was playing standards in a standard kind of way.

"There she is."

In a room with a preponderance of good-looking women, Janice Melville held her own. In a career in which avoiding attention was a good idea, her looks must have made that difficult. She was very blond, very white-skinned, with the blackest eyes in such an expanse of paleness that Moretti had ever seen. There had been an actress in the seventies in a television series to which his mother was addicted with similar colouring, he remembered, with the same long, slanting eyes.

Janice Melville saw them and waved without any discernible change of expression. As they came over to the table near the bar, Moretti got the feeling of distance, detachment, as if she had an invisible force field around her, separating her from the rest of the room. A glass of red wine stood on the table in front of her.

"Hi, Peter. You must be Ed Moretti."

"You must be Janice Melville. An honour to meet you, ma'am."

One thin, dark eyebrow went up. "Retired. No more ma'ams, please. Jan."

Janice Melville had worn the years well, especially taking into account the nature of those years. She had to be in her mid to late fifties, but looked a decade younger. She wore black, presumably because she liked black, because she was whip thin, her small breasts beneath the clinging jersey fabric heightened by the narrowness of her ribcage. Her only piece of jewellery was what looked like a very pricey gold watch, with diamonds on the bezel.

"Do sit down, and let's talk. I won't want to talk once they start playing. Are you eating? The chicken curry's good."

She had a light voice, higher up the vocal scale than Moretti would have expected. On the phone she would sound two decades younger.

Moretti and Walker ordered the curry and two beers and, as soon as the waiter moved away, Moretti said, "Peter's told you why I'm here, but I've had some more information since then from my sergeant."

"Go ahead."

She listened in silence, sipping her red wine, waiting to respond until after the beers arrived.

"So. Sounds more like some sort of coup d'état to me, as opposed to terrorism, in which case I couldn't have helped you. Those doors are closed, even to me, now I am an outsider."

"Coup d'état? Would whites be involved in something like that in, say, Africa?"

"If there was something in it for them, and they were the money men."

"A change of government for mercenary, rather than idealistic reasons."

"Exactly. One is not talking about orange revolutions here, although even orange revolutions have been known to benefit the power brokers and their corporations. Naïve to think otherwise."

"Money. A familiar theme in Guernsey. But in this case the coup d'état would have to be about something produced by the country, and the cash would be the by-product."

"Except that the cash is what it's all about for the white guys in this case. And power, of course, but money is power."

The curry was good, as she had said, West Indian as opposed to East Indian.

There was a pause in the conversation, and then Peter Walker spoke. "Diamonds?"

"Very possibly." Moretti noticed Janice Melville did

not meet Peter's eyes when she replied, as she had with him. "A messy, dangerous business, but I've no need to tell you that. *If* it's diamonds. The problem with diamonds is that they're easily obtained — no need for huge capital investment in many cases — but it's very difficult to secure the source. Might not, therefore, be diamonds, or diamonds may be only part of whatever this is."

"Diamonds are not a power broker's best friend."

"Diamonds are a fairweather friend and an unreliable lover."

This time Janice Melville looked straight into Peter Walker's eyes, and Moretti watched him flinch.

This was getting off the rails. The coup d'état theory was useful, but he hadn't come here for theories he'd probably have arrived at himself eventually, and a good chicken curry wasn't enough reason to subject himself to Gypsy jazz just to endure the banter and barbs of two star-crossed ex-lovers. It was beginning to look as if he'd been conned into this for the sake of Peter's love life, rather than anything more useful. Moretti put down his knife and fork and leaned back in his chair, allowing his impatience to show.

"Coup d'état somewhere in Africa, with wicked white men raping the dark continent yet again. Even this plodding copper might have eventually grasped that much." Moretti started to get up. "Can you help me with contacts, names, Ms. Melville? You can, but will you? Otherwise let me leave you two to your own devices, whatever those may be, and get out of here before the entertainment."

"Too late. The entertainment is about to begin."

Janice Melville was laughing. "Hang about, plodding copper. Let me hear the music, and then I'll give you what you want. Then you can leave us two to our own devices."

She was, apparently, amused by his outburst, but from the look in those black eyes when she said "devices," giving Peter what he wanted was not part of her plan. At least, not without much further negotiation. Janice Melville turned her chair around and gave her full attention to the stage, now vacated by the piano player after a smattering of applause.

The man who came on stage did not look like a Gypsy. Long, lean, fair-skinned, and fair-haired, he looked to be in his twenties. He wore wraparound dark glasses, a black shirt and black jeans, and the guitar he carried was the *petite bouche* style of instrument favoured by jazz *manouche* guitarists. He was followed by another guitar player and a bass player, both of whom looked more likely to have sprung from one of the birthplaces of Gypsy jazz. Their set-up was blessedly brief, and they opened with a melody Moretti didn't recognize, the bass underlining the melody, the rhythm guitarist providing the familiar repetitive boom-chick *manouche* beat.

The blond was good, a gifted player, his style in this number closer to traditional Gypsy music than the jazz-influenced Parisian sound. When the unfamiliar piece was over, the group moved directly into one of the jazz *manouche* standards, "Les Yeux Noirs." Black eyes. For a split second, the lead player looked toward their table, then back to his guitar.

Moretti turned to look at Janice Melville. Her own black eyes were closed, her face slightly upturned, as if she were sunning herself, her slim body pressed against the back of the chair. Not so much a devotee of the music as a devotee of the musician, was the thought that crossed Moretti's mind, as she suddenly shifted in her seat, one hand smoothing her skirt over her thigh. He turned to look at Peter Walker, and it was clear that the same thought had crossed Peter Walker's mind. Not so much crossed, as hit him like a ton of bricks between the eyes.

"La Gitane," "Besame Mucho," Django Reinhardt's beautiful "Nuages." In spite of himself, Moretti surrendered to the moody, bluesy playing of the band, briefly putting to one side what had brought him to this unlikely place. That was the beauty of jazz for him, there was nothing he could do about Peter's angst anyway, and all he could hope for was that the antagonism she obviously still felt for her ex-lover did not rub off on him.

Applause, some whoops and bravos, and the band left the stage, the lead guitarist briefly acknowledging the audience on his own, his eyes moving again to their table. Janice Melville smiled.

"He's good, isn't he?"

Peter Walker's smile was warm and wide. "Actually, Ed can't stand Gypsy music. He says he grew out of his Django Reinhardt phase years ago."

You bastard, Moretti thought. *If you're sunk, then so am I, is that it?* He turned to Janice Melville. "You want to talk about this now? Otherwise, I'm off."

"Good. Meet me here at ten o'clock tomorrow

morning." She took a pen and a slip of paper out of her tiny black satin purse, wrote something on it, and handed it to Moretti.

Her next remark was addressed to Peter Walker. "Piss off, Peter. I wanna be alone."

Only she wouldn't be. This evening, set up by Peter, had given Janice Melville the perfect opportunity to settle an old score, and was a complete waste of time for Moretti's purposes. He could only hope that Falla was coming up with something, since it looked as if he was coming back with nothing.

"I'll piss off with pleasure, but first I'm pissing off to the gents." Walker stood up. "Meet you at the door, Ed."

As Moretti got up to leave, Janice Melville put a hand on his arm.

"Wait a bit. Give me your mobile number."

Moretti did so, pulling out his notebook to write it down.

"No need for that. I'll remember it. And no need to tell Peter about this. In fact, don't, okay?"

"Okay."

By the time Walker met Moretti at the door, Janice Melville was gone.

"Sweet fucking revenge, wasn't it. Public, with a witness, and another musician to boot."

"You said she was bright, ruthless, and driven. Why are you surprised? I'm only surprised she said she'd give me information. Unless I'm walking into a set-up of some kind as an extension of the lady's payback scheme."

"Doubt it. That's the icing on the cake for her, isn't it? You get what you came for, and I get to go home empty-handed."

They were sitting in Walker's living room, drinking brandy. Above Walker's head Gillray's *Sad Sloppy Weather* seemed apt enough for the moment.

"Where are you meeting her tomorrow?"

Moretti took the slip of paper out of his pocket. The handwriting was unexpectedly florid, with looping, twisting, capitals. Nothing in the least reserved or austere about it, hardly a clean line anywhere.

"Looks like a private address," he said, handing it to Walker.

"Near the river. Chelsea. Not hers. Could be a safe house, or an ex safe house more likely. Unless it's the pseudo-Django's pad."

"Unlikely. I doubt she tells him much. Retired she may be, but old habits die hard in her business, as I don't have to tell you."

As Walker gave the paper back he said, "Watch your back, Ed. You don't know whose toes you may be treading on with this investigation."

Opposite Moretti on the wall, a portly gentleman was losing his footing. *Very Slippy Weather* indeed.

Just before going to bed, Moretti called Falla's mobile. There was no reply.

Not surprising. It was late, and any emergency call would be made to her home phone number. As he thought of Falla's sitting room in the little flat on the Esplanade, Moretti felt a twinge of — what? Nostalgia? Surely not. Anxiety? About what? Resisting the train of thought that might lead to enlightenment, Moretti got out his *London A to Z* and checked the address on Janice Melville's piece of paper with its convoluted script. As he did so, his mobile rang.

"Moretti."

It was Janice Melville, as though his thoughts had summoned her. "You alone?"

"Yes."

"Tomorrow, leave as though you were going to the ten o'clock appointment. It could be a long day, so if you can manage to bring a change of clothing or at least a toothbrush without attracting attention, do so. Go to Kensington High Street Tube station, and wait outside the entrance. Someone will meet you there."

Before Moretti could say anything in reply, she rang off.

Chapter Eleven

Day Six

Outside the window of Peter Walker's living room the sun shone on the young spring leaves of the plane trees. Bird sang and, in the street below, a young man was walking a string of dogs of various breeds and comically variegated sizes. They fanned out across the pavement like a flotilla, scattering pedestrians in their wake, none of whom seemed unduly put out, smiling at them and their escort as they passed. It was that kind of morning.

Peter's head emerged from behind the newspaper he was reading as much to avoid conversation, Moretti felt, as anything else.

"I heard your mobile last night, didn't I? Anything new?"

"Not much, so my sergeant says. At least no one has got themselves killed in my absence. Yet."

"Right. You taking a taxi to Chelsea?"

"I'll try for one on the High Street. Failing that, the Tube, so I'll leave in good time."

Walker put the paper down and removed his spectacles. His unshaven face in the bright morning sunlight looked a decade older than the smiling, boyish visage of the day before. Returning from the bathroom after his phone call, Moretti had heard the sound of the heavy glass stopper of the whisky decanter being removed. From the look of Peter's face, it had been lifted a few more times in the night.

"Call this sour grapes if you will, Ed, but you realize that this is more likely to be about getting information from you rather than the other way round."

"I don't trust ex-MI5 operators to come bearing gifts, if that's what you mean. But I do hope to do some trading. And call this sour grapes if you will, Peter, but have you ever really believed I'd get anything from them? This was all about rekindling old flames."

"Not entirely, so let me vent a little, you cynical bastard." Walker got up and poured himself another cup of coffee from the pot on the table. "This was about killing two birds with one stone — lousy metaphor in the circumstances, but it'll do. I spent much of my time on that pleasant speck in the Atlantic deciding what I was going to do with the rest of my life, and getting in touch with Janice Melville always came out on top of my list. Then you came over and asked for my help. It seemed like a gift from the gods. Ex-MI5 operators may not often bear gifts but, just occasionally, the gods do."

"Not often in my pantheon. I hope yours are kinder. Sometimes it's better not to stir up old fires."

"I'd agree with you, but this one's already stirred." Walker raised his coffee cup in Moretti's direction. "Here's hoping one of us gets what he wants."

"That was a cheap shot, saying what you did about my tastes in jazz."

"Very childish of me. I was surprised at myself. Hell hath no fury like a retired copper scorned. Brought out the vengeful ten-year-old in me, and I had no idea he was still in there."

"I should be off."

"Good luck. I mean it, believe it or not."

Back in the bedroom, Moretti put a change of underwear, shaving tackle, a toothbrush, toothpaste, and his mobile charger into his briefcase. It didn't bulge too much, because he really had very little in it. His case notes, and a series of numbers taken from Baby Mothball's computer.

He was a bit early for his rendezvous with whoever, but he didn't have to wait long, jostling the motley crowd of Tube-takers in their two-piece suits, their gaudy florals, their ubiquitous jeans, their hairstyles ranging from chrome domes to dreadlocks to multicoloured, multi-gelled creations, stunning as tropical birds. Moretti stood for a moment, wondering at which side of the entrance to the underground he should position himself. A baby passing in a stroller clutched at his trouser leg and he started, pulling away from the contact. He was more on edge than he realized.

"Mr. Moretti."

The man who addressed him looked like the perfect waiter. His voice was bland, even toned, his expression slightly ingratiating, with a glimmer of a smile, the slight bow of his back suggesting obsequiousness. Gord Collenette would have hired him on the spot. When he tried to remember his escort's face afterward, Moretti would have trouble remembering a single feature.

"Yes."

"This way, sir."

Moretti followed the man around to a small cul-de-sac quite close to the underground entrance. In an area marked NO PARKING stood a black BMW with diplomatic licence plates. The man unlocked the car as they approached and held open the passenger door at the back.

"I'll sit in the front."

"Very well. Do you want your briefcase with you, sir?"

"Yes."

As his escort shut the front passenger door, Moretti saw it had no interior handle, and felt the tension in his body twist tighter. When the driver got in he asked, "Are you afraid I'll get away from you?" He indicated the door.

The man laughed. "Not you, sir. Others, yes."

The driver backed out of the narrow alleyway with some speed and with considerable skill, and Moretti remained silent as he did so. Once out in the High Street he asked, "Why the diplomatic plates? Is that what I'm supposed to be?"

Again, the light, deprecatory laugh. "If you wish, Detective Inspector. The plates make it easier to park in the city without producing identification. That's it, really."

"I see. Am I allowed to ask where I am going?"

"Sussex. It should be a pleasant drive in this weather."

The BMW slowly made its way through the southern outskirts of the city, its diplomatic plates giving it no advantage in the dense traffic, its driver silent as he negotiated what clearly was a route he knew well.

Somewhere beyond Croydon, as continuous city began to break into pockets of built-up areas interspersed with countryside, Moretti spoke. "Where in Sussex? Or is that classified information?"

His escort smiled. "The Weald, sir. Between the North and South Downs. There'd be little point in not saying if you know this part of England well. Do you?"

"Not well." Actually, he didn't know it at all.

"Nice area, if you like unspoiled countryside. Not that parts of it will remain that way much longer. Do you like gardens, sir?"

"Of course. Who doesn't?"

"Then you're in for a treat. The rhododendrons will be in bloom. And the azaleas. A bit early for some of the roses."

Surprised by the horticultural bent of the conversation, Moretti lapsed into silence. If this was some concrete bunker concealed in the depths of the Sussex countryside, it promised to be an unusually herbaceous one.

Beyond the tinted windows of the car, the landscape now rolled by with little interruption from urban sprawl. Small villages appeared and disappeared, and the road became narrower, twisting, enclosed by hedgerows. It was the countryside of the travelogue, the England imagined by overseas visitors that still existed between the beautiful cities and the industrial cities, much of it threatened by encroachment and development.

"Here we are."

The driver took a mobile out of his pocket and spoke, briefly.

"Five minutes."

The car turned off the narrow road into what seemed at first to be an even narrower lane that quickly widened into a solidly tarmacked surface, still enclosed by high hedgerows. So the appearance of the house ahead of them was sudden, as was the large sign just before the heavy, wrought-iron gates: CADOGAN HALL HOTEL.

"A hotel?" Was this another wild goose chase?

"Of a sort. Mostly used for conferences, that sort of thing. You won't find it in the tourist guides, and we have — special arrangements here."

"What do you do with the casual stranger who might wander in?"

"Fully booked, one says, and then recommends a couple of local establishments. Quite simple."

The rhododendrons were indeed spectacularly in bloom along the driveway, their glorious reds, purples, and pinks diverting the eye from the tiny cameras that looked down from among their towering foliage. Beyond a stretch of mauve azaleas and a wide border of multicoloured perennials Cadogan Hall appeared, like something out of a Merchant Ivory film, a splendidly gabled, many-turreted, profusely ivy-covered manor house.

"Some concrete bunker."

"Isn't it. Hiding in plain sight is often better — well, somewhat plain sight, I'll concede. If you don't mind waiting, sir, while I check in."

The driver brought the BMW to a halt in front of the main entrance, got out, and went up the steps to the door which, unusually for a hotel on a mild early summer's day, was closed. He disappeared inside, apparently without knocking or ringing a bell, and was back almost immediately.

"Just around here, sir, where someone will meet you."

They drove around the side of the manor and pulled up at a flight of steps leading to a French window that was open. A man stood there, arms folded across his chest, waiting. As the driver opened the car door on Moretti's side, he came down the steps holding out his hand.

"Detective Inspector Moretti, welcome, you made good time. I'm Derek Lang. Come in."

No Jan Melville, unless she was somewhere inside. Moretti turned around to thank his escort, but he was already in the car and driving off around the back of the house.

Moretti followed Derek Lang up the steps and into a large room set up for the sort of conferences and meetings his driver had said was the principal purpose of the building. A long mahogany table stretched the length of the room, with about twenty upholstered chairs around it. At one end there was a laptop and some papers, coffee, and sandwiches. Lang made his way toward them and pulled out a chair.

Unlike the horticulturally minded driver, Lang's body language did not suggest that Moretti was his superior. Ruddy-faced, with a thin slick of grey hair cut close to his skull, he looked to be in his early fifties, with a slight corpulence beneath his navy suit that suggested a desk job rather than a career in the field.

"Would you like something to eat first, or would you prefer to go to your room? After a two-hour journey, probably the latter."

"My room?"

"Didn't Jan tell you? You'll be staying here tonight. She'll take you back tomorrow."

Jan to Derek Lang, so definitely not a minion.

"My room then."

Lang took a card out of his pocket and handed it to Moretti. "This'll lock and unlock the door."

His room turned out to be what was apparently part of the same suite, beyond a door that led directly off the conference room itself. It was no different from any high-quality hotel room, with windows that didn't open, and a spy hole in the door that probably worked both ways, Moretti suspected. When he returned to the meeting room, Derek Lang was sitting eating a sandwich.

"Coffee? Help yourself. I hope you like prawn sandwiches." He watched Moretti pour himself a cup of coffee, then said, "Let's get down to business. Jan has filled me in, so there's no need to go through all that again. I understand you may have something for us."

"I have something, but whether it's of use or not —"

"We'll determine that. So let me fill you in on what we think we know about your case." The way in which Lang was going through the sandwiches, picking them up delicately and then demolishing them in one gulp suggested that his embonpoint was likely to increase exponentially over the passing years. "As you may know, we have an outfit, GCHQ, that listens in on all kinds of electronic communication — what the Americans call chatter. Emails, phone taps, faxes, whatever. Over the past few months there have been recurring messages from the same group of sources that initially interested us, because we suspect some of the participants have terrorist links. As the information came together, it became evident that this particular scheme was not to do with terrorism, but with something entirely different. A possible coup d'état somewhere on the continent of Africa. A wide choice of possibilities, of course, and the chatterers are extremely careful about stating precisely where. And they don't need to, because they all know where they're talking about. Then, suddenly, the exchanges stopped, and since there has not been a coup d'état on the African continent, we assume one of three possibilities: that the planning is completed — unlikely from what we were picking up — or that the conspirators have reason to suspect their messages are being intercepted, and have found another way to communicate with each other."

"Or that the plan has been aborted." Moretti poured himself another cup of coffee and took another sandwich. "Good prawns."

"Aren't they? Exactly, that's what we assumed, until we heard about the arrival of Masterson on Guernsey. Such an unlikely concatenation of circumstances, and one always takes note of unlikely concatenations."

"So Masterson was one of the chatterers."

"From time to time. Mostly he was talked about, so we hadn't tapped into his computer. We should have done, because his name has come up in connection with others we are more interested in."

"The financing of terrorist organizations would be right up his alley. He also has expertise and connections in armaments, some of them perfectly legit."

"Yes. He'd be useful because of his being apparently above board in that area."

Moretti thought back to his conversation with Ludo Ross. The world is crisscrossed with a vast, intertwined chain connecting drugs, gun-running, you name it, he had said. All grist to the mill of a man like *Bébé Boule à Mite*.

"Now, Detective Inspector, I understand you have some numbers for us."

Lang polished off the last of the sandwiches and wiped his hands carefully on one of the white linen napkins provided. "Pity they didn't give us anything sweet. I always like a taste of something sweet, don't you? Now, Detective Inspector, I have some names for you, and I understand you have some numbers for us. post office box numbers from Masterson's computer, I gather."

"That's what they look like." Moretti pulled out the list from his briefcase, glad that he'd just unpacked it, thus avoiding rummaging around in his underwear. "Tough and time-consuming to check mail if you don't know from where and to where it's going."

"And these chappies may have resorted to snail mail to escape detection, yes." Lang held out his hand.

There goes my trump card, thought Moretti as he handed over his sheet of paper. Hopefully the Jan Melville connection ensured something in return.

"They may be safety deposit boxes. As you can see, there are initials after groups of letters — suggest states or cities to me. Could be names."

"Thank you." Lang took spectacles from his pocket, looked for a minute or so at the list, but made no comment before opening a dispatch case on the table near him, putting the list inside and relocking it. "Now. The names. They were using pseudonyms most of the time, but they were decipherable, and sometimes they were careless. Apart from your victim, three names recurred. First, Leo Van der Velde, a South African mercenary with many years of dubious experience in Africa, who uses the cover name Double V. Not very clever, and he's used it before. We've had an eye on him since a rather iffy sale of helicopters to a certain African country. He flew out of Cape Town about a month or so ago, and then we lost track of him. Possibly he was the unseen man who spoke in a whisper. We think it was Van der

Velde who brought Masterson into the group. They call him Baby?" Lang paused and looked enquiringly over his glasses at Moretti.

"Baby Mothball."

"Quaint. The next chap is probably the French-speaking African your witness heard. Patrice Adeheli. Not his real surname, but one he has used quite openly for years. It is the name of an African sun god, so I'm told, and reflects the ambitions of the user, who sees himself as the sun king of a small west-African country called Maoundi. Adaheli fled the country about a decade ago, and now lives in exile in Paris. They call him Sol, not too original." Lang turned on the laptop and pointed at the screen. "There it is: Maoundi. A tiny chunk of real estate off the Gulf of Guinea, worth its weight in gold."

"Gold."

Moretti waited for Lang to say what he knew he was going to say.

"Black gold, Detective Inspector. Oil, vast reserves of it, virtually untapped, certainly underexploited. That's what this is all about, of that you can be sure. What the numbers you have given me have to do with this I cannot imagine, because it is far more likely their money is in one of your Guernsey banks rather than safety deposit boxes in America. And why they would visit their stash is beyond me, but I presume it was something set up by Baby, God knows why."

Moretti looked across at Derek Lang, who was putting his glasses back in his pocket. "But you said three names. Van der Velde, Adaheli, and —?"

Derek Lang had a very small mouth, which now almost disappeared as he sucked his lips together before he replied. "I am going to give you the third name, Detective Inspector, against my better judgement, and because it is thought by various people that you, as an outsider, have a better chance of nailing this bunch. However, for reasons that will become clear, I would suggest you keep this one to yourself. It is the third name that has made this investigation tricky, without any real evidence to go on, and this particular conspirator is still in South Africa, as far as we know."

"A South African?"

"No, sadly. I wish he were. He is as British as I am, son of a pillar of society with deep pockets, a litigious reputation, and more connections than an octopus has tentacles. The son is a playboy, a risk taker, and completely unprincipled, unlike his father, whose blue-eyed boy he is. He is Norman Beaufort-Jones, only son of Sir Hugh Beaufort-Jones, ex-chancellor of the Exchequer, and ex-owner of the Beaufort Brewery chain."

"Good God."

"Absolutely. He has been in more scrapes than a pye dog has fleas, and Poppa has bought him off every single time. If you can bring your murderer to justice without using his name — and since he is not in Guernsey, that looks possible — you'll stand a better chance of success. Otherwise you'll have one of the Beaufort-Jones' lawyers hanging around your neck, night and day."

"So they killed the money man."

"It would appear so. Looks like Baby was being naughty, doesn't it? Anything else you can think of that might be useful?"

"Masterson had done extensive research into *hawala*, but there was nothing specific about what he was doing with the information."

"Ah. Looks like he was having problems moving money without having it traced. We are getting better at following the money trail."

Lang stood up, brushing the crumbs from his jacket as he did so. "Hope this is helpful, Detective Inspector."

"It is. Do you by any chance have photos? Beaufort-Jones should be easy, but Van der Velde and Adaheli might take time."

"I can get those for you before you leave. The rest of the afternoon is your own, and Jan will join us for dinner tonight. We have an excellent chef on staff at the moment, because we have a major conference with American colleagues shortly." Derek Lang's pale face flushed in anticipation.

"Sounds good. I'll check in with my sergeant and see how things are going."

"Of course. I'll leave you to it." Lang picked up his dispatch case and laptop. "The door you came in by can be used if you want to go outside, but best not to leave the property itself. There's a drinks cabinet in your room, and Internet access. Do you need anything else?"

"No thanks, but I'll take the coffeepot with me. By the way —" Moretti picked up his cup "— did Beaufort-Jones have a nickname? You didn't say."

Derek Lang grinned. "He did indeed. They call him Game-Boy. Very apt, no?"

"You think he's just in it for the kicks."

"Not entirely. Game-Boy has expensive tastes and an expensive wife to keep happy. She's Russian, ex-model, beautiful, a very greedy girl. This coup would outstrip the Beaufort Brewery millions, and make him rich beyond the dreams of even his wife's avarice."

"Money and sex."

"Heady stuff, yes. One often acting as an accelerant to the other. I must say it has a sweet old-fashioned ring to it, compared with the motivations we are now dealing with. I feel quite nostalgic thinking about it."

"Money and fanaticism."

Derek Lang didn't respond to Moretti's observation. "I'll leave you to it then, Detective Inspector. Jan will contact you. She should be arriving this afternoon, I believe." He smiled, turned, and left the room through an interior door that presumably led to the rest of the hotel. Or whatever Cadogan Hall really was.

Moretti sat among the rhododendrons and pulled out his mobile. He had finished the coffee in his room, but there was something claustrophobic about that sealed space with its observation peephole, and he decided to make his phone call outside. After checking the suite for bugs and listening devices, none of which he found, and none of which he expected to find, he took himself out the French windows and down the steps into the gardens.

Around him in the sunshine bees buzzed busily in the pink and mauve flowers, the thick green foliage towering above his head. The grass beneath him was warm and slightly damp, and his mother's generation would have warned him about scarlet fever, arthritis, and the danger of getting piles.

"Falla?"

It was a relief to hear her voice.

"Guv. I was just going to try to get hold of you. How are things?"

"Helpful. I'll fill you in later. Is Hanley kicking up?"

"No more than usual. Later being —?"

"Tomorrow evening, I hope. Any developments?"

"Yes. You were right to say take a look at Nichol Watt's time in America. Looks like he knew Masterson there."

"Well, well. Save the details for when I get back. Does Hanley know?"

"Yes, Guv. I had to tell him to calm him down. Well, to calm him down about you, and to give him something else to get worked up about. He wants further proof before making any moves."

"Just as well. Don't do anything yourself until I get back, Falla, I don't want anyone scared off right now. Are you still keeping an eye on the boat people?"

"We are, but Hanley's whining about how it's stretching us thin, which it is."

"Anything else?"

"Not really." He heard hesitation in her voice. "Nothing that can't wait."

"Okay then. See you tomorrow."

As Moretti put the mobile back in his pocket, he heard a rustling sound in the bushes, and Jan Melville emerged from behind a bed of aggressively red rhododendrons.

"Hello, Ed."

She was wearing patched jeans and an olive T-shirt, sandals on her bare feet, toenails as bright as the blooms behind her. As she sat down, a faint scent of vetiver drifted toward Moretti, and he thought of past loves and Sandy Goldstein.

"Wise move," she said, pointing at the pocket that held his mobile. "The walls here have ears."

"The motivation was claustrophobia rather than paranoia. I hear you are my ride back to London."

"So I gather."

In the daylight she looked older, the pale skin of her forehead and her cheeks furrowed, her neck above her olive shirt lined, softened with age.

"You've known Peter a long time he tells me. Longer than I have."

"On and off, a long time. That was a dirty trick you played on him. Did he deserve it? What's the point, after all these years?"

"The point is, Detective Inspector, there is no point. I don't know if he deserved it, but I did. I had my little revenge, and I've had my little joke. Let me laugh now."

Which she did, throwing her head back and laughing uninhibitedly until the tears came. Moretti sat and waited for her to stop.

"That sounded more like an exorcism than a little joke," he said.

The tears in Jan Melville's eyes made them seem darker than ever. "Let me show you something." She stood up and took a photograph out of her back jeans pocket and handed it to Moretti.

It was a snapshot of Jan Melville and the blond guitarist, arms around each other, smiling into the camera. Without the dark glasses over his long, dark eyes, the resemblance was striking.

"Good God. He's your son."

"He's my son."

Moretti handed back the photo, and Jan Melville put it back in her pocket and sat down again beside him.

"He's not —?"

"No. I wish. His father was a shit, but he gave me a very nice child, so no point in regrets."

"And you produced a musician."

"I did, piano player, I did. And I called him Peter."

Nothing came to mind that wasn't either sentimental or trite, so Moretti said nothing.

"He is an important part of my life and I can enjoy his company more now than I could, sadly, when he was growing up. My career made that — dicey." Jan Melville tapped Moretti on the shoulder. "Speaking of which, do you mind if we get out of here in the next little while?"

Moretti turned to her in surprise. "I'd love to get out of here in the next little while, and I'd love to know why you suggest doing so."

"Look, Ed —" the tone of her voice had changed "— you'll have gathered by now there's someone involved in this business of yours who's got friends in high places.

Some, or one, of those friends is on the inside. Lang won't tell you that in so many words, but I will. He also won't tell you that one of the chief reasons for agreeing to talk to you is not to get your list of numbers, but because you may be able to nail Beaufort-Jones for him."

"Actually, he said just the opposite, but now it makes sense. The only sense I could make of it before was that Peter had arm-twisted to reconnect with you."

"Which he did, but getting Derek to agree was because of Game-Boy, not because of any clout I still have. And Game-Boy's mole is the reason for all these theatrics, bring you out here instead of to the Yard or MI5 headquarters. That's why I'm the one driving you back. Your driver this morning, Jekyll, is hopefully reliable, but we can't be too careful."

"Jekyll?" Moretti laughed. "Is that a code name? I've been hearing those most of the afternoon."

"No, his very own. His great-great-aunt was Gertrude Jekyll, the celebrated gardening expert. He's the gardening consultant for this place. Among other things."

Which explained the tenor of the conversation in the car. "Here's hoping he isn't going to morph into Mr. Hyde," said Moretti. "I'll go and get my things right now, but shouldn't I tell Lang? I'm going to miss a good meal, apparently."

"All the more for Derek. No, I'd rather no one knew officially that you have vacated the premises. I'll deal with that later, after we've gone."

"Lang was going to get some photos for me."

"I have them."

Jan Melville pulled a package out of the pocket in her T-shirt. Moretti opened it and took out the three pictures inside. One was of a stunningly handsome African, another was of a laughing, fair-haired man in his thirties, smoking a cigarette, and the third was of an unsmiling middle-aged man, his skin deeply tanned and lined, his fair hair bleached white by a tropical sun.

"Interesting," said Moretti.

Shades of Melville and her guitar-playing, look-alike son — there seemed to be a theme going here. He was looking at an older, more shopworn version of that experienced, so-called German yachtsman, Hans Ulbricht.

Chapter Twelve

Liz Falla had always liked this part of the island. Ensconced between four parishes — Castel, St. Andrew, Forest, and St. Pierre du Bois — St. Saviour's had the feel of being part of a larger entity than Guernsey, separated as it was from the sea. Yet, if you wanted to remind yourself that you were on an island, you could walk down Petit Bot Valley and be on one of the prettiest coastlines in minutes. If ever she got a little more money she would buy a cottage here, but it would take a lot more money than Detective Sergeant Falla presently had in her piggybank.

Dorothy Watt lived in a converted fifteenth-century farmhouse in a valley that ran behind St. Saviour's Church. As happens so often on the island, the distant past meets the more recent past at St. Saviour's, the largest of the island churches. Below the stone bench in the churchyard on which a feudal lord once held court, run the tunnels constructed by the Germans on the principle that they were unlikely to be bombed in a sacred place.

Liz Falla turned the police car through the gate, which was open, and stopped outside the heavy stone-framed entrance to the house, which formed an *L* shape around a well-maintained cobbled courtyard, not unlike Coralie Chancho's home. To the right of the front door was a large French window, obviously a modern addition, framed by rose-covered trellises, and behind the window stood Dorothy Watt. As Liz got out of the car, her mobile rang.

It was Moretti. Concisely as she could, she updated him, watching Dorothy Watt watching her. As she said, "Good luck, Guv," Nichol's ex threw the window open and called out to her.

"Come in this way. I've just finished my workout."

The first Mrs. Watt was a tall, strong-boned brunette in her forties who, from what Liz could tell through the folds of the towelling robe she was wearing, was in excellent shape. The knee-length garment exposed strong calf muscles above bare, tanned feet, from which she was kicking a pair of pricey-looking trainers. Presumably she had been using the treadmill on the tiled deck. Beyond her stretched an azure-tinted swimming pool beneath a canopy-shaped roof, the structure obviously an addition to the original farmhouse. The wide, tiled surround fairly sprouted mini palm trees and massive flowering plants in tubs. The arrival of big money on the island had heralded the arrival of a plethora of experts in the installation of every luxurious mod con the well-heeled considered essential.

"You're not what I expected. You remind me of someone." A pair of shrewd hazel eyes surveyed Liz Falla.

"Really?"

Who knew what Dorothy Watt was expecting, and perhaps best not to suggest, "Probably your ex-husband's present squeeze."

Dorothy Watt sat down on a sofa covered in a pale creamy velvet fabric that almost matched her robe, giving Liz the feeling she was interviewing a disembodied head, arms, and legs.

"My children will be back with their nanny any time, so let's do this. I try not to talk about their father in front of them if I can help it. He's enough of a problem for them as it is."

"Of course. Do you mind if I take notes?"

"Go ahead. Sit down." Dorothy Watt picked up a glass from a table beside her. "Can I get you anything?"

"No, it's fine, thank you." Liz sat down on a straight-backed chair opposite Dorothy Watt and took out her notebook. "When we spoke on the phone, you mentioned the business of the MRI machines when you and Dr. Watt were in America. Perhaps you could fill us in a bit more, and I'd appreciate it if you kept this to yourself."

"Not tell Nichol, you mean." Dorothy Watt clearly found this funny. "Only too happy to — but how much do you already know?"

"Well," Liz prevaricated, "I think it best I don't lead you, but leave you to tell things as you see them, Mrs. Watt."

"Ms. Le Huray. I use my maiden name. Isn't *that* a laugh, maiden name." To judge from Ms. Le Huray's expression, this, just as clearly, was not funny.

"You're an islander. I didn't know."

"Why would you? When Nichol ran into problems I suggested we come here. I even thought he might straighten up in other ways too, but the leopard's spots and so on. Anyway, you didn't need to learn about Nichol the skirt chaser. The whole island knows about that, but I never thought the MRI business would come back to haunt him." Dorothy Le Huray took a good swig from her glass. "It all started at a medical convention in Canada. Nichol met a man whose business was the leasing of medical equipment to health centres and hospitals, very expensive equipment, chiefly magnetic resonance imaging machines. When Nichol heard the kind of money that could be made — millions of dollars — he wanted in on it and, being Nichol, didn't bother himself too much with the — niceties, shall we say. He was to be the contact man in the States, using his name and the name of the hospital where he was working as references. To cut a long story short, there was, in fact, only a banking company with a fancy name and there were no MRI machines. The police told us it was not just a fraud bringing in millions of dollars, but a cover for the laundering of dirty money. In fact, the only legitimate business this fellow had was the international arms business." Another swig of water. "God, we were terrified. Nichol was the only one on the hook, because his name was attached to just about everything. The clever bastard who conned him had kept clear by saying to Nichol that it was his standing as a medical man that was important. Too true!"

"Was Dr. Watt arrested or charged?"

"No, but he was questioned on and off for days, and it cost us a fortune in lawyers' fees, while the crook who had done all this got out of the country. I'm not sure where he is."

In the hospital morgue, thought Liz Falla. She watched as Dorothy Le Huray poured herself another glassful from a jug on the table beside her. "Do you remember the name of the man, Ms. Le Huray?"

"I most certainly do, because we only discovered afterward it was not his real name."

"What did he call himself?"

"Letourneau. Buddy Letourneau."

The name of the so-called housekeeper.

"Oh," added Dorothy Le Huray, "that reminds me. He had a wife, Adèle. Smooth bitch. Nichol being Nichol, it was not just the millions that drew him in, she was put up as bait."

"Put up as bait?"

"Yes." Nichol Watt's ex-wife leaned forward. "My louse of a husband was sucked in by French knickers, Sergeant, not just Yankee dollars." The faint fragrance of vodka wafted toward Liz Falla as Dorothy Le Huray picked up a large and spectacularly glittering watch from the small table beside her. "My children will be home soon with their nanny. Can we call this a day?"

"Yes, thank you. What you have told us will help in the investigation, Ms. Le Huray."

"Investigation? So you think this is in some way connected to what happened on that yacht?" The shrewd hazel eyes surveyed Liz Falla. "What can Nichol's MRI contretemps have to do with that? I can understand why the dead body outside Mona's place might be connected. Murder is not a common crime here, as I don't have to tell you. We may *feel* like it, but we islanders go in for smaller stuff, like smoking a joint or stealing a neighbour's wife — oh my God!" Dorothy Le Huray leaned forward, her breasts threatening to break free of their ivory velour confines. "It's him, isn't it? Letourneau? *That's* why you're here, isn't it? And Nichol has been called in, and told you he recognized him — oh my God!"

Oh my God indeed because, of course, Nichol Watt hadn't said anything, and Liz Falla was now as anxious to leave as Dorothy Le Huray was to get rid of her.

As she said her goodbyes and thank-yous, a car turned into the driveway. Through the windows she caught a brief glimpse of a small face pressed against the glass. A hand came up and waved at her and she waved back, her mind momentarily shifted from Dorothy Le Huray's revelation by the little boy's smiling face.

As she drove through St. Martin's and St. Andrew's toward the coast road, Liz tried to recall how Nichol Watt had behaved when he came to the yacht, and remembered that neither she nor Moretti had seen or spoken to him then. Only by phone, later. She waited until she had driven back into the courtyard outside the police station and tried to contact Moretti. There was no reply. Disappointing, but not unexpected. Now that her boss was — well, wherever he was — it was unlikely she would be able to speak to him.

As she got out of the car, she saw Constable Mauger coming down the steps. She remembered he had been one of the first at the scene of the crime.

"Constable Mauger, a word."

Mauger bounded toward her, eager to help. "DS Falla?"

"Were you in the cabin when Dr. Watt arrived to examine the body?"

"Yes. Why?"

She had to do this carefully, or Mauger would be yapping about it all over the station, and up the chain of command it would go to Chief Officer Hanley.

"Just something that came up in Dr. Watt's report that needs clarification. Did he seem — put out about anything? You know, anything out of the ordinary happen?"

Constable Mauger thought a moment, then said, as if the memory had taken him by surprise, "Well, it was a bit weird, DS Falla. He took one look at the deceased and said, loudly, 'bloody hell.' Just like that. 'Bloody hell.' Then it was pretty much business as usual. Since there wasn't much blood, I thought he was just surprised at a gun being involved, that's all. Why are you asking?"

"Like I said, clarification. And that clears it up. I'll pass it on to DI Moretti."

Hopefully the mention of a superior officer would keep the constable quiet. Just as she could only hope that Dorothy Le Huray would take heed of her final warning. "I cannot give you any information as to what Dr. Watt has told us, but it would be best if you did not discuss this interview with him."

So much now depended on whether Dorothy Le Huray preferred her revenge hot as Dwight's vindaloo, or as a meal best eaten cold.

Which made Liz think of food. She debated whether to go to the police canteen or to head for home, and it was the thought of bumping into the chief officer rather than what was on the canteen menu that guided her decision. Still, she planned to return later in the day to use the police computers, and take advantage of Moretti's absence to do some checking on Sandra Goldstein. The woman's hostility seemed puzzling, and she wanted to take a closer look at the possibility of some sort of criminal activity. Such a level of paranoia because Goldstein was interested in Moretti and saw his DS as a threat seemed unlikely.

What do you care? she thought. *He's a big boy. He's single, he's attracted. Or seems to be. What do you care?* Not finding an answer to her question, she did what she usually did in similar circumstances. She filed it away for future consideration.

Liz Falla finished the last mouthful of her cheese omelette, put the plate in the sink, poured herself another cup of coffee, and changed CDs. The otherworldly voice of Loreena McKennitt now filling the space. Oh, how she had wanted to nail Nichol Watt for the murder, but she knew that the likelihood of Masterson's killer merely and spontaneously exclaiming "bloody hell" was remote. Watt had been taken by surprise, then pulled himself together.

Damn. She finished her coffee and checked her messages. There was one, a text message. It was from Moretti. It said: *Don't let Ulbricht and Baumgarten go anywhere.*

"Why?" she yelled into the phone as she dialled Moretti's number. "Why?"

Still no response. She put a call through to the Esplanade Hotel, which was answered by Betty Kerr.

"Oh, hello, DS Falla, and many thanks. We really needed those rooms."

From the CD player came the sound of Loreena singing her version of the "Lady of Shalott," and Liz Falla's warm little room suddenly turned chilly.

And moving through a mirror clear that hangs before her all the year, shadows of the world appear.

"Where are they, Ms. Kerr?"

"Didn't you know? Chief Officer Hanley said it would be all right if they returned to the yacht. They went with a police escort, and since there's a full-time guard on the pier, he really didn't see the need for me to be inconvenienced anymore." Betty Kerr gave a little laugh. "And you needn't worry about Mr. Rossignol, Sergeant. I'm holding on to him. He's a super cook, and he's scared stiff about going back to that lot."

Liz wasted no time in replying, hung up, and put a call through to the police station to find out who was on sentry duty. The desk sergeant put her through to

PC Brouard. The sound of his voice was not reassuring, its normally strong baritone muted and uncertain.

"DS Falla, I was just about to contact you. Those two Germans went to pick up supplies, and I didn't worry too much because we've got their passports, haven't we, but they've been gone quite a bit now."

"How much is quite a bit?"

"Hours. Well, all day, and the Letourneau woman is really pissed off —"

Liz cut PC Brouard off in mid-sentence, turned off the CD player, grabbed the keys of the police car, which she had, thank God, held on to, and left the room.

So the Letourneau woman was pissed off, was she. She wasn't the only one.

Moretti's head hurt. Badly. A lump had come up on it almost immediately, and now it was throbbing to its own internal beat. Boom, boom, boom.

A sympathetic crowd gathered, giving advice and comfort. "I've called the police ... you need to get an icepack on that ... a bag of frozen peas'll do the trick ... you should see a doctor in case your brain swells ..."

A passing taxi slowed down and pulled over to take a look, and Moretti stuck out his hand, stumbling into the seat by the driver. He had to get away before the police got there, before he had to answer any question, got taken to the police station, or even the hospital. And he had to hope the convenient taxi was not part of whatever this was. As he gave the cab driver

Peter Walker's address, a Greek chorus of warnings and advice drifted through the window.

"Blimey, mate, what happened?" The cabbie seemed genuinely shocked. "You was mugged?"

"Yes."

"Did they get anything?"

"My briefcase."

"Least it wasn't your wallet. Anything of value?"

"Not much."

Some clean underwear, some shaving tackle and, more annoyingly, the charger for his mobile. But the numbers from Masterson's computer were safely with Lang. If indeed they were safe. And the photos were safe also, tucked into a moneybelt worn against his body.

"Bit of luck then. Sure you don't want me to drop you off at a hospital?"

"Sure. My friend will take care of this."

"Right you are, Guv."

Guv. Liz Falla. Thank heaven for texting, eliminating the sound of the human voice. Moretti pulled out his mobile. His hands were trembling, which surprised him. He must be suffering from shock, but he didn't want his "friend" to be at home to take care of anything. He no longer knew whom he could trust.

He was in luck. The house was empty, and he tottered upstairs on shaky legs and into the sitting room. He put the key down on the desk, went into the kitchen, and ran the cold water tap, wet a tea towel, and wrapped it around his head. It hurt and kept slipping, so he took it off, poured himself a glass of cold water instead. He found a bottle of aspirin in Peter Walker's bathroom cabinet, took two, then put the bottle in his pocket.

He had to get away before Peter got back. Had he followed him? Was he in cahoots with Jan Melville? Perhaps shock was making him ridiculously paranoid, but that's how he felt. Paranoid. After all, Jan Melville had dropped him off at the Tube station, and then whoever it was had come out of nowhere, hit him, and grabbed the briefcase.

In big cities, people got mugged every day. But most people didn't get mugged with a voice hissing in their ear, "Back off."

It was the last thing he remembered before dropping to the ground and feeling the briefcase being wrenched from his hand. Clearly the wrencher assumed he carried a laptop, and did everything electronically, as most people did these days.

"Aha," he said out loud. "You forgot you were dealing with a plodding copper from the back of beyond."

Even talking was painful. Moretti winced, went into the bedroom he had used, repacked his bag, went downstairs, and opened the hall closet. It was chaotic, as hall closets tend to be, but eventually he found what he was looking for. He extracted a watch cap of black wool that Peter Walker used on his sailing and birdwatching visit to Herm — was that in fact what he *had* been doing? — and pulled it over his contused skull. Moretti, as his father had, was holding on to a full head of dark hair, now edged with grey, but the bump was visible and he wanted no comments or curiosity.

He took a moment to consider whether he should leave a note saying something innocuous like, "Called back urgently. Will be in touch." But only a moment. Picking up his belongings, he let himself out of the house and flagged down a passing cab.

At some point on the way to the airport, he left another message for Falla, and the aspirins started to kick in.

PART THREE

Exposition

Chapter Thirteen

Day Seven

"That's a real pigeon's egg, Guv. Have you got an icepack in your fridge? If not, frozen peas will do."

Moretti started to laugh. "Ouch. There's an icepack, I think. In the door."

Liz found it, wrapped it in a tea towel, and handed it to Moretti. "No, seriously, the peas mould themselves to the shape of —"

"I know. Peas were included in the advice I got from my London sympathizers. Thanks, Falla."

Moretti leaned back in the armchair and held the pack to his head. "Okay, so tell me the worst."

"The worst is that the two Germans have flown the coop. And there's more."

While she filled Moretti in on her interview with Dorothy Le Huray, Liz looked around at her boss's home. She had been here before, on their first case as partners, when she was assigned to protect a witness in that case. Not just a witness, but the ballerina wife of the murder victim, who subsequently was involved romantically with Moretti. It had broken up fairly swiftly; she didn't know why.

The place seemed unchanged, very much still the home he had inherited when his father died. Liz knew Moretti had lost his mother when he was still quite young. She also knew the two most significant objects in the room were the family piano and her boss's truly antediluvian record player that, he maintained, reproduced the best and purest sound. She saw there was a new acquisition on the wall, a watercolour in among the Guernsey prints and some fine old black-and-white photographs, and she recognized the female figure in the painting, a nymph called Arethusa. She only knew that because her image had come up in the earlier case, which meant this was a gift from Moretti's ex-lover. Which made her think of Sandra Goldstein. Perhaps she'd have time to do some digging later at Hospital Lane.

"You should eat something," she said. She got up and went into the kitchen. "You've got some cold chicken here in the fridge," she called out, "and some bread. I'll make you a sandwich." She came back, carrying a tray with chicken, bread, a plate, and a couple of knives, placing everything on the dining table in the corner of the sitting room, pushing aside a pile of records to make a space. "Do you think it was just a mugging, Guv? A coincidence?"

"No." There was something remarkably comforting about Falla's slim fingers dexterously cutting bread and slicing chicken. Some time he really must go and hear her sing, watch those slender fingers playing her beautiful Martin guitar. "Not with 'back off' lovingly murmured into my ear. I think one of our problems is that there are any number of red herrings, most of them supplied by that jack of all trades, Masterson. He had so many irons in the fire and most of them were — well, fishy. If an iron can be fishy. Yet they are still all linked to the main reason he was killed, and it is a very dangerous main reason. He was playing with some very big, very unpleasant men who will stop at nothing to get what they want. What I don't know is whether he was trying to stiff them, or whether things just didn't work out. Or both. He made money on the MRI scam, but it fell apart, and I suspect the same thing happened with the offshore-haven scheme. The Mounties and the taxman got on to that one before the really big money was made."

The sandwich was good and he was hungry. Liz Falla put down a glass of orange juice on the table, sat down opposite him, kicked off her shoes, and folded her legs up beneath her. She looked even younger like that, and Moretti felt ancient, and weary, and sore. Thinking straight suddenly became difficult. "Okay, Falla," he said, "my addled brain is having problems. Whodunit, Detective Sergeant? Who have we got in the frame?"

Liz Falla leaned toward him and counted them off on her fingers. "First: Coralie Fellowes. Yes, her Baby Browning didn't do it, but she was there, I'm sure. Second: Nichol Watt, although his 'bloody hell' would suggest not." She looked across at Moretti and saw he was smiling. "I know, I know, I'd just like it to be him. Okay, not likely him. Looks like he was being used as a patsy by Masterson, doesn't it? Then there's the bloke who ended up dead on the Amsterdams' front lawn, the bodyguard. And there's Garth Machin and, possibly, his wife."

"Ah yes, the fair lady of sorrows. But the most likely killer, or killers, are the ones the little shit warned him about. The ones who get you when your back is turned, your own."

"The so-called housekeeper and the so-called Germans. Given he was shot with a Glock, the most likely, and now the two principal suspects are on the lam. But this is a small island, Guv, and we've got all available personnel out looking for them."

Moretti drank the orange juice, finished his sandwich, and put the plate down on the oak chest he used as a coffee table. "Falla, you did the right thing, but it's too late now. Ulbricht and Baumgarten are probably long gone, and not via the airport or by the regular ferry service."

Liz Falla looked at him, but did not reply. She picked up the remains of his meal and took them back into the kitchen. Moretti reached into his shirt and pulled out the body pack, extracted the photographs Jan Melville had given him, and put them down on the oak chest. He watched in silence as she came back into the room, sat down, and picked them up.

"That looks like —"

"Poppa Ulbricht, don't you think? These, I am sure, are the three people Melissa Machin overheard that day, and it is fortunate she had the good sense to stay hidden. I am going to tell you what I was told about these three, and the only other person who gets that information is Hanley."

Liz Falla listened in silence as Moretti filled her in, then asked, "Do you think the little shit ignored his own advice, tried his hand at blackmail, then was shot by one of them?"

"Yes. Probably Ulbricht. My feeling is that Baumgarten is the point man, and watches his back, but Ulbricht is the hit man. A loose cannon, Martin Smith, and he became a liability."

Moretti was startled by his partner's sudden yelp, as if she were in pain. "*Now* I remember what was bothering me, Guv, about Melissa Machin's account. I couldn't put my finger on it at the time, but she said, 'Bruiser? That's what his shirt said, wasn't it?' There is no way she could have seen that from inside the house and, besides, it was getting dark. I think she went outside and she saw something. She'd been cooperative right up to the end, and then she became almost hostile. She'd been so frank it never occurred to me she might have withheld anything."

Moretti got to his feet. The icepack slipped off unheeded into the armchair as he took out his mobile. Liz could hear the sound of a phone ringing, somewhere.

"Answer it, answer it, pick the damn thing up — Mrs. Machin? This is Ed Moretti. I'm coming right over. Do you have a spy hole in your door — yes? Keep back from the windows, but watch out for me and the detective sergeant you met a day or two ago. Open the door to no one else, not even Garth — I'll explain when I get there."

Moretti put his mobile away, picked up the photographs from the table, and repacked them in his moneybelt.

"To state the obvious," he said, "Melissa Machin is in a whole lot of trouble, because we don't know if the Germans are off the island. We'll take her first to Hospital Lane and then, Falla, to your place. After dark."

Liz Falla was already at the door, car keys in hand. She was smiling as she turned back to Moretti, and he remembered that her brains were matched by her coolness under fire, a metaphor he hoped would remain only a turn of phrase.

"I'm babysitting again. Right, Guv?"

"Right. And you can put those car keys away. We'll take my Triumph and leave the police car here. Someone can collect it later."

His partner's smile broadened as she replied. "Brilliant. With that head injury, I'd better drive, hadn't I?"

Melissa Machin packed a small bag as they waited, then walked between them to the Triumph. Moretti had let Falla do the talking, and she had said the right thing.

"Mrs. Machin, please come with us. For your children's sake, please don't delay, just come with us."

"But, Garth —"

"Leave him a note saying you are on the mainland," Moretti said, adding, "but don't say where. I'll talk to him."

Moretti watched the window as Liz Falla went up the stairs with Melissa Machin. On that pristine, featureless landscape, whatever Garth's wife had seen would have stood out like — a dead prizefighter. And he thought he knew what she might have seen.

"At first, I didn't really think it was odd. They were not out of place, because they were well-dressed, and their car was in keeping with most of the cars around here."

"What kind of car?" Moretti asked.

Melissa Machin gave a faint smile. "I couldn't tell you what make, I'm afraid. It was black, shiny. I'm not good on cars."

"So there were two of them?"

"Yes. They had such cheerful expressions, looked as if they were dropping in on the people next door. And they made no attempt to hide, so it never occurred to me they were dangerous. Not at first, not until I heard this popping noise. Like a cap gun, sort of, after I'd walked away from the window. Then I heard the sound of the car leaving, fast — the brakes squealed, something like that. I looked out the window and saw what looked like next door's gardener lying on the lawn, only it wasn't his day, and that was odd. I thought maybe he'd had a heart attack or something, so I ran out of the house to help him. Then I saw the wound and knew. Just knew."

"That it might be something to do with what you overheard?" Liz Falla interjected. "You'd told me so much, why didn't you tell me everything, Mrs. Machin?"

Melissa Machin shook her head. "Panic, I think. I don't know, I really don't. Fear of implicating Garth any further in — whatever this is all about."

"Did you see the two men or the car?" Liz Falla asked.

"No. Just the body on the lawn."

Maybe it was his sore head, but Ed Moretti felt irritation rising inside him. He was tired of being nice. "Is this the full story now?"

"Yes. I promise you, I saw nothing."

Melissa Machin was shaking visibly, but Moretti felt only exasperation.

"See, the trouble is, Mrs. Machin, you have put yourself and Garth in greater danger, which could have been avoided if you had told DS Falla the truth."

"I didn't lie!"

"You withheld information, the two men you saw are killers, and we don't know where they are."

As the tears started to run down Melissa Machin's cheeks, Liz Falla stood up and put a hand on her shoulder. "Which is why, Mrs. Machin, you are going to spend the night at my place."

Wiping away her tears, Melissa Machin turned round in her chair, and looked up at Liz Falla. "What about Garth?" she asked. "Mightn't they come looking for him?"

Before Liz could answer, Moretti replied. "They might, and if your husband chooses to tell me what is going on, we may be able to save him." He stood up, pushing his chair back with unnecessary vigour. "A word with you, DS Falla."

Outside in the corridor, Moretti took Liz by the shoulders, which surprised them both. As she looked up into his eyes, Liz remembered Moretti being compared once to someone called Dirk Bogarde. Some time she must ask him who Dirk Bogarde was. She felt his hands tighten on her shoulders, then release, as if he suddenly became aware he was touching her.

"First, before I leave here I'm going to arrange for Adèle Letourneau to be held in police custody overnight, preferably longer. That will free up an officer to be posted full-time at the Machins'. I don't think Letourneau is of great importance in the grand scheme of things but, if she *is* the brains, then they made a mistake cutting her out. She may yet talk. But I could be wrong, and I'm worried she may be able to swim her way out of police custody. One of those wetsuits was — wet, remember? Second, I've arranged a meeting with Chief Officer Hanley. He needs to know about my Cadogan Hall meeting, and the international ramifications of this case. He is less likely to get upset if I break the rules, and less likely to blow a gasket if islanders are not involved. We'll take the Triumph to your place, and then I'll drive it back home."

"What about Garth Machin?"

"I'd love to set him up as bait, but for tonight I've told him to stay at the office, and that his wife is safe with us. One more thing —" even in the deserted corridor, Moretti lowered his voice "— I believe the Cadogan Hall mob have thrown us to the wolves. They didn't help me in return for a few post office box numbers, but because we may bumble around and flush out these characters, and if we are killed in the process, too bad." He held out his hand, and grinned at Liz. "You really think I'm going to leave my Triumph sitting on the Esplanade for joyriders? Come on, Falla, hand over that key."

Reluctantly, Liz Falla took the key out of her pocket and mentally added a sports car to her wish list. As Moretti took them from her, she remembered her plan to check out Sandra Goldstein. It would have to be put off, again.

It should have been awkward, but it wasn't. Melissa Machin was as easy and compatible as any of her woman friends, and it was that thought that led Liz Falla to another.

What woman friends? She had no close friends in the force, and many of her former school friends were no longer on the island. Two had gone into the financial sector, and they had drifted apart, largely because neither could understand how bright Liz Falla could have chosen being a bobby over being a businesswoman. And she was not big on coffee klatches, hen parties, and their modern counterparts, tweeting and texting. At least, not as a solely female undertaking. There were women on the force she liked, but her rapid rise to detective sergeant had put a space between them and her.

With whom did she share the things that were important to her? Some members of her family, maybe. Then, of course, there was her band, Jenemie, but she really only shared a love of music, and playing music, with them.

As they ate their frozen dinners, she and Melissa Machin talked about art and books, and Melissa Machin returned more than once to the impossibly difficult separation from her children, which was, apparently, something set in stone by the class into which she had married.

As they talked, Liz came to the conclusion that she only spoke at any length to whoever was in her bed, and that included Brutus. And Moretti. But that was mostly about work, and for sure not in bed. Her boyfriends were rarely that interested in talking when they shared her bed, so perhaps that was why she had been attracted to Ludo, for all his advanced years. And Moretti had put up barriers between them, barriers that had as much to do with his personality as with their professional relationship.

"The class into which you married? I'd have thought you and your husband came from the same background, Mrs. Machin."

"Melissa, please!" Melissa Machin finished the last of her meal and put the bowl down on the table. "That was really good curry. Did you make it?"

Liz laughed. "No. And I'm Liz. The drummer in the Fénions makes them. His vindaloo is amazing, could blow up a battleship, but I thought the butter chicken best for tonight."

"Dwight." Melissa looked at Liz questioningly. "Are you and he —?"

"Once. Not anymore. Dwight likes to move on, and I was okay with that."

Liz got up and took the bowls over to the sink. "So, this whole class thing. On this island you've got to get it right, or you tread on the wrong toes."

"Everywhere, I think. I met Garth when he was playing sax in a Paris club. I was there studying art on a scholarship. My family are all in the arts one way or another, so money is tight. We were crazy about each other, Garth and me, but I think part of the attraction for him was my family's bohemian attitude to life. I didn't meet Garth the financier until after I realized I wanted to spend my life with him, have children with him. The sax player never completely went away, but the money man came out ahead of him. Money is so seductive, Liz."

Liz thought of her wish list, and her own reluctance to sit behind a desk. "I know. I'm in the police force to put curry on the table, but I would love to play my guitar and sing for a living."

Melissa Machin looked delighted. "You play that lovely thing? I wondered if it might be purely decorative."

"Perish the thought!" Liz took a bottle of wine from her small wine rack near the sofa bed that would be her guest's that night. "I don't like drinking wine with curry, but I love it afterward. Let me guess — bohemian family — red?"

"You guessed right." Melissa was laughing as she got down from her chair and on to the floor, to sit cross-legged on the pretty little tribal rug that Ludo had helped Liz choose in happier days. Just as he had guided her with her wine selection. "Then you'll play and sing for me, Liz?"

"Try and stop me."

She began with "Plaisir D'Amour," and watched the tears drift unchecked down Melissa Machin's face.

Plaisir d'amour ne dure qu'un instant
Chagrin d'amour dure toute la vie.

Moretti let himself out of Chief Officer Hanley's office with a sigh of relief. The briefing had gone surprisingly well, and he was reminded of his superior officer's best qualities, which came more readily to the fore when Hanley did not have to concern himself with island politics or island personalities. Hanley had listened, allowed him to talk, asked the occasional question, then picked up the phone. By the time he put it down again, Adèle Letourneau was in custody and on her way to Hospital Lane with PC Brouard, who was only too happy to oblige. His feet were hurting, and he was fed up with being sworn at in a language he didn't understand, although the gist was quite clear. What's more, the Letourneau woman came quietly, which was unexpected, an added bonus, and almost as if being in custody overnight was not that unwelcome.

Moretti unlocked the Triumph and drove out of the police car park into Hospital Lane. The throbbing of the bump on his head had now turned into a more general headache radiating in a tight band just above his ears. On an impulse he turned away from his normal route home and drove toward the harbour, to Le Grand Saracen. Maybe he would feel better if he had something to eat, and Deb Duchemin's lasagna travelled well. It was almost as good as his mother's. Emidio's was busy, and he was able to get in, pick up what he wanted, and get out again without having to talk too much. His head was too sore for an exchange of pleasantries, witticisms, or customers enquiring when he was playing again downstairs.

If only, he thought. *If only.*

The image of a witch in black and silver floated through his mind with the music that was always there, as he headed for home. So it was not surprising he thought her a figment of his imagination when he saw her outside his house, sitting on the step, her coat folded up beneath her.

Chapter Fourteen

"What are you doing here? Is something wrong?" Moretti called out the car window, as Sandy Goldstein stood up and came toward him. She was holding a small package in her hand and she was smiling. Under the porch light her teeth shone, incredibly white.

"Waiting for you is what I am doing here, and the only thing wrong is that I am freezing." She gave a mock shiver. She was wearing a black turtleneck sweater and black pants, but the coat on his doorstep was scarlet. "And in case you're wondering how I found you, Gwen told me where you lived. I have a gift for you, a thank you for the phone."

Gwen indeed. Very few called Gwen Ferbrache by her first name.

"That wasn't necessary."

Charming, he thought. What an impression I must be making, and why did this delectable woman appear on my doorstep when all I want to do is to crash with the help of an aspirin or two. Or three.

"Very gallant, Detective Inspector." Sandy Goldstein was laughing.

Moretti climbed out of the Triumph, retrieved the lasagna, picked up the red coat from the step, and unlocked the door.

"Come in."

As she walked by him into the house, the fragrance she had worn at the club drifted in after her, and he followed in its wake.

"This is a pretty place. Your parents' originally, Gwen tells me."

She is so at ease in her skin, he thought, watching her put down her package, walk over to look at the prints and photos on the wall.

"Yes. You have left Julia on her own? In the circumstances, I feel I must ask."

"Yes. She is so happy and secure here, and this is from her as well. More than from me, as a matter of fact, because it is one of her watercolours. We had it framed in town."

She sat down and gestured to Moretti to do the same, as if she were in her own place. Inside the package was a rectangular painting in a simple frame.

"Wildflowers. Julia chose the muted tones. We had no idea what your place was like, or your tastes, but Julia felt this was — well, you."

"She was absolutely right. Thank you."

Sandy Goldstein came over and stood beside him. "See, she identified them all on the back. Fennel, hogweed, coltsfoot — we are becoming quite experts, Ed — some reeds and a touch of yellow. Ragwort, Julia loves yellow — aah!"

With his frayed nerves, her muted shriek sounded like the harbour siren in his ear, and Moretti jumped violently.

"You've got a helluva bump on your head. What happened, Ed?"

"I was in the wrong place at the wrong time, so let's just leave it at that."

"Oh my God, and you come home and find me on your doorstep. Unasked for and unwanted. What timing. I'm so sorry."

"How were you to know?" He was thinking much the same thing, only unwanted wasn't on his list. He felt her body against his side, then her lips against his head.

"Oh, Ed, you poor baby," she said.

How things unfolded from there he could never quite remember afterward, and he put it down to the bump on his head. Loss of memory, loss of judgement, above all, loss of control. He hated losing control, most of the time.

She had a silver stud in her navel with a diamond in it, and around the diamond was a tattooed flower that bore no resemblance to any Guernsey wildflower whatsoever, of coastline or marshland, of wasteland or watermeadow.

Moretti had read somewhere that men had two and a half times the sex drive of women, but clearly Sandy Goldstein had not been one of the female subjects of the study. At some point they had got upstairs to the bedroom, but the lasagna had not got as far as the fridge. Much later on that night he realized he had completely forgotten about his headache and his hunger.

Ah well, he thought, in one briefly sane moment. She wasn't a witness, or a potential suspect. She wasn't married to anyone else. She had nothing to do with yachts, or gun-running, or MRI machines. Or murder. And it had been such a long, long time.

Day Eight

They were making breakfast and laughing together when the phone rang. It was wonderful to laugh with a woman with whom he had just spent the night.

"Must you answer it?"

"Yes, I must."

As he picked up the phone, Sandy Goldstein put her arms around him, and kissed his ear.

"Guv? I think your mobile's off."

It was Liz Falla. A wave of guilt washed over him, followed by anxiety. He should have checked in with her the night before, made sure everything was all right.

"Falla? Are you okay?"

Moretti felt Sandy Goldstein stiffen, then move away from him.

"I'm okay, and Mrs. Machin's okay. But there's been another murder."

Moretti's anxiety heightened. Christ, he should have moved Garth, but his annoyance with him had clouded his judgement, leaving Garth to take his chances.

"Garth?"

"No. I just checked in with PC Le Marchant, who was on duty overnight, and nothing happened."

That left one prime target, and Moretti knew who it would be.

"Coralie Fellowes, Guv. Mrs. Evans just arrived and found her."

"I'll meet you there, Falla."

Moretti put down the phone and turned to look at Sandy. She was not laughing anymore.

"I know. You gotta go, right?"

"Yes. I'll order you a taxi to take you back to La Veile."

She was already in the sitting room, picking up her red coat. Moretti noticed it had a hood. Which probably made him the big, bad wolf. Certainly he was being made to feel like it.

On his way to St. Martin, Moretti made another call to Falla.

"Where is Melissa Machin? Still at your place?"

"No, Guv. I thought she was safer now back with her Fort Knox security system and a police guard. Was that right?"

"That was right."

"Oh, and I think we've got the car they used to go to Fort George, Guv. It was rented at the harbour by the crew members and returned later that afternoon. All above board and no attempt to hide. Said they wanted to take a look at some of the fortifications."

"They are cool, those two."

Moretti rang off, phoned Hospital Lane, and arranged for Garth's wife to be taken to the airport and put on a plane to the mainland.

Then he gave some thought to Sandy and her hostility after the phone call. She was the one who had come bearing gifts, not the least of which was herself. Surely she knew he was a policeman, she knew he was on a case, so why the animosity? Could it be it had more to do with Liz Falla than his abrupt departure? And why would that be? After all, they were not "an item."

Later, Moretti would wonder if he had deliberately blinded himself by thinking only about female rivalry, and not about other, more disturbing possibilities. At the time his only concern was that his night with Sandy might turn into a one-night stand, and that he would not be treated to a repeat performance. A kaleidoscopic vision of a diamond-centred tattoo flowering beneath magnificent breasts whirled dizzily through his tired mind.

"Why did you leave her overnight?"

Mrs. Evans, who had been sobbing uncontrollably, became indignant. She looked up at Moretti from the kitchen chair on which she sat, and fairly spat her answer back up at him. "I've got a home of my own, and a family of my own, and my son was sick of going over to let the dog out and walk him. He really only obeys me, and can be very uppity with other people — the dog, I mean, not my son. Though goodness knows he's been difficult enough — my son, I mean —"

Moretti cut her off in mid-flow. "Of course, Mrs. Evans, perfectly understandable. Now I want you to tell me exactly what happened, from the moment you walked in."

Mrs. Evans pulled herself together with a rolling forward and backward movement of her plump shoulders, took a sip of water from the glass on the kitchen table, a deep breath, and began. "Well, I walked Rambo and got here about eightish. Lady Fellowes is not an early riser, and I know better than to disturb her, so I got her breakfast together — well, black coffee and some toast, eats like a bird — then I heard it."

Mrs. Evans gulped, and looked over at the police-woman standing by the kitchen door.

"I could do with a nice cup of tea. Steady my nerves. Tea bags are in the canister by the cooker. Milk and two sugars, love."

Moretti nodded at the officer, who crossed to the stove and put the kettle on.

"Heard it, Mrs. Evans? Was someone in the house?"

Mrs. Evans shook her head vigorously. "No, they weren't, but I didn't know that, not right then. Oh, I thought, she's got visitors, bless her. She hardly ever has people come to see her, and never at that hour in the morning. Usually I'd take the tray upstairs to the bedroom, but this time I picked up the breakfast tray and went through to the sitting room. And oh my Lord, there she was, and you'll find the tray too, where I dropped it."

Just as the kettle started to whistle, Mrs. Evans began moaning, and the two sounds crescendoed together in an unearthly harmony.

"Heard what, Mrs. Evans?"

The policewoman handed the cup of tea to the housekeeper, who took a noisy sip and looked up at Moretti. "The music, Inspector. That's what I heard. The music."

SOC were already there, shrouded in their ghostly working whites, figures of death in the midst of Coralie Fellowes's rose-lit mausoleum. Jimmy Le Poidevin was leaning over Coralie's body, which lay on the chaise. The voluminous fringed shawl that Moretti remembered from his earlier visit was folded around her, exposing her tiny feet in stiletto-heeled shoes. As he came into the room, slipping the shoe covers by the door over his own shoes, the head of SOCO looked up.

"Christ, you look terrible. Worse than the deceased. Thank God you've finally got here. We can switch the frigging music off."

Moretti stepped over the shards of china and slices of toast from Mrs. Evans's breakfast tray. The spilled black coffee had created a new pattern on the carpet, ebony on rose. He pulled a pair of gloves out of their plastic package, put them on, and went over to the tape player on the ormolu-topped table near the window. How many times had the music of Coralie's heyday played and replayed through the last night of her life? He turned the player off and removed the tape. It must have been made for her, because it had no commercial label. When he came in, it was playing something easily recognizable: Charles Trenet's "La Mer."

"I'll need to listen to this at some point."

"Not right now. We could all do without an encore, thanks very much."

Moretti joined Jimmy Le Poidevin by Coralie's body.

"Looks peaceful, doesn't she?" Jimmy straightened up and groaned, holding his back.

She did. Coralie Chancho looked as if she had lain down for a moment for a nice rest, and had gone to sleep. There was little skin discolouration, and her kohl-rimmed eyes stared back at Moretti with what looked like a touch of amusement. Even in death, her maquillage was perfect, as it had been when he and Falla first interviewed her. So that had no particular significance, because she had not been expecting them, and Mrs. Evans said she had few visitors. The makeup was for her, Coralie Chancho, and her alone.

"Looks like a natural death, but I gather it's not."

"Nope. She was smothered, probably by that." Jimmy Le Poidevin indicated an overstuffed silk cushion on the carpet near Coralie's deathbed. "It's red, but you can see the lipstick smear on it."

"You'll check that, of course."

"Of course. They sent someone from the hospital when the housekeeper phoned emergency, a new young hotshot who just arrived on staff."

"He's gone? Wish he could have hung around a bit longer."

Moretti spoke with mild irritation, and Jimmy Le Poidevin snapped back. "Wish you could have got here sooner. But your DS couldn't get hold of you, and the hospital's understaffed at the moment. Dr. Watt has taken sick leave, apparently. The young hotshot hinted at a nervous breakdown, which seems unlikely in Nichol's case. That giant ego of his usually makes him bulletproof."

Moretti did not respond to Jimmy's barb. He was right, of course. So, even Nichol had his breaking point, and such a collapse at this precise moment put him squarely back into the frame.

"Does the hotshot have a name, and will he be doing the autopsy?"

"Yes. Dr. Burton, and you'll know more then. But he did say there's something odd about this. She's a frail old bird, and would have died quickly, but he'd still expect to see more signs of resistance, if not a struggle, and I agree. Natural human reaction to fight back when someone is trying to smother you."

"No signs of a struggle?"

"Nothing. *Nada.*"

"Time of death?"

"Burton thought after midnight, more like the small hours of the morning, rather than earlier."

"Any signs of a break-in?"

"None that we saw, but you'll double-check that, no doubt."

"Was the shawl draped over her like that when you first saw her?"

"Yup. Like she'd been laid out by the murderer. The doc moved it a bit to examine her, then replaced it."

Moretti looked around the room. It seemed exactly as he remembered it, with its plethora of photographs in their gilded frames.

"Wait a minute."

On a low table by the window, the only photo on it was knocked over, lying on its face. Moretti straightened it up. It was one of the nude portraits, Coralie smiling with a huge feathered fan in her hands, strategically placed over her hips.

"There's one missing."

"How can you possibly tell? The place is littered with them, like mice droppings."

"Because I have been in this room before. Definitely one missing."

"A souvenir, a trophy. Quite common, isn't it?"

"Guv." Liz Falla had come quietly into the room and joined him by the table. She looked across at Coralie Fellowes' body. "Poor woman." There was a quaver in her voice. "Not even golden lasses are spared, are they, Guv?"

His partner's emotional reaction took Moretti by surprise, then he remembered Falla singing with the former Folies star. "La Vie en Rose." Almost certain to be on the tape someone had compiled for her.

"Falla, I'm sure there's a photo missing from this table. Of her, of course, but can you remember anything more?"

His DS looked at him, surprised. It was not often he had to rely on her memory. Probably the head injury. He looked terrible.

"Yes. Nude. No fan in this case, and it was signed, with some sort of message. I remember that, but I didn't get close enough to see what it said. It had faded, after such a long time."

"Can I get on now?" Jimmy's familiar plaintive cry filled the room.

They left him and his cohorts and returned to the kitchen, where Mrs. Evans still sat, nursing her third cup of tea.

"Oh, I know you," she said to Liz Falla. She dabbed her eyes and mouth with a tissue, then added, "Well, I know your mum. She says you've got the power, but you don't want to know about it. Be useful in her job, I said, save a lot of time, second sight would, I said —"

Liz Falla broke into the housekeeper's flight of fancy, her earlier emotions on seeing Coralie Fellowes nearly getting the better of her. "Solid police work and investigative techniques are what I was trained to use, Mrs. Evans, not ignorant superstition."

"Well, I never." Mrs. Evans returned her empty cup noisily to its saucer.

Smothering a wild desire to laugh, which he could only put down to lack of sleep, Moretti pulled out the chair opposite Coralie's housekeeper and sat down.

"Mrs. Evans, can you answer a few more questions for me?"

"For you, yes." A pointed glance at Moretti's DS.

"Was the cushion on the floor when you found Mrs. Fellowes, or did you remove it from — anywhere else?"

Mrs. Evans shuddered. "It was on the floor beside her. I thought she was asleep at first, and I went over all cheery to wake her up. Then I saw her staring up at me, and I dropped the tray."

"To your knowledge, did Mrs. Fellowes have a will?"

"Oh, yes." Mrs. Evans perked up and beamed at Moretti. "I was one of the witnesses. Me and the gardener, Ted Priaulx. He's always done the gardening and odd jobs for her and Colonel Fellowes. She hadn't made a will since her husband died, she said, and she suddenly decided to make one. She's left both me and him — Ted, that is — a nice little something for our trouble." Mrs. Evans suddenly became flustered. "But that doesn't mean I'd harm a hair on her head, Inspector. I'll never be able to get another job like this one."

Moretti leaned across the table and touched the housekeeper's hand, still clutched around the tissue. The gesture brought on a fresh bout of sobbing. "Of course, and I believe you, Mrs. Evans. So there were a number of bequests. Was there also a principal beneficiary?"

"Yes, there was." Mrs. Evans expression softened, and she started to smile. "He was so good to her, he was, really her only visitor. Made her laugh, talking about the old days. A real gentleman, not like some."

"And his name?"

Mrs. Evans's smile was warm and tender. "A real gentleman," she repeated fondly. "Bit of a ladies' man, I suppose you might say. Professor Ross — do you know him? Ludo, she called him. Darling Ludo, she used to say to me, my oldest, bestest friend."

Any wild desire to laugh instantly abandoned Moretti. He turned to see Liz Falla had moved, and was now standing next to him.

"I need to speak to you, Guv. Urgently," she said.

Moretti stood up, feeling his calf muscles shake at the effort. No point in thinking about sleep. Sleep would not be knitting up his ravelled sleeve for quite a while, the way things were going.

"When did this happen? After the Masterson murder?"

They were on their way to Ross's, having arranged for Mrs. Evans to be taken to the station to make a written statement, after which she had been assured she would be given a lift back to her home and to Rambo duty. Moretti had also set up a search of the property, looking for signs of a break-in, but both he and Liz knew how easily she let complete strangers into her home. Perhaps loneliness had made her open the door to her own death.

"Yes." Beside him in the Triumph, Liz Falla groaned. "It was when I went to see him, to ask him why he hadn't said anything to you about that business with Mr. Machin. I got nowhere — of course. That man knows how to keep a secret, said it had nothing to do with anything, was a personal matter. But, see, I just don't buy Ludo as some lonely hearts confidant. I was just gobsmacked when he went for me like he did. Losing control is not Ludo's thing, is it?"

"No." It was a characteristic he and Ludo had in common, but it was amazing what women and sex could do with that one. "I have to ask you this, Falla. Might it not be because you —?"

"Gave him the push? Could have been, but what he did really put any chance of *that* out of the window, didn't it, and he's one smart cookie, is Ludo."

"True. So he got very angry when you made certain comments about Coralie Fellowes."

"Yes. Got personal. Trashed me and, what's worse, trashed my music."

"Your music?" Moretti turned to look at Liz Falla. She was looking out of the car window and he couldn't see her face. "That's serious stuff, and I know it's not true. You bowled him over, Falla, so we've caught him out in one lie, at least."

"Thanks." His DS turned back and smiled at him. Moretti returned the smile, feeling suddenly a lot better about everything, although why he was not sure.

"Here we are. And he's not expecting us, so watch out for those hell-hounds of his."

As if on cue, the two ridgebacks appeared, followed by their master. He was smiling as Moretti wound down the window.

"I recognized the Triumph," he said. "To what do I owe this unexpected — double — pleasure?"

Chapter Fifteen

Ludo Ross sat hunched over on his elegant red chaise, weeping.

Not what he had expected, this collapse. Women and sex, yes. Oh, yes. But Coralie Fellowes? She had to be at least a decade older than Ludo.

Liz Falla made a move toward the chaise as if to comfort him, but Moretti restrained her. He did not want to give Ludo any chance to recover his equilibrium.

"You knew her well?"

"In the old days. The very old days, when the world was young. I was still a virgin, and had the unbelievable luck to have La Chancho as my first lover." Ludo Ross looked up and it was at Liz Falla he was looking. "Not like your generation, where sex is available à la carte from early puberty to all and sundry. I left my boarding school to do my degree, and was recruited straight into the secret service. I'd been heavily petted

and that was it, until Paris and Coralie. And no guilt!
Just sex. God, what a baptism. What an initiation."

Moretti interjected. "This was during the war?"

"Almost." Ross was pulling himself together.
Perhaps it was a grimace, but he seemed to be smiling now. "My service really started when mushroom
clouds were going up and iron curtains were coming
down. But France after the war was in chaos, and it
was difficult to tell at the time who were the bad guys
— apart from the Germans, of course — because many
had collaborated. Inevitable, when your country is
taken over for five years. It happened here in Guernsey.
People just want to survive. And they fall in love."

"What was Coralie Fellowes's role in that chaos?"
Moretti went over and sat down beside Ludo Ross.
There was no advantage to be had now in distancing
himself. "It could be important. People have long memories, and some are passed on to the next generation."

"Which is why I was detailed to get her out of
France. Coralie was one of our agents, but to most
of her countrymen she was a traitor who slept with
the enemy. Which she did. Coralie's pillow talk with
top German officers gave us invaluable information
throughout the war, but once it was over she was in
danger from her own."

"You mean to say —?" Liz Falla got up from the
chair opposite the two men and walked toward the
window that overlooked the courtyard. Below her,
crouched on the flagstones, Benz and Mercedes looked
back up at her. She could see they were growling, lips
drawn back, angry they had been separated from Ludo

when he had visitors. *Just as well,* she thought, *with him crying like that they'd tear us limb from limb.* "You mean to say that top brass went to all that trouble sparing an agent to smuggle a Folies Bergère *showgirl* out of Paris? She was no use to them anymore, was she? So why would they do that?"

Ludo Ross sprang up from the chaise with such force he knocked Moretti sideways. He strode over to the window and swung Liz Falla around to face him. In his face she saw the fury that had been there before, when she spoke disparagingly about Coralie Fellowes.

Here we go, she thought. What she wanted, to see this "ladies' man," to use Mrs. Evans's phrase, losing it. Losing control.

"Why? Because her British contact had been Ronnie Fellowes, and he would have given his life to get her out. But, as *you* said, once her usefulness was over no one would lift a finger. Coralie was in jail in Paris, and the charges against her were serious. Ronnie was terrified she would be shot."

Moretti interjected. "Why didn't Ronald Fellowes handle this himself? He would have had more clout, surely, than you."

Ludo looked at Moretti and smiled. "It didn't take clout, Ed. It took arm-twisting, bribery, and, above all, it took the kind of ruthlessness you have when you are still a teenager and think you can do the impossible. I was twenty years younger than Ronnie, and I broke every rule in the book. Ronnie knew I had done very well in my — training."

"You killed to get her out."

"I killed to get her out."

"And then you got lucky."

Liz Falla's jibe got the response she had expected. Ludo Ross put up his hand as if to hit her face, and Moretti pulled Falla back. The antagonism between them was as palpable as the lightning strike from a Taser. *If looks could kill they'd both be lying on the Kirman,* thought Moretti. As Falla turned away from Ross to look at him, she raised her eyebrows, almost quizzically, and he saw she meant this to happen.

Moretti raised his voice. "DS Falla, keep this professional, or I'll drop you from the case. The pair of you are behaving like squabbling six-year-olds." Moretti released Falla, pushed her in the direction of the chair behind him, and turned his attention back to Ludo Ross. "Sit down, Ludo, answer my questions, or I'll take you down to the station and we'll do it there. So you got Coralie Fellowes out. You kept in touch?"

"No." Ross had regained his usual self-possession, tears and anger gone as if they had never happened. He picked up his pipe and pouch from the table beside the chaise, and the room filled with the delicious aroma of honey and Turkish latakia. Ambrosia. Liz saw Moretti's hand go into his pocket and touch the lighter he always carried. She smiled. So far his talisman was working well for him.

Ross lit his pipe and continued, his tone measured. "I got out of the service, got on with my other career, and then, years later, saw Ronnie's obituary in the *Times*. There was a bit about Coralie in it and, God, the past came flooding back. It also mentioned they lived in Guernsey, and it came at a time when I was thinking of retirement. So, here I am and, because I imagine you are going to ask, it was never again a physical relationship. We could talk about things we could never share with anyone else. Coralie married Ronnie for his money, and then found she loved him."

Old mortality, the ruins of forgotten times. Moretti watched the smoke from Ross's pipe float by him on the air, like smoke from a funeral pyre.

"We now know that Masterson cheated Ronald Fellowes, and Lady Fellowes is the only person of interest picked up on the CCTV cameras the night of Masterson's murder. But the gun retrieved from the harbour, the gun she threw into the water, did not kill him. She was there, Ludo, we know that. And now she is dead, you no longer have to protect her. Was that one of the things you could share, what happened that night?"

Ludo sat with his head tilted back. Moretti could not see his expression, but he doubted there was much to see, not now.

"No," he replied. "It was not." He leaned forward, his tone confidential. "But I'll tell you this, if she'd got there first, he would be dead, so my feeling is he was dead already, and she got out of there."

Liz Falla looked up from her notebook. "Then why throw the gun away? There was no need to do that, was there?"

"Disposing of anything incriminating had been drummed into her during those war years. Habit, I imagine."

"But she slipped up," said Moretti. "She left lip-stick on a champagne glass."

"Might not have been Coralie. Masterson liked his babes." Ludo Ross looked over at Liz and smiled, no antagonism now in his expression. "Don't we all."

Falla smiled back at him, sweetly, then turned to Moretti. "I forgot to tell you, Guv, but the analysis came back. The lipstick is a discontinued brand. Helena Rubenstein. With that blast from the past we really don't need a DNA match, do we?"

Ludo Ross sighed deeply, and put down his pipe. "Oh, my dear Coralie," he said. "Almost certainly shocking pink. Her favourite colour. She loved to shock. Nothing more to be said, is there? She must have been there, and that's why she died."

"That's why she was murdered, yes. And you, Ludo, are the main beneficiary in her will."

Moretti expected anger, but Ross started to laugh. "Look around you, Ed," he said. "You've spent enough time with me to know I don't need to murder a frail old lady, who was my friend, for her money. And now —" he picked up the tobacco pouch again, fiddling with the clasp, his eyes hidden "— I think we should talk about Garth Machin, don't you? Before someone else is killed."

The three photographs lay on the table between them. Moretti watched Garth's face.

"Leo Van der Velde, Patrice Adaheli, Norman Beaufort-Jones. Double V, Sol, and Game-Boy. The trio who were going to make your fortune, and theirs. More importantly, theirs. I doubt you would have survived to play your trumpet for very long."

Garth Machin swore, tried to bite another chunk off his non-existent thumbnail. "Fucking Ludo," he said. His office was cool, but he was perspiring, and the smell of his sweat reached across the desk to Liz Falla.

He stank of fear. He was in over his head and he knew it. Liz thought back to the interview with Ludo, and his apparent breakdown.

She didn't buy it. It was all calculated, a performance. The only genuine emotion came when she'd ridiculed La Chancho and he lost it. On their way to interview Machin she and Moretti had discussed Nichol Watt's collapse, which seemed to put him back in the frame for the murders. Which she was all for, and she was only too happy to send Brouard to remove the doctor's passport. But there was more, much more, to be said about Ludo.

"Fucking Ludo, indeed," replied Moretti. "If he hadn't behaved like a priest in the confessional, we might have these three under lock and key by now. Or, certainly, their accomplices. The silence that was supposed to keep you and your wife safe has put you both in danger."

Anguished, Garth Machin looked at Moretti. "Where is Melissa? I can't reach her."

"No, you can't. She is safe."

Liz looked up from her notebook. "Doctor Watt's ex-wife told me about the MRI machines. You told DI Moretti that your disagreement in the club was about his behaviour toward Mrs. Machin and, given Dr. Watt's reputation, that made sense. But was it about Masterson?"

"Yes. Nichol can knock it back, drinks like a fish. In a drunken moment he told me about Masterson and how he was duped. Swore he'd get him. Maybe he did. That's what I wanted to talk to him about."

"So the idea for how to make big money —"

"— really big money, fuck-off money, get out of this jail money —"

"— came to you after you heard about Masterson?"

Garth Machin looked surprised. "No. They approached me, those three in your holiday snaps. Perfectly legit, it seemed, through our website. They wanted to discuss financing the development of oil in a small African country. They needed a lot of cash, and they offered me a humungous payback. That's when they had me, of course, because much of the money would line my pockets and not those of Northland. I met them first in London, not here."

"Besides being paid through the back door, when did you first realize everything in the oil patch was not hunky-dory?"

"After the first payment, when they had proof of my involvement. When I discovered the oil development would involve the overthrow of the legitimate government of Maoundi. Assassination. They were going to run a puppet president, a buddy of Adaheli, now living in exile in Paris, pocket the profits. And, you know, at first, they had me persuaded it was no big deal, that one African president is much like another.

Greed made me as unprincipled, as racist, as those bastards." Garth jabbed a finger on the face of Double V.

"When did greed change into cold feet?"

"When they came close to home, and arrived in St. Peter Port. When they told me they wanted me to carry a lot of cash for them that was arriving with Masterson. When they told me Masterson had fucked up, and was going to be eliminated. Their word. Eliminated."

"Why Guernsey? Because you were here?" Liz looked up from her pad and flexed her right wrist.

"Only in part. It was Masterson's idea. He has island roots and had, apparently, run a successful operation of some sort from here before. 'At the back of beyond,' he said to them. 'No one will recognize you there.'"

"What were you to do with the cash?" Moretti asked.

"Deposit it in our bank, all above board, because I would be doing it, and I am above suspicion." Garth gave a hollow laugh. "God, I could do with a drink," he said, taking out a handkerchief and mopping his brow and upper lip.

"Then the money would buy arms? Helicopters? Mercenaries?"

Garth shook his head. "Not directly. Even Beaufort-Jones was nervous about that, and he has major protection. MI6 and the FBI have got good at following the money trail."

Moretti and Falla looked at each other. Liz was thinking about Masterson's research into *hawala*; Moretti was remembering Jan Melville's observations about post office boxes.

"Diamonds," he said. "Because you are above suspicion, you were to buy diamonds for them."

Both Falla and Machin looked at him, surprised.

Garth gave another of his vacant laughs. "Got it in one, piano player. Me, a stupid, jazz-playing banker in that world of sharks. I'd have lasted five minutes, and I knew it. More to the point, so did they. I wasn't made for international skulduggery, Ed. They would have got what they wanted out of me, and then I would have been — eliminated. Just like Masterson."

Moretti stood up, suppressing a groan. He really must take up Don Taylor's invitation to join him on his runs across the island before he fell apart physically. But that would have to be put off, again.

"Set up a meeting," he said. "Say whatever it takes to get them over here. Can you do that? Tell them it's urgent. Tell them agents of theirs are about to be picked up by the police, and are to be flown out for questioning by MI6."

Garth Machin leaned back in his chair. There was a damp patch on the leather seat back. "Easy. Van der Velde and Beaufort-Jones contacted me last night on my private email here. Adaheli is in Harare. Since you lot found the stash on the yacht, they are on their way with more. All they need is a safe place, because they know my house is under surveillance since that bodyguard had to be — yes, that word again — eliminated. They'll be coming in by private plane."

Moretti thought fast. A little more time would be nice, but he didn't have that luxury. "There really is only one place, and they may need convincing. You'll have to play the dumb-copper-in-the-back-of-beyond card and hope they buy it. Tell them we have a small police force of limited skills. Tell them that the yacht is unguarded since we took Masterson's housekeeper into custody, and that the harbour is not well policed at night. They may be able to use their meeting place as their getaway vehicle. Ulbricht said it could almost run itself."

"But how do I explain how I got on the yacht?"

"Difficult," said Moretti, "but this might work. Tell them you will take the dinghy from that beloved wooden boat of yours over to the yacht. Tell them you noticed that the divers looking for the gun had left a ladder down that side of the yacht, and you'll break the glass door to the main salon and get in that way."

"I've done that," said Garth eagerly. "Had to break in through our patio door once —"

Moretti interrupted him. "Don't embroider, Garth. Say as little as possible. As you said, you're a stupid jazz-playing banker in a world of sharks, and they might pick something up." He was scribbling on a piece of paper as he talked. "Here is my mobile number. When the meeting is set up, give me the details, and dispose of this."

Garth took it. "You're tethering me like a sacrificial goat, aren't you?"

Moretti stood up. "Yes. Climbing up rope ladders in the dark is not my idea of a good time, and I, fool that I am, will be tethered with you."

He turned to Liz Falla. "*Just Desserts*. Perhaps it will finally have a chance to live up to its name."

***

It had started to rain hard while they were at the Northlands offices. In the confined space of the Triumph, Moretti heard Liz Falla humming under her breath.

"'Plaisir D'Amour.' You're thinking of Ross and La Chancho."

"No. I'm thinking of Melissa Machin." But she did not elaborate. After a moment, she said, "Did you buy Ludo Ross's act?"

"Not entirely. The grief over Coralie Fellowes was genuine enough, but he used it as a shield against revealing himself further."

"Do you think he could have used what Garth told him to get involved? Not for the money so much as the thrill, the kicks?"

"Once a player, always a player, you mean. I hope you're wrong, Falla, but I was reminded of something today I should have realized before. Ludo Ross is charming, personable, brilliant, became an academic but, before that, was just as much a killer as Ulbricht or Baumgarten. What I don't know is whether he still is."

They made the rest of the drive in silence. As the car passed through the old gateway, Moretti said to Liz Falla, "We don't have much time before this all gets underway, because they are going to have to improvise, and the fact that Adaheli is in Harare suggests they were hoping to move soon, or they wouldn't risk showing their hand too far in advance."

"What's our next move, Guv?" Liz got out of the Triumph and stood on the doorstep. Moretti appeared to be taking a look around the courtyard.

"I'm going to leave a message for Hanley, the harbour authorities, and — some other people. Then I'm going to crash. We could be short of sleep over the next little while. I'll get someone to pick you up. Come in."

Inside, Moretti saw Falla's glance take in the two wineglasses. Her eyebrows shot up in that look of surprise that made them disappear under her bangs. A drop of rain shivered like an exclamation mark on the slick of dark hair that curved around her left ear. He removed the glasses from table and took them into the kitchen.

"You know where the phone is," he called out.

"It's okay, Guv," was her reply. "I'll use my mobile." There was a slight pause and then she appeared in the kitchen doorway. She was holding the lasagna in its foil package.

"Has this been out all night, unrefrigerated?" she enquired. "In that case, you shouldn't risk eating it. You'll have to throw it away." She was smiling.

Moretti took the lasagna from her, depressed the foot pedal of the bin with unnecessary force, and threw it away.

Chapter Sixteen

Day Nine

The sound of the water lapping against the *Just Desserts* was soothing, even under these circumstances. Moretti could hear in it the rhythm of Dwight's drums, the wizardry of Gene Krupa, the brilliance of Benny Goodman's clarinet. Slap, slap, slap. Sing, sing, sing.

"I feel sick. Why did we have to come so early?"

Garth sat on a sofa opposite Moretti, drinking Masterson's excellent Scotch. In the dim light from a table lamp Moretti could see the tremor in Machin's hands, the tic in one eyelid. The only change he was aware of in his own body was the acceleration of his heartbeat, disconcertingly out of sync with the sound of the water.

"You're lucky I didn't make you swim. Of course we came early, soon as it was dark. We still don't know where the two sham Germans are. Hopefully not around, but something tells me they will be around somewhere. Let's go over this again. What did they tell you, and who did you speak to?"

"Game-Boy. He thinks we speak the same language, glad to have me on board because I talk posh. He actually said that, laughed. He sounds a bit of a wacko to me. They agreed without much persuading about the yacht, and I think they've had to cut corners because of Masterson, so they're pushing it. 'Not how we usually operate,' is what Game-Boy said. I am to leave all doors unlocked, and to expect them when I see them. I said I'd come by water and wait in the main salon, as you suggested. They are bringing the cash, instructions as to how to buy the diamonds, and where they are to be deposited." Garth looked at Moretti. "I have it all on tape — isn't that enough?"

"No, it isn't. We must have the transaction take place, and then we can move in."

"We?" Garth's voice shook. "Don't mean to be insulting, Ed, but by 'we' do you mean the likes of PC Brouard, and that pretty sidekick of yours? You've told me nothing."

"No, because I don't trust you." Moretti cut off Garth's wail of protest. "Why do you think I'm here risking my own neck? Sergeant Falla — I presume that's who you mean by my sidekick — is coordinating everything, back at Hospital Lane. I will be contacting her soon. And you are right, this is far too tricky to handle by myself, so I have involved some experts in this sort of thing. Less you know about them the better. In the next few minutes, I'll be leaving you here to meet your pals, and hiding on the yacht. And you needn't have bothered to tape your conversation, because your office, your phone, everything, is now bugged."

As Moretti stood up to leave, his mobile rang.

His first reaction was annoyance, because he had arranged with Liz Falla that he would contact her. She was in direct touch with those running the operation, and they had not been happy about his "pretty side-kick" being the point person. He had assured them she would follow instructions to the letter, and here she was, breaking the rules.

"Falla. What —?"

"Had to do this, Guv. There's a fly in the oint-ment." He could hear the anxiety in her voice.

"A fly in the ointment? What fly?"

"Who, Guv, who. I know where the South Africans are, and I know who sent them there. Trouble is, we don't know if your visitors know, but they probably do."

"Who sent them where?" The gentle motion of the yacht strengthened into something more intense, as if the wind had come up, or a vessel was approaching. "Quick, Falla. We may be about to have visitors."

"The fly —" Falla's voice quavered "— is Denny. Denny Bras-de-Fer."

Denny Bras-de-Fer loved a big story, and was quite willing to invent one, if necessary. It had got him into trouble in the past. This time there was no need for creativity, just ingenuity and cunning, and those were qualities he had in spades. Already there were stringers and freelancers sniffing around the yacht murder, but the fact that Masterson was a Canadian, operating outside the British Isles, had slowed down the interest of the fourth estate. Denny could smell big money — by his standards — if he could beat everyone to the punch.

Masterson's connection to Beaufort-Jones was only known to a handful of insiders, and Denny Bras-de-Fer was jumping in the deep end of a very murky pool without a lifebelt. But intelligent analysis had never been Denny's strong point. He acted on instinct, charm, and self-interest, with self-preservation as a top priority.

Besides, he did not like being rejected by women, and when Liz Falla told him to get lost, he became even more interested in the *Just Desserts* murder as a matter of principle. The satisfying furor caused by his article in the *Guernsey Press* had spurred him on to continue his investigations and, since he had no police contacts — quite the opposite, in fact — all he could do was keep an eye on the yacht.

After hours spent on a bench overlooking the *Just Desserts*, to the detriment of his beauty sleep and his social life, he was finally rewarded. He watched the arrival of a glamorous older woman and two young men, delivered by police car, and his first thought was to target the woman. His speciality, after all. But she disappeared out of sight into the bowels of the vessel, and never reappeared. Just as he was considering walking up the gangplank and presenting himself as a reporter for the *Guernsey Press,* the two men emerged. They were talking together, relaxed and cheerful, carrying what looked like shopping bags. They exchanged a joke of some kind with the solitary policeman on the pier, who appeared to be pointing them in the direction of the shops. Denny decided to follow them, which would require wheeling his Vespa along with him.

Denny loved his Vespa, a powder blue LX 50 4V. He had chosen powder blue, because it went down well with the birds — only blokes with machismo were unafraid of such a feminine shade. In his mind it created the image of a debonair, continental member of the paparazzi, the sort of sophisticate who always said "Ciao," like he did, and never "Cheerio," or "Goodbye." To be sure, this model was not very powerful, but who needed that on an island this size, and it was the iconic image that mattered. He had no intention of leaving it unattended, and he soon saw that having wheels was a stroke of luck.

The two men continued along the Esplanade and, to his surprise, did not turn up any of the streets that would lead them to the shops. When they reached the foot of St. Julian's Avenue, they hailed a cab and got in. After a moment's delay, presumably as they gave the driver directions, the taxi set off up the avenue. Quick as a flash, Denny was on his Vespa following them.

Denny Bras-de-Fer was in his glory. Here he was, acting out in real life his childhood dreams and grown-up fantasies, in pursuit of his quarry. Who the quarry was, he did not know, but it was clear they had misled the copper on the pier, so possibly he was tailing the bad guys. What a coup for him if he tailed them to their hideout! Certainly they had come on the yacht, but this was no scenic excursion. Maybe they had accomplices. At some point he would phone the cops, but he wanted to see this through to the end.

The taxi turned off Les Gravées and headed south, twisting and turning along the narrow lanes, through St. Andrew and into the parish of St. Martin. The bends in the road made it tricky for Denny not to lose sight of them, so he risked following more closely, and he had to come to an abrupt halt when he saw the taxi had stopped outside the sort of gussied-up cottage only the well-heeled could own. Getting off the Vespa, he tucked it under the hedge and waited for the taxi driver to deliver his fares. A few moments later the two men emerged, and started walking up the driveway to the front door of the cottage. He could now hear them talking, casually, relaxed, in what sounded like German.

Denny waited for the taxi to leave. Then, stealthily creeping along against the hedgerow, he turned into the driveway. He was going to have to risk exposure, because there was no hedge up to the house, so he waited until they had rung the bell, and the door of the cottage opened. He heard voices, a yell, then the sound of the door closing, and silence.

The yell was worrisome, but Denny hesitated only for a moment, then started to creep up the exposed driveway, scurrying from bush to bush. When he reached the cottage he was panting, sweating, his heart beating like a bass drum in his chest. Crouching beneath the windows, he crept along the wall until heard voices. They were coming from a corner room to the right of the front door, and the windows on the side of the house had bushes close to the wall, which afforded him some cover. He scuttled around the corner, squatted beneath the window, and listened.

It was not hard to hear what was going on, although the man doing most of the talking kept his voice low. But the man he was questioning was doing the exact opposite, he was screaming, and Denny could hear every word he was saying. Over and over between the screams he was saying, "No, no, I know nothing — I killed nobody — no, I don't know who did — Christ, I'd tell you if I knew, I'm no hero — what woman? Her? — I didn't kill Masterson, and I didn't kill her — aaah!"

At this point, Denny decided he'd had enough. But, before sneaking back down the driveway and reaching the safety of his beloved Vespa, he risked a quick look through the window, raising his head a few inches above the sill.

The man screaming was a mess. His arms were tied to a chair with what looked like his trouser belt, but in spite of his bloodied face and broken nose Denny recognized him. He had seen him often enough with some dolly-bird or other in the jazz club. He was a doctor, or a surgeon or something. Nichol Watt, that was his name. Before Denny ducked down, the interrogator struck Nichol Watt again, so hard his head smacked back against the chair on which he was strapped.

But where was the other man?

He had barely formed the thought when he felt a cold, hard pressure against the back of his neck.

"Get up. Make a move and I pull the trigger."

The pressure against his neck increased. Denny had often said to his coterie when laughing about some jape or other, some trick he had pulled on some unsuspecting sucker, "I nearly peed my pants." It was not an expression he would use lightly again.

He was nudged in the direction of a door near the back of the cottage, and pushed through. Inside he found himself in the same room as Nichol Watt and his interrogator, who was lighting a cigarette as if nothing out of the ordinary was happening, which, for these two men, was probably the case.

"Here," said his escort to the other man, then something in what sounded like German, but wasn't.

The blond man smiled. "A word of advice, you who are about to die. Only amateurs tail professionals on shiny baby-blue bikes. Who are you?"

His escort shoved him from behind toward the other man, and Denny's knees gave way. He fell on the ground, and started to grovel. "Please, I'm just a reporter, I'm not with the police, I'm only trying to get a story. I'm good at keeping my mouth shut, if you just let me —"

He was silenced by a kick in the small of his back, the pain travelling the length of his spine.

"We don't have time for this." The tall, fair-haired man smiled through the cigarette smoke at him, and the dark-haired man kicked him again. This time his back went numb. "We need to know before we leave what the doctor knows about who else is — in on this. We cannot have that. Too much to lose. Come, reporter — what do you know?" The fair-haired man inhaled, hard, until the end of the cigarette glowed, and held it out.

It was with terror that Denny realized he had nothing he could tell them, because he knew nothing, and he was sure Nichol Watt would have spilled his guts if he knew anything. He couldn't even fabricate who killed who, because he had no idea what woman they were talking about. Coralie Fellowes? The papers had been told it could be natural causes, but it had to be La Chancho. Unless he could think of something, their ignorance would be their death warrant.

At that point, Denny's creativity and, above all, his instinct for self-preservation kicked in.

"I know who's behind it," he trilled, his voice an unrecognizable falsetto. "It's not him. It's another man, a guy who was in the secret service. He's been in on the case from the beginning. If anyone killed anyone, it's him, and not him." He pointed to Nichol Watt and was rewarded with a blow from a gun butt around the back of his head.

"Cut to the chase, reporter."

"He lives close by, and I can take you there, get you in the door, past his dogs. They're vicious, but there's no need to worry about him, he's an old man now. His name is Ludovic Ross."

Just before they left the room, the fair-haired man took the dark-haired man's gun and smashed it against Nichol Watt's head so hard that he and the chair fell sideways. He lay on the floor without moving. As the interrogator pointed the gun at Watt's body, the other man said, "No more bullets. We have no more bullets."

The interrogator nodded, bent down, and took Nichol Watt's car keys from his pocket.

Benz and Mercedes were restless. Ludo Ross could hear them moving around the house as he sat listening to Brubeck playing *The Last Time We Saw Paris* with his quartet. He remembered they had disbanded shortly after recording the album.

Shame that all good things have to come to an end. Outside, the island was bursting into bloom after its gale-swept winter, but Ross had the feeling of things ending, rather than beginning.

"The sere, the yellow leaf," he said out loud. "Coralie, Coralie."

I'd better stop drinking, he thought, *or I'll be crying again.* Perhaps the dogs sensed his mood. Perhaps that was all, but, like them, he was restless. It was like the old days, he felt as if he was being watched. Paranoia, a familiar bedfellow.

The thought of bedfellows brought Liz Falla to mind. Not that she had been in his bed, and he'd ruined any remote chance of that by his egregious insults. Some time, the next time he saw her, he would tell her what he felt about her voice. Magic.

There be none of Beauty's daughters with a magic like thee.

Such a pity that desire never left, never let you sink gently into that good night. Or so it had been for him. He reached out his hand for the bottle on the table and, as he did, he heard the two ridgebacks making their warning growls. They were trained not to bark full throttle immediately.

"Benz, Mercedes."

But they did not come to him. They ran past the sitting room and up to the next floor, and he followed them. They were not heading for his bedroom, but for the narrow, foot-long spy hole set in the windowless wall overlooking the lane behind the house, and the sealed door that had at one time led on to the second-floor balcony. Benz was standing on his hind legs, pawing at the wall.

Ross took his old Zeiss binoculars from the hook by the spy hole, where he always kept them, and looked out. Just visible on the lane below was a car, and someone was getting out of it, from the back seat. Which meant that whoever it was had been driven there. With the two dogs snarling beside him, he watched as the passenger started to walk, quite openly, around to the front of the house. He waited a moment, and saw who had driven his unknown visitor. Getting out of the car were the two crew members of the *Just Desserts*.

Ross ran to his bedroom, took a gun out of his bedside table drawer, and slipped it into his pocket. Then, taking the two dogs by their collars, led them back downstairs.

One of the ways Ludo Ross had passed the hours that hung heavy on his hands was training the two ridgebacks for the kind of situation he never, in his saner moments, thought would actually happen. The knowledge that they were what he had made them comforted him in his paranoia. He knew for certain the two crew members were trouble, and that a decoy was going to ring his doorbell at any moment. The advantage he had was that they would also have to come in through the front door, but the disadvantage was he needed the decoy alive, to find out what the hell was going on.

As he reached the hallway, the doorbell rang.

Ross let go of the dogs' collars, bent down, stroked them, and whispered, "Wait. Wait. Wait until I say the word."

The dogs crouched down beside him.

Pulling the gun out of his pocket, Ross exhaled deeply, threw the door open, and hauled his unknown visitor inside, throwing him to the floor as he wailed, "Don't shoot, don't shoot."

"Shut up."

He barely had the words out of his mouth when he saw the two crew members running up the driveway, one of them carrying a gun. As a bullet whistled past him he shouted at the two dogs, just one word: "Kill."

He watched as they did exactly what he had trained them to do, all those years. Unerringly, flawlessly, they went for the jugular, dropping the two men in their tracks. He heard them screaming as Benz and Mercedes finished their task.

At school Ludo Ross had always loved the short stories of Guy de Maupassant, and the one about the old Sardinian widow avenging the murder of her son was his particular favourite. He had never forgotten it, never thought he would have the opportunity to try out her chosen method against her son's killers. In what strange and unforeseen ways a good education can come in useful. He turned to the whimpering figure on the floor.

"Not a move, not a sound, until I call off my dogs. Then I have a phone call to make, and you and I are going to have a little talk."

Chapter Seventeen

One advantage Moretti had was that he knew the layout of the yacht and they didn't. Crouched down in the dining area, with its sliding glass door open into the main salon where Garth waited, he knew he had a chance of getting out. A tethered goat is what Garth had called himself, and that is what he was, with about as much chance of escaping. Not that he would be killed immediately. His co-conspirators still needed him, after all. But Peter Walker and Janice Melville had made it clear there were to be no heroics and, once SIS were involved, they were just as likely to finish him off, if he got in the way. Garth's fate meant nothing to them. It was Van der Velde and, above all, Beaufort-Jones they wanted.

But good horn players were hard to find.

All he could do now was wait. The most likely scenario was that they would arrive beyond the harbour limits and transfer to a smaller vessel, and SIS's plans were to pick up the waiting boat as well as Game-Boy and the South African. Chief Officer Hanley had briefed the harbour master, so there would be no unwanted interruptions from harbour security.

In the open dining area he heard them when they arrived, the small boat bumping against the side of the yacht, a muttered curse in an English accent, so probably Beaufort-Jones, the posh talker. They were obviously in very good shape, slithering up on one of the ropes over the side, landing lightly on the deck, close to the doors from the salon. So maybe they knew the yacht's layout, after all. No surprise they had come prepared. Moretti could not see them, but he heard an exclamation from Garth, quickly suppressed.

Moretti strained to hear what they were saying. Both men sounded dangerously edgy. Masterson's dabbling in many pies had exposed them, and this particular high-wire act was not part of their pre-ferred way of doing business. They seemed to want information as to where Garth was planning to buy diamonds, and Moretti knew he had been provided with some names.

Top of the list was a Toronto-based South African who had recently designated himself as head of a min-ing company by the simple process of removing the names of its directors on a government database and substituting his own. Chances were that Game-Boy and Double V already knew about him, and it would give Garth credibility. Assuming, that is, that the con-spirators did not yet know Interpol was on to him.

He heard Garth answer, at some length, and then say, "Thank you," like the well-mannered banker that he was. Presumably they had handed over the cash.

The yacht shifted suddenly, and there was silence from the salon. Moretti heard Beaufort-Jones say, "What was that?" He sounded jumpy. Garth's reply was unclear, but he gave a laugh so full of terror it seemed to infect his two visitors.

"What's wrong with you?" Van der Velde's voice.

Beaufort-Jones's voice: "We leave first. You wait thirty minutes before you leave."

Van der Velde spoke again. "How do we know you haven't set us up, Machin? Maybe we should take a look around."

To his horror, Moretti heard Garth start to stutter.

Christ almighty. Garth's improvisation under stress was a talent limited to his horn-playing. Van der Velde repeated his question, this time accompanied by what sounded like a fist in the face. Garth cried out.

Moretti was unarmed. His choice, but also that of the experts, who wanted to know how recently he had fired a weapon. His answer had confirmed their decision, but now he wished he had one. How long could he crouch there, doing nothing, while Garth got beaten up trying to protect him? As Garth moaned again in pain, Moretti started to get up.

As he did so a hand came out of the darkness across his mouth and, with it, the faintest whisp of a familiar aroma: apricot essence and honey, a touch of Turkish latakia.

A familiar voice muttered in his ear. "No."

Ludo. Ludo, wet and smooth against his body as a seal, reeking of harbour water.

"Wait."

He pushed Moretti away and down, and started to move toward the open glass doors, his body flat against the floor. A moment later, it was all over.

"I could do with some of that, Garth. Pass me the bottle."

Ludo tossed his gun on to the coffee table and started to strip off the wetsuit he was wearing. Garth, hand shaking, held out the bottle to him.

"For God's sake, Ludo," Moretti protested, "SIS must have heard the shots. They could be here any minute."

Moretti looked at the two bodies lying on the floor. Beaufort-Jones's face was turned toward him. He looked as if he were grinning. *Joke over, Game-Boy,* thought Moretti, *he had you both in seconds.* What a killer Ludo must have been. Still was.

"Not likely. They'll be waiting for these two SOBs to come to them. Yes, they'll have heard the shots, and they'll be thinking it was Garth dead, or you dead, or both of you. They'll wait a bit before they do anything they haven't planned, which is why I want you both to shut up and let me talk. Okay?"

Moretti shrugged his shoulders, the tension in them making them feel like lead weights. The bump on his head was hurting like hell. "Whatever you want. You're the guy with the gun, and you're the one on the firing line, so to speak. You had the gun under the wetsuit? Risky."

Ludo took a swig from the whisky bottle. "That's good stuff," he said, sounding as relaxed as if the three of them were in his sitting room. "Yes, but their wetsuits are superb quality, so I left mine here and took one of theirs on my earlier visit."

"You *were* here before. I wondered."

"I know you did. You got some of it right, and some of it wrong."

Ludo ran a hand through his wet, rumpled hair and over his face. Moretti could not see his own face, but if he looked anything like Garth he had aged a decade. Ludo, on the other hand, looked years younger, the dark shadows under his child-bright eyes erased.

"What did I get wrong?" he asked.

Ludo laughed. "Motivation. All this —" Ross swept his hand around the room, gesturing at the two bodies on the floor "— is not because this gang couldn't shoot straight, or because money is the root of all evil, or —" looking at Garth "— a horn player's greed. All that might well have worked out just fine in the end. These are all by-products of two big mistakes made by Masterson."

"Coming here would be one of them."

"Exactly. Nowhere in this world is the back of beyond any more."

"And his other mistake was to underestimate the power of memory." Moretti stretched across the table and took the bottle. Drinking good Scotch with Ludo was something they had both enjoyed. "I think I got that right, Ludo. You killed Masterson for Coralie. That looks like a Glock to me." He indicated the gun on the table between them.

"It is." Ludo appeared delighted. "Almost, but not quite, Ed. Right about the power of memory, but much too unsatisfying to do it myself. Too easy. It was like the old days, planning to kill him."

"How the hell did you find out he was coming here? I knew, because I was supposed to collect the money from him, for the diamonds." Garth's voice was slurred, but he seemed more under control, looking Ludo straight in the face as he spoke, no longer huddled into the corner of his chair.

If anyone looked in the window of the salon, it would look like three chums together, sharing a bottle of Scotch, and a few good stories. If you overlooked the bodies on the floor between them, that is.

"Chance. I was talking to the harbour master — he's a bird watcher, like me — and he happened to mention the *Just Desserts*, and Masterson. I knew who he was, because Coralie had told me about him. When I told her, she said, 'If this was still the war, I would kill him for killing Ronnie.' So I said, 'Why not?' I knew how I could get on board without being picked up by the CCTV cameras, but Coralie was the problem. Swimming in a wetsuit was impossible for her, of course."

"What was all that with the Baby Browning?"

"Her idea. Hiding in plain sight was something she did so well in the bad old days. We planned it to the second, the visit to the Landsend, the area on the dock where she could get on board the yacht outside the camera range. Those cameras focus on the pier, not the gangway."

"And, within the range of the cameras, she gave one of her finest performances," said Moretti. "A frail old woman, frightened out of her skin, throwing the wrong gun into the harbour."

"Didn't she though!" Ludo stood up suddenly, and startled his audience by picking up his gun and starting to pace about the salon. "She even planned her wardrobe carefully. 'My Poiret,' she said. 'There's no mistaking a Poiret.' She already had the Baby Browning, a gift from Ronnie before he died." Ludo laughed, and waved the gun with cheerful abandon. Garth shrunk back again into the corner of his chair.

"Did she just turn up at the yacht?"

"No. She had a note hand-delivered, with her phone number. Masterson called her back, tried to warn her off, then agreed to see her that night. I assume the meeting with these boyos —" indicating the two men on the ground "— was much later on, and she threatened to screw everything up. I imagine he hadn't planned to stick around after the meeting. He was already in their bad books from what he said to her before I came on the scene."

"Then you handed over the gun to her. I guessed that."

"You guessed right, Ed — and, guess again whose gun this is?"

Ludo did not give Moretti time to reply. He was pacing around the salon, reliving the moment when he and Coralie Fellowes had orchestrated the final act of

Masterson's life. "I arrived in here, much as I did just now. Masterson was spinning his Glock around as if he were Clint Eastwood. 'Silly old bitch,' I heard him saying. Such a pleasure to see his face when I caught the gun in mid-flip and handed it over to Coralie." Ludo chuckled. "Candy from a baby, Ed. Candy from a baby mothball."

"How did you get him to the bedroom, and why?"

Ludo laughed and sat down again, resting his hands on his knees, cradling the gun. "Simple. She backed him up into his bedroom, the old lecher, and shot him there. Always loved to add her own original twist, did Coralie, and bedrooms were her battleground, where she fought the enemy, in the old days. She asked me to say some last words over him, as he lay there begging for his life. So I did."

"What did you say, Ludo?" Garth reached out for the bottle again, and drank the last drop. He seemed genuinely interested, drunk enough now to be calm.

"*The grave's a fine and private place. But none, I think, do there embrace.*" Ludo laughed again. "Coralie loved it. 'Perfect,' she said. Then she shot him, clean as a whistle. I was amazed she could still hit the target from that distance."

"Then you came back in here and drank champagne," Moretti said. "Wasn't there the danger his visitors would turn up?""

"Yes." Ludo smiled. "It added to the moment, for both of us. Then I watched her leave to do her performance for you all, swam back to where I had left my car, drove it to our prearranged rendezvous, and took her home." He was reliving the moment, the adrenalin rush. "She was tired, but happy — God, it was such *fun*!"

"The lipstick stain was deliberate, I assume."

"Yes. She wore gloves, but the lipstick was a nice touch. 'Coralie was here, Ronnie,' she said when she pressed her lips against the glass. 'Coralie was here.'"

"What happened to her gloves and her bag?"

Ludo's smile was tender. "A gift for me, a memento. A souvenir."

A souvenir. A blank space on a small table, a photograph of a glorious, naked Coralie, a faded inscription.

"It *was* you." Moretti stood up. In the distance he could hear an approaching craft of some kind. "You took the photo off the table."

"Yes. She wanted me to take it, after I did what she asked me to do. It was one of Ronnie's favourites. She was very tired, very sleepy when she phoned me." Ludo was still smiling, stroking the gun as he answered.

"You loved her, Ludo. How could you?"

"How could I not, Ed? I could never refuse her anything."

Ludo also seemed to become aware of sounds outside. He put his hand into an inside pocket of the zippered jacket he was wearing under the wetsuit and pulled out an envelope. "This is for Liz. Give it to her, would you? Not much time left, but she knows what happened at my place and can fill you in, and that there's a young idiot there, locked in my very secure bathroom. There's a key in the envelope, and a safe combination. And something I want her to do."

Moretti took it, put it in his pocket. Garth began to sob, and Ludo went over and knelt down in front of him. Speaking gently, as if to a child, he said, "Not to worry, Garth. Being a decoy for MI6 can be used in your defence, a good lawyer will see to that. And I have saved them the problem of disposing of these two, without a public enquiry. But that still makes me a triple murderer."

"Ludo —" Moretti looked at the two bodies lying between them "— no need to say you killed Coralie Fellowes. We have two likely suspects who cannot answer."

"No." Ludo sounded angry. "I don't want that. Don't ask me to explain."

"You don't have to. It was her last wish, what she wanted from you. You could never refuse her anything, and it would be a betrayal. Here —" Moretti held out his hand "— give me the gun. You don't need that anymore. Best not to be holding that when SIS arrive."

Ludo hesitated, then handed the gun to Moretti. "I thought of ending it all myself, the final, grand gesture, but I am not as brave as Coralie. I think I'd rather face the music, Ed." He grinned. "Should be fun, and fun is in short supply in my life."

Moretti took the gun from him, checked it, removed the remaining bullet. "I know who the idiot in your bathroom is, but how do we get past your hounds? What are the secret commands you use with them? We'll need to know."

"No secret commands, Ed. Like me, they were trained to kill when asked, and that's all I needed to say to them. Kill. You won't need to worry. I've seen to that. They would never have obeyed anyone else."

Even in the soft lamplight of the salon, Ludo now looked like a very old man, his face worn and creased with pain.

"One of the hardest things I have ever done in my life," he said.

Then he walked out of the salon, hands in the air, and faced the music.

Chapter Eighteen

The aftermath seemed to take forever. In actual fact, it took about a week. Intelligence services do not like hanging around in public places while onlookers stare, comment, and, worse still, take photographs. The bodies — all the bodies — the yacht, Adèle Letourneau, and Ludo Ross were swiftly removed from the scenes of their crimes. No one was happier about that than Chief Officer Hanley.

But for Moretti, there was one loose end he was anxious to clear up, a loose end that was of no importance to either MI5 or MI6, but that was nagging him.

Offshore Haven Cred.

The dead could not speak, and Ludo insisted he had not pulled the brochure from the magazine rack.

"Not even to provide us with a red herring?"

"Never entered my mind, Ed. My word of honour," he said, which had made them both laugh.

Which left only Adèle Letourneau.

"Yes," she said, "I removed it."

Sitting in his office, just before she was to leave the island, she looked her age. More than that. She looked empty, almost vacuous, a sense of loss clinging to her. Finally, the jig was up.

"Why?" Moretti asked.

"Because it was yet another of Bernard's grand schemes that had put us at risk. You'll put us in an early grave, I told him, more than once. Ulbricht and Baumgarten were our babysitters, keeping an eye on us for those three bastards and, as far as I knew, they didn't know about Offshore Haven and I wanted to keep it that way. But he'd talked about it to that cretin, Martin Smith. Just before I left the yacht that night, I pulled the brochure out of the magazine rack and destroyed it. I thought then he had a chance of making it through, because they needed him, and it would take time to — replace him." Adèle Letourneau laughed, her face contorting with what looked like grief. "What I didn't know was that he had set up a meeting with a madwoman. And a madman."

"But he didn't know about the madman, did he?"

"No. That was Bernard's trouble. He had balls of brass, and the foresight of a baby, my *bébé boule à mite*." Her voice was caressing. She leaned toward Moretti, confidentially. "And she — she did what she was always good at, she got a man to do what she wanted."

Moretti thought about Ludo's words. *It was just like the old days.* And, more chillingly, the murder of a woman he had once loved. *I could never refuse her anything,* he had said.

Masterson's housekeeper shrugged her shoulders. "He was mad, you know, that Ross. Like Ulbricht and Baumgarten, he was a killer. That was not about love, Detective Inspector. That was not about love."

Moretti and Falla sat drinking coffee in the Commercial Arcade after a lengthy debriefing at Hospital Lane, prolonged by Jimmy Le Poidevin's complaints about lack of cooperation, lack of foresight, and lack of input. He had finally been silenced by Chief Officer Hanley himself.

"I suggest, Jimmy, that you take your complaints to MI6. I have no names, but I can give you their address."

It had given them both something to laugh about in the car, but neither of them had felt much like laughing since then. Liz was unusually quiet in the cafe, looking out of the window at the shoppers and the first tourists in the arcade, the warm, beautiful day reflected on the cheerful faces passing by. In a month or so, the tourists would return en masse.

It was Moretti who broke the silence. "How is Nichol doing? Have you spoken to your cousin?"

Liz smiled, and took another bite of her chocolate-filled croissant. "He's doing well, considering what they did to him, and how long it was before he got medical help."

Moretti nodded. "From what Bras-de-Fer says, they were holed up there a while, while Ulbricht and Baumgarten — or whoever they really are — tried to make contact for instructions on what they should do next."

"Yes. They just left Nichol for dead on the floor. Dr. Burton says he must have a skull like concrete, but myself I think he's suffered brain damage. Apparently he has found God, so one of the nurses tells me, and is trying to get back together with his wife. My cousin is weeping and wailing — she has no idea how lucky she is."

"God help the ex Mrs Watt, but perhaps she has more sense than your cousin. How *is* the idiot in the bathroom? They knocked him around pretty badly."

Liz groaned. "Considering what a blubbering, weak-kneed cretin he is, he's doing brilliantly. He's regrouped, and reinvented himself as the hero of the moment. All kinds of women are lining up to lick his wounds for him. He's the man who saved the day, would you believe?"

Moretti laughed. "Denny Bras-de-Fer will come out of most of life's hornet's nests unstung and smelling of roses."

He looked at Liz across the table. She was running a finger around the rim of her cup, her head bent forward, so he could not see her expression. There was a sadness about her today that was totally out of character, and he assumed it was not about Denny.

Tentatively he asked, "Ludo's 'something I want her to do for me' — is that giving you a problem, Falla? Is there anything I can do?"

"No." She looked up and Moretti saw to his dismay there were tears in her eyes. "Yes. Guv, I wish I could talk about it, but I'm supposed not to do that. When I've done — it, I'll make my own decision."

Moretti would have been only too happy to stop asking questions at that moment. His and Falla's was a working relationship that — well, worked, and he wanted to keep it that way. A quiet time professionally would suit him nicely for a while, as he decided what to do about Sandy Goldstein.

He knew what he wanted to do about Sandy Goldstein. It kept him awake at nights. But the devil, as usual, was in the details. And the most disturbing detail of all was Julia King. Sandy would never move in with him, never leave her friend and colleague on her own. But perhaps that was what he wanted in a relationship, and certainly his ex-partner back on the mainland would say it was. All sex and no commitment, Val would say. Since he had not slept around while they were together, and they had been living under the same roof, he was not sure what she meant. She seemed to want from him something more, something of himself he could not give.

So maybe Sandy Goldstein was the answer.

He was brought back into the present by a question from Liz Falla. The tears, thank God, were gone.

"Double V and Game-Boy never did get to meet Masterson, did they? Not the first time?"

"No. Remember, Masterson reserved two nights 'in case' at the hotel, and I think that was why Ulbricht and Baumgarten got anxious about Coralie's death. They were around the yacht that night, saw her command performance, felt someone else was involved who killed Masterson. They may even have seen Ludo's car at some point, which was why they believed Denny's story. They knew it wasn't Double V or Game-Boy, because they had warned them off."

"Guv, how much of Ludo's story was true, do you think? Was most of it moonshine?"

"God knows, Falla. That's the advantage of being sworn to silence, you can make up anything you want. And I never questioned even his qualifications, just bought his story. His age was always a mystery, and when I really thought about it, I realized he must have missed most of the war. When we went to see him about Coralie Fellowes, he modified his story from the one I was originally told. I suspect she had been in jail for some time until Ronnie Fellowes found himself a young agent who was prepared to break the rules for him."

"Did you always think he was involved?"

"Not always. At the beginning I thought the answer lay outside Guernsey, in financial cyberspace, with bad guys in Montreal, or the sun king of a small west-African country. But the motivation was closer to home. In the end, the one who remained was the truth."

"Shape-shifter, that's what he told me he was called, and that's what he was. Melissa Machin called him a man's man, and Mrs. Evans called him a ladies' man. He was whatever he needed to be."

"No man, everyman." Moretti realized there would be a hole in his life without him.

"I'll miss him, you know," Liz said, as if reading his mind. "He taught me a lot, a bit like Eliza Doolittle."

"He was your Svengali, and you were his Trilby."

Falla grinned, her joie de vivre returning as swiftly as it had gone, another sign of youth. "Svengali I know, but I thought the other one was a hat," she said. "I'll have to look that up — that's what Ludo would tell me to do. I'd better make a move." She pulled out her pretty little smartphone and manipulated it with a speed and deftness that made Moretti feel very old. Old age was not an absolute, such an individual matter, and as he watched his partner's sleight of hand he felt older than Ludo Ross who, in Moretti's memory, would always seem ageless.

Falla looked at him across the table. "I've got a gig tonight, and it's been a while since I played with them." As she stood up, she said, "I'm going to need some time off, Guv. To get this — thing — out from under my feet."

"Of course. We're both owed some time off, and getting back to the club is top of my own list."

Apart from Sandy. He had already left a message on her mobile, which she hadn't returned. A twinge of apprehension struck him. Perhaps he should head straight out to Verte Rue and see how things were.

They were leaving the café as Moretti's mobile rang. Pulling it out he said to Liz Falla, "Have a good one tonight."

"Thanks, Guv."

As she walked away from him, he answered his call. "Moretti."

"Ed." It was Chief Officer Hanley. "Could you come right over here?"

"Is there a problem?" No big surprise, because there were any number of loose ends still to tie off before the case was closed.

"You could say that." Moretti could hear what sounded like astonishment in his superior's voice. "There is an American gentleman here in my office, who has told me quite a story. His name is Sam Meraldo."

Ellie looked very much like her father. Sam Meraldo had dark eyes and hair, film-star good looks, and a trace of an accent. It was easy to see why Julia King had been crazy about him.

"Detective Inspector, I am told you are the man who can help me."

Moretti was about to open his mouth and say "over my dead body," or something similar, when Chief Officer Hanley leaned forward and said, "This has to be done discreetly, Ed. We checked the property records, and saw that the property in question is owned by your aunt, Gwen Ferbrache."

"She is not my aunt, sir, but she is a close family friend."

"Exactly. So you may be able to handle this, without undue —" Hanley hesitated, then went on "— risk, to those involved."

This was not how Ed Moretti had planned to spend his first free day after wrapping up the *Just Desserts* affair, sitting across the table from Sam Meraldo, of all people. He was tired, he was frustrated, but above all, he was angry. He exploded, a reaction so out of character that Hanley visibly jumped from the seat of his chair.

"How you have the gall to come here, Meraldo, spin Chief Officer Hanley a pack of lies, expect me to lead you to a woman you have terrified, and a child — your own child — you have threatened, and involve the island police force in finding them, is beyond belief!"

Before Hanley could untangle his tongue into words, Moretti pressed on across his chief officer's outraged spluttering. "You should know, sir, that Mr. Meraldo's wife, her daughter, and her close friend sought refuge from him here. I have no intention of leading him to them, and I think you should hear how he has persecuted them."

Before either man could respond, Moretti went through the catalogue of harassments and abuse listed by Sandy Goldstein in Gwen Ferbrache's sitting room: the dolls with ropes round their necks, the X-rated videos, the phone messages, the photographs, the stalking. By the end of his recital, he noticed that Hanley had moved his chair further away from Meraldo, his attention now turned in the American's direction.

"This is — unconscionable, sir. What have you got to say about all this?"

Meraldo did not reply. Instead, he bent down and pulled a handful of papers from a briefcase on the floor, and handed them out, like a class assignment, some to Hanley, and some to Moretti.

Moretti found himself looking at the sort of material Sandy Goldstein had described, clear evidence of harassment and persecution. The crucial difference was that it was directed at Sam Meraldo, by Sandy Goldstein herself.

"Oh my God."

Sam Meraldo smiled, wearily. "Got quite an imagination, has Sandy — heck, she's a writer. Not the first time, Detective Inspector, I've been through this. Very difficult to deal with, when a child is involved. And, frankly, I don't care a flying fuck what the relationship is between those two, but I do care about my daughter being removed without warning. I never wanted to take her away from her mother — besides, in my job I cannot care for her full-time — but I may have to do just that." Meraldo held out another document to Moretti. "Here are my divorce papers and custody agreement with Julia, in case you need further proof."

Moretti took the papers, but did not look at them. Instead he asked, "Why did this take you so long? We did check for any report of a missing child called Ellie King, or Ellie Meraldo, but the officer found nothing. They have been here a few weeks now."

Sam Meraldo reached out and took the papers back, put them in his briefcase. "Because I was away on business in central Mexico, and out of touch. I am Mexican by birth, now an American citizen, and I work for a big mining consortium undertaking exploration in the mountains near Saltillo. My fault, I shouldn't have trusted, not after what has happened. But I have to make a living, officer."

It was Chief Officer Hanley who answered. "Mr. Meraldo, how do you want to go about this? You think there may be a risk for your daughter if we just — rush in?"

Meraldo shrugged his shoulders. "I don't know, but given Goldstein's crazy behaviour, perhaps." He turned to Moretti. "You seem to know the situation. You have met Sandy Goldstein?"

"I have." Inadequate would suffice for the moment.

"Or your aunt perhaps? Could she help us?"

Moretti pushed back his chair and stood up. "Not Miss Ferbrache," he said. "I wouldn't want to involve her in this. I'll do it. If they see me, they'll not — well, they'll not fly off the handle. Or Sandy won't."

From the other side of the desk, Sam Meraldo looked up at Moretti. He was smiling and shaking his head.

"Isn't she something?" he said. "She and I were involved, which is how I met Julia. We fell in love, got married, had Ellie. Sandy never forgave me. She and Julia were professionally associated, but I never grasped the complexity of the relationship."

Svengali and Trilby. The hypnotic controller and the dominated follower. If Sandy split from Julia and stayed, would he become her new lapdog? Moretti knew what his answer to that would be.

***

It was an easy drive up to Verte Rue in the spring sunshine, for which Moretti was grateful. He was driving his Triumph, and he winced as the suspension grazed over the ruts and bumps in the lane. Ahead of him he saw an upstairs window was open, heard Ellie laughing, caught a brief glimpse of Julia King through the window.

If luck was on his side, Sandy was downstairs. He knew she had taken a little room at the back of the house as her workroom, and he supposed, hoped, she was there. He decided to sound his horn as he approached. If Julia and Ellie came out, he'd put them in the car. If Sandy came out, he'd cut off her retreat back into the house. He came to a halt, sounded his horn, and Sandy came running out. Moretti got out of the car to meet her, and she flung herself into his arms.

Just at that moment, an over-eager PC Brouard bounced up the lane, with Sam Meraldo sitting by him in the front seat. Moretti felt Sandy freeze, and he held on to her before she could break loose.

"Sandy, this is not a social call."

"Fuck you, Ed."

As she struggled to break free, PC Brouard brought the police car to a shrieking halt, skidding on the stones and gravel, leaping out with complete disregard for what they had planned at the station. At least Sam Meraldo stayed in his seat, as agreed.

"Stay!" Moretti shouted, and Brouard thundered to a halt like a well-trained canine.

"It's over, Sandy," he said.

"It already was." The fight had gone out of her. She turned and gestured at the little house, the watchpost in the middle of nowhere, where she had secreted the three of them. "I've had enough of this place. I'm bored out of my skull, I can't write here, and you are useless as a lover. Great in bed and lousy at being there, if you get my drift."

He did.

Sandy turned toward the police car where Sam Meraldo sat. "He can have them both. Julia's getting antsy, says she wants a life. I thought we had one."

On your terms, thought Moretti. "Julia even started suspecting me," she had said. Maybe Trilby was beginning to think for herself.

Sandy pushed him away. "She phoned him," she said. "Julia phoned him, betrayed us on my own cellphone. And I thought we were safe here, out of sight and out of mind. But nowhere is, is it, Ed? Not any longer."

Moretti did not feel the need to reply.

Chapter Nineteen

Paris

Charles de Gaulle Airport was chaotic, but the sun was shining, she had only her carry-on, and was quickly out of the terminal, walking along passages and tunnels to the train station. The queue for tickets for the RER train service into the city seemed particularly long, considering it was not the height of the tourist season, but time was not an issue. Around her the cacophony of languages calmed rather than assaulted her senses. Liz thought of Ludo and Coralie and the task ahead of her with anticipation now, not anxiety. Past loves, past lives. *Plaisir d'amour, chagrin d'amour*. Both belong here.

Besides, she had her instructions. It was like an old TV program she had seen in reruns — "Your mission, should you choose to accept it." She had accepted it, chosen to be Ludo's messenger. *Let's hope the messenger does not get shot for her pains,* she thought. Metaphorically, hopefully, in this case.

Finding the right train was not easy, and she had dragged her suitcase up and down various escalators before locating it close to where she had bought her ticket. The clerks at the guichets seemed overwhelmed by the crush of humanity, her French was not that fluent, and, even after she had boarded the train, she was not entirely sure it was the right one.

"*A Châtelet?*" she asked two beautiful black girls sitting in the seat opposite, dressed in long, flowing robes of many colours, and they assured her, "*Oui.*" Liz thought of Dwight and what a rarity he was in Guernsey. Here the opposite was true. She looked at those around her. She was the one in the minority.

Outside the train window the graffiti-covered walls of the banlieues flashed by, depressing in their monotone ugliness, the hellish circles that surround so many cities. Inside the long carriage a golden-earringed Gypsy plied her trade, holding out what looked like horoscopes printed on little cards. A young woman brought around pieces of handmade jewellery, held them out to her, discreetly. Liz shook her head, and they smiled and moved on. They did not push or persist, so presumably this carriage commerce was tolerated up to a point, as long as passengers were not pestered.

The train slowed again, as it had done before, but this time one of the girls pointed out the window. "*Châtelet.*"

Liz thanked them, said "*Au revoir,*" and got out on to the platform.

Her instructions were to take the Métro next, toward Porte d'Orléans, getting out at Saint Sulpice station, but she decided to disobey, just a little. She would take a cab, stay above ground and watch Paris pass by in the sunlight.

Outside the station she stood in the street, and waited for a cab to pass by. None did. An elderly woman sitting on a bench watched her with interest. Liz went over and asked her where she could find a taxi, or a taxi rank. The woman said, with a note of triumph, *"Pas de taxis,"* and something else in which Liz caught the word *Grève*.

Strike. No wonder the trains had been so busy. Liz got out her street map, and pointed to the rue Cassette, where her hotel was. The woman consulted it, then pointed across the road.

"Jardin du Luxembourg," she said. *"Vous pouvez marcher."* She pointed to Liz's case. *"Ça roule."* You can walk, that thing has wheels.

The taxi strike was a blessing. Sunshine and roses, long tree-lined allées, children lining up for donkey rides, the fine gravel crunching beneath her feet. Near the Fontaine de Médicis a woman and child were feeding pigeons. On an imposing set of steps close to the Palais du Luxembourg, a bride was posing for photos, laughing at her new husband as he ran along the terrace, talking to anyone and everyone who stopped to watch. Liz Falla and her rolling suitcase were of little interest, nothing out of the ordinary, part of the Paris landscape.

From the exit near the orangerie it was only a short distance to the hotel that Ludo had chosen for her. What he had said about it in his letter to her ran through her head. "This place has memories for me, and I will enjoy thinking of you there. It was a convent in the eighteenth century, and there is something piquant about putting you and that voice of yours into an ex-nunnery."

Apprehension filled her as she turned into the Rue Cassette. What should she expect — sackcloth and ashes and straw mattresses? Charm was only one of Ludo's qualities; he could be cruel. Very cruel. She trundled herself and her suitcase along the narrow pavement of the twisting street past a wall that was tall enough to hide what lay behind it, and turned in to an entrance screened with a wrought-iron gate, into a hidden courtyard.

A delightful courtyard, with cobblestones and statuary, flowers and ornamental trees blooming in giant urns, a feeling of serenity protected from the bustling street behind the convent walls. Inside, soft lighting and a soft-spoken receptionist, the lobby open to an elegantly furnished salon and, beyond, a lounge and dining area, its wall of glass leading to a secret, bird-filled garden behind high, ivy-covered walls.

No sackcloth and ashes, no straw mattress in her tastefully decorated bedroom, looking over the courtyard. *Just as well Ludo is paying for all this,* was Liz Falla's reaction, as she tipped the porter. It'd be sackcloth and bread and water for me for the unforeseeable future, otherwise. The porter handed her the key to the door — an impressive piece of heavy brass with an elaborately tasselled handle, more bordello-like than convent — and departed.

She tidied up in the well-appointed ensuite bathroom, went down the curving staircase to the dining room, ate a giant *croque monsieur* outside in the walled garden, fortified herself with a coffee and a glass of wine, asked for directions at the desk, and set out beyond the convent walls on her mission for Ludovic Ross.

The meridian line crosses Paris where Liz Falla walked, past the church of St. Sulpice, with its enigmatic gnomon outside. Liz was not that much of a history buff — she believed in living in the present — but she had read *The Da Vinci Code*. The past was with her as she walked, but it was Ludo's past, and Coralie's past, and she was curious to meet the reason for her pilgrimage. A few steps from the church, in a side street off the Rue de Canettes, with the four ducklings for which it was named still in place over one of the seventeenth-century houses, she reached her destination, rang the bell, identified herself, and was admitted.

He was expecting her, she had made sure of that, but he was not what she had expected. She had wondered which parent he would look like, but he did not remind her very much of either Ludo or Coralie. He had the slender build of both, but there the resemblance ended. He was, she knew, about sixty years old — surreal thought that Ludo had been a teenage father — and his wary eyes surveyed her from behind spectacles perched on a strong beak of a nose. His thinning hair was grey, neatly trimmed, at odds with his clothing, which was well-worn, almost threadbare, as if he were making a statement about the insignificance of her visit.

Liz looked around her. Décor and design were obviously not important to him, but the place was comfortably furnished, overflowing with books, magazines, newspapers.

"Mr. Renaudie, you know who I am and why I am here."

Ludo's son gestured to a chair, relatively free of paper and periodicals. "Please sit down, madame. I know who you are, you are a detective sergeant from Guernsey, but I don't understand the need for this visit. I was happy enough with my adoptive parents, and I was not happy when my father came back into my life, although I appreciated the financial support. It set me free to do what I wanted. But our contacts are few and far between, and we have only met twice."

His English was fluent, just a trace of an accent.

"What is it that you do?"

"I have a bookshop near the Place de l'Odéon."

"The visit is necessary because your father's circumstances have changed. Not financially, far from it. In fact, he is turning over his property and most of his assets to you."

"Why?"

"He will be going on trial, and will almost certainly spend whatever is left of his life in prison."

Charles Renaudie sat down, abruptly. It was the only emotional reaction Liz saw as she told him what had happened on the *Just Desserts* on two nights in April. He did not interrupt until Liz had finished. Then he asked two questions. "Why? I thought spies, even ex-spies, got away with murder."

"You were wrong. He is no longer in the intelligence service, and he took the law into his own hands."

"He and my birth mother together planned and executed the first murder — why?"

"The man they killed had cheated your mother's husband, Sir Ronald Fellowes."

"So they sought justice on behalf of the man for whom my birth mother deserted me."

There was no denying that. From her backpack, Liz got out the packet of papers Ludo had left for her in his bathroom safe, and put them on the table in front of her.

"This is what your father asked me to bring to you. Some of the papers are about legal matters, and there is a personal account as well."

"You can keep the personal account."

Liz looked across the table at Charles Renaudie. "Take it or leave it," she said, "I've done what I said I would do." She stood up, and Charles Renaudie stood up also.

"You know what?" she said. "Ludo didn't desert you. He looked until he found you. Enough of the self-pity. Get over it, Mr. Renaudie." Liz picked up her backpack from the table. "I'll see myself out," she said.

* * *

Back behind the convent wall, Liz lay on the bed in her hotel room for a while. The passive hostility of Charles Renaudie had left her feeling drained. She wondered if Ludo had asked her to do this in the hopes that his son might react more warmly, with some show of feeling.

"Wrong, Ludo," she said out loud to her reflection in the mirror across the room. She needed to talk to someone, anyone. She pulled out her phone.

"Moretti."

She felt suddenly warmer, more optimistic, the blood circling again in her veins.

"Guv, it's Falla. I'm in Paris."

"Ah. So tell me."

When she had finished, there was silence at the other end for a moment. Then Moretti said, "I wondered. Remember when I went to Italy after our first case together?"

"Yes. Was it something like this?"

"In a way. War casts a long shadow." But he didn't elaborate. "How did he take the fact that his father killed his mother?"

"I didn't tell him."

"You spared him."

"Oh no, not spared him, Guv." Liz shook her head vehemently, as if Moretti was in the room with her. "I think he would have enjoyed it."

"You'll have to get a new stereo, Guv. Ludo left you his music collection. And his wine cellar, actually."

When he met her at the airport, she looked tired, and she sat in the Triumph with her head resting against the back of the seat, her eyes closed.

"Nice of him. What about you? Or did he consider this pilgrimage on his behalf a gift?"

"No. He left me La Chancho's Poirets and Delaunays. Spooky. I'm going to sell them on eBay."

Moretti could think of nothing else to say, so he changed the subject. "PC Mauger says thanks, but it really should have been your collar. You told him to take a look at someone called DeBiase? Gord Collenette's maître d'? Dealing cocaine, I believe, as a side order with *coquilles St. Jacques*."

"Wicked!" The news seemed to have revived her. A minute or two later, he heard her humming under her breath, and after a while he said, "What's that? I don't recognize it."

She turned her head toward him, and he could hear amusement in her voice. "You wouldn't, Guv, it's not your kind of music."

"Try me."

So she sang to him and, no, it was not his kind of music, but the emotional impact of her voice was everything Ludo Ross had described. He had been critical of her lousy choice of lovers but, in that respect, were they really that different?

"It was written by a Celtic singer from New Zealand. I like it. I'll be singing it next week at — but you'd not be interested."

"I'm interested," Moretti heard himself saying. "I'm interested."

Herm

"I am surprised you brought her here."

"I am surprised she agreed to be brought here," said Peter Walker. "She is not at all a country girl, or a beach girl. A creature of big cities, Janice is."

"So why here?" Moretti pulled off his loafers and felt the warm sand beneath the soles of his feet, the sun on his upturned face. "This place is so tiny you could hold it in the palm of your hand. Could be scary for a creature of big cities."

"Because this is where it all started. Coming here, meeting you again, you asking for my help. Janice knew the policeman and the musician. The policeman is long gone, and I needed her to see a part of me she never knew, this old fart with binoculars and a song in his heart, watching the fulmars on their nests. How long this will last, I don't know, I can only hope, but I needed to be here with her."

"And she came with you. A good start, I'd say. Here she comes."

Walking toward them over the curve of the beach from the hotel, Jan Melville called out, "I'd forgotten what a savage game croquet can be. I won! Here —"

She handed over two of the three cans of beer she was holding, took a hearty swig from hers, and sat down close to Peter.

"What a competitive person you are."

Peter Walker touched her cheek with the chilled can, then his own, and Jan Melville's slanting black eyes gleamed, and she laughed as if he had said the wittiest thing in the world.

"I must be off." Moretti got up from the sand, brushing down his jeans, slipping his feet back into his shoes.

"Are you playing tonight?" Peter asked. "We could come across with you, stay overnight in the big metropolis."

"I'll be at the Grand Saracen tomorrow night, although it'll be strange without Garth. Still, it looks like his horn-playing days are not over, thanks to his lawyer and a certain eagerness among the power brokers to get this whole business over ASAP."

Janice Melville laughed. "And, thanks to Ludovic Ross, there are more bodies than bad guys to stand in the dock. What a storyteller! Looking at the case notes, I have wondered if Coralie Fellowes was killed by person or persons unknown. Hard to believe Ross did it, when clearly she was the love of his life. He liked to kill, that man — or was he just bragging?"

"Oh, no." Moretti shook his head. "Ludo did it. Only Ludo would have put her to sleep, playing for her the tape he made her, the music of their time together."

Chagrin d'amour dure toute la vie.

"If you don't have plans for tonight, why don't you stay and have dinner with us?" Peter pulled Janice to her feet, held her close against him.

"I have plans. Not my music, but someone else's. It's something I have been meaning to do, but it never seemed the right time."

Jan looked quizzically at him. "What makes it the right time now?" she asked.

Moretti smiled. "I heard the siren singing," he replied.

Acknowledgements

Warm thanks once again to the Guernsey Police for their help with the structure of the force and the unique administration of laws on the island. My thanks also go to Ros Hammarskjold — my ex-co-headgirl at the Guernsey Ladies' College — and her husband, Frank, for their friendship. Grateful thanks to my meticulous editor, Cheryl Hawley, and to Michael Carroll, associate publisher and editorial editor at Dundurn, for giving me the pleasure of seeing Moretti and Falla on the printed page. Kudos to designer Jennifer Scott for her moody and atmospheric cover design. Appreciative thanks go to "Nick," whose anonymity I will maintain, who gave me useful insights into the internal power struggles in local government and the impact of the financial presence on the island. To Bill Hanna, my agent, goes my gratitude for all his efforts on my behalf. Sadly,

Frances Hanna, my long-time agent and friend, did not live to see this book in print, and I have dedicated it to her memory. I shall miss her sharp editorial eye and conversations with her about politics, the arts — and cats. Thank you to my stepson, John, for his help with sound systems and firearms. Loving thanks as always to my husband, Ian, for his support, and for revisiting his skills as a geographer and cartographer to make a map of Guernsey for the book.

Also by Jill Downie

Daggers and Men's Smiles
978-1554888689
$11.99

On the English Channel Island of Guernsey, Detective
Inspector Ed Moretti and his new partner, Liz Falla,
investigate vicious attacks on Epicure Films. The international production company is shooting a movie
based on British bad-boy author Gilbert Ensor's best-
selling novel about an Italian aristocratic family at the
end of the Second World War, using fortifications from
the German occupation of Guernsey as locations, and
the manor house belonging to the expatriate Vannonis.

When vandalism escalates into murder, Moretti
must resist the attractions of Ensor's glamorous
American wife, Sydney, consolidate his working relationship with Falla, and establish whether the murders
on Guernsey go beyond the island.

Why is the Marchesa Vannoni in Guernsey? What
is the significance of the design that appears on the

daggers used as murder weapons, as well as on the Vannoni family crest? And what role does the marchesa's statuesque niece, Giulia, who runs the family business and is probably bisexual, really play?

Visit us at
Dundurn.com
Definingcanada.ca
@dundurnpress
Facebook.com/dundurnpress